KU-453-939

LE PROJET

Serret

C · P · SERRET

DIE
THE
VILLAIN

TEMPEST & GAYLE,
PHŒNIX,
MMXXIII.

Published by
Tempest & Gayle
PHOENIX

Die the Villain is a work of fiction. Names, characters, places, and incidents either are the products of the author's imagination or are used fictitiously. Any resemblance to actual persons, living or dead, businesses, companies, events, or locales is entirely coincidental.

Copyright © 2020 by C. P. Serret

The moral rights of the author have been asserted.

All rights reserved. For permissions and other queries, please contact
gayle@gmx.fr

Design by C. P. Serret

ISBN: 978-1-7343234-5-0

LCCN 2019919131

for the lives of silenced desperation

Deep in my soul that tender secret dwells,
    Lonely and lost to light for evermore,
Save when to thine my heart responsive swells,
    Then trembles into silence as before.
        LORD BYRON, The Corsair: A Tale

THE FALL,
I.
★

N ᴇᴡ ᴍᴇssᴀɢᴇ. He smiled at the brusque salutation: *kitsune*, like old times. But Ane-san was former geiko; she was elegant, even when curt – even on a darknet mail client that encrypted to the subject line. He wiped his lenses with the hem of his black tee.

The blustery rain was breaking up. Didn't matter though, it was all grey through the window wall beside his table, the midrise across Third a skyless wall of glassed concrete. Cars and cargo trucks trundled across his spectral reflexion while posh passers-by hunched against a whirling gust and the lash of dead leaves. He turned the glow of his laptop screen away from the spattered glass.

Ane-san needed leverage on two Diet Members; she wanted it all: emails, bank records – even disk images – for them, their wives, and assistants. Find connexions; follow the money; find the dirt. He'd returned to the U. S. over a year ago – withal at her fingertips. He began typing confirmation but paused mid-keystroke.

Black pumps, slim heels, despite the wet. Her dark hair was wind-tousled over a black café-racing jacket and red scarf, a violet midi dress under her unzipped leather and a matching tote in the crook of one arm; she was Lady Purple in spades – a neoteric Murasaki no Ue. Smileless behind her Jackie O sunglasses, she stood out at the end of the line among the uptown coffee bar's ambient selection of book-club reads, bibelots, and blonde woods.

He was as conspicuous but invisible, the other metal-base plywood tables crowded with backlit apples, patched jeans, and rain gear. Alone among flatline mouths. Tense linéaments.

Exclusivism was tacit; there'd been few ᴡʜɪᴛᴇs ᴏɴʟʏ signs here in the northeast, even at the interbellum peak of de jure apartheid – the ɴᴏ ᴅᴏɢs–ɴᴏ ɪʀɪsʜ signage further back, ɴᴏ sᴘᴀɴɪsʜ out west. Hollywood's hot-blooded señorita would be other: an exotic collectable fit for display. Lady Purple, likewise, but girls like her came and went, branded paper cups in hand. He'd prefer that to the hot seat and the piped Top 40, but he tacked a random course through the city's Wi-Fi footprint, and there was parking.

He turned back to his inbox, a graphical window into Hobbes' "warre of all againſt all" – delete that gift horse unopened. Information flowed through a distributed subterranean network. Virtual bullion changed pseudonymous hands. Ane-san's request required two compartmentalised teams, and he priced it as such. Never let anyone connect the dots – not even the players doing the dirty work. He hit *Send* and started at an unfamiliar female voice close by:

—Can I sit here?

Lady Purple was beside his table in her spotless patent pumps, sleeved cup in manicured fingers. Spotted his Hanshin Tigers cap? He nodded. She settled in without another word or glance, setting her slouchy tote across from him: HERMÈS, &c. in fine silver logotype on pebble-grained leather. All that glittered was gold, but she held a glamour beyond her fin-de-sièclism of coruscant luxury – that je-ne-sais-quoi cliché you couldn't put your finger on.

Furtive gazes trailed her as she sat, then, enviably, fell away, like the Shining Wall, above approach. The pushiest string of gods-gift guys had hit on him over the past week, the last a tasteless conformista in a Ché tee. Hadn't been easy not to shoot that one.

She lifted her dark lenses unto crown, retrieved a starship-grey MacBook Air from her tote, then texted on her iPhone. Up close, the sheen of her skin was more glasslike than porcelain.

—I've seen you here before, haven't I?

—Don't think so, he replied. Not a regular.

She looked up from the screen, her dark eyes taking his in. Opaque behind their gleam, their delving deepness was an exquisite, thrilling trill. She pointed at the encircled "A" on his black 'n' white varsity jacket.

—You don't go to school around here?

—No, this isn't from a school; got it online. I finished B-school a couple years ago. Working now.

She lowered her phone.

—Really? No offense; I thought you were a high-school girl skipping class.

—Really. Turned twenty-four last month. I skipped a grade and didn't take a gap year before college or B-school.

—H'm. I don't turn twenty-four till next August. Maybe it's the glasses; they might be a little big for your face. You must get carded everywhere.

—Bartenders I'm friends with card me just to be dicks.

She leant closer.

—Green eyes. Where… ?

He had half-dozen evasions on tap, but he gave her the reductive answer:

—Cuban-Irish.

—Glad I didn't try to guess. You look like one of those Brazilian models.

—It would take an hour to explain my dad's side of the family – he has some Irish, too – but the Caribbean's a melting pot like Brazil. Too bad for me I'm not Brazilian supermodel–tall.

She offered a hand, her short fingernails lacquered a pale pearlescent blue; it was cool in his.

—Chloë. So you speak Spanish?

—Finn. No. My mom's a militant Irish speaker; she made us speak it at home for years – even my dad learned some – and Spanish kind of fell by the wayside. I understand a little, but a lot of my relatives only speak Spanish, so…

He was of both worlds and neither but never dredged this stuff up. Most girls were content to talk about their goings-on as he'd listen, but Chloë was cagey. She scattered a few unconnected puzzle pieces, deflecting most of his questions with counter-questions like an operative in a spy novel, trained to resist interrogation – or any girl well-practised in eluding pushy guys.

—But Finn's your first name?

—Well, Cris. Cris Finn.

—No Ó or Mic with your Finn?

—No, just Finn.

Chloë didn't speak Japanese but said not to give her shit; she was third-generation. A Kennedy dropout dressed for the red carpet or Instagram, she'd been coerced into an office gig by hovering parents – a black sheep with a trust fund. Flunked out after coasting as an undergrad? He didn't ask.

—But specifically, she reïterated, why an MBA? Not afraid of the glass ceiling?

—I work for myself now, but the MBA was s'posed to be my leg-up. My edge. I saw what it was like for my mom to be a middle management apparatchik; we all did, and my aunt told me, "Because you're Spanish, you'll have to work twice as hard to get equal credit" ¶. I didn't expect it to be any different in Japan than here when it comes to discrimination; I'm not naïf. I did land an internship and *naitei* – early recruitment in advance of graduation – but my MBA only got me in the door. Company culture is more important than anything you bring to the table. I had to play dumb, follow the old-man rules, and keep my mouth shut. That's when I got it: all of us, we were slaves. Now that I'm on my own, no ceiling, no chains.

—Ballsy.

—It took a little time to get off the ground, but I have an outsourcing and consulting company. Small business supply chain. One-man show ¶. I travel around the city every day, dealing with clients. Spend a lot of time in places like this.

—Your parents must be prouder than mine.

—Well, we don't talk anymore. Haven't in years. They don't know anything about my business or even that I'm back in the U. S.; this isn't where I grew up ¶. I looked around some at first, but it was all kind of samey – one generic city after another – so I stopped here: Generic City, USA. Ever read Hillier or Koolhaas in class?

—No. And sorry, I didn't know you were estranged.

—No big. You here on a business trip?

Chloë pointed back over her shoulder, at the land of multimillion-dollar brownstones.

—No; I moved into the neighbourhood recently, but my wireless isn't up yet. Such a drag.

Finn made a sympathetic noise. She took a sip of coffee and checked her phone. If she lived here, then she was sitting in a coffee bar noonish on a Thursday and not at her undefined job. Some corporation.

—What do you do for fun around here? she asked without looking up. I don't know the local club scene.

—Nightlife – the club scene – isn't my thing, sorry. I'm kind of a homebody: I read; collect vinyl; and I, uh, watch baseball, obviously. Sometimes I stop for a drink at the end of the day. Happy hour?

—That's cool.

Chloë's tone conveyed the opposite, and a pall of silence fell while she texted. Didn't matter though; it was a pop-up tableau – the city's strata collided sometimes. He sank behind the parapet of his laptop screen. A sinking feeling. Shouldn't matter, but he drew a blank, his fingers at rest on the kana keyboard. He pulled up the latest extraits from the Agency's *Studies in Intelligence*, too aware of her to apprehend what he clicked through, till a glass-on-wood thunk. Phone set down, she smiled.

—Want to do lunch? I'm hungry, but I need real food, not pastry; it's not my cheat day.

He blinked, baffled but curious. Who is this person?

—OK, how 'bout Cuore Vuole? Venetian bistro, wine bar…

—Sold.

She slipped the Air back into her tote, one eye on her supine phone. He shut down and pulled his Live USB, the counter-forensic key to his amnesic workstation; otherwise, a workaday T-series loaded with intermodal logistics software, a naff bit o' electrical tape over the webcam. She offered to drive but was parked at her place, a couple blocks away. He stood, shouldering his grey messenger bag, and picked up his stick umbrella.

—No; I'll drive. I'm in that garage right there.

They pushed out through double doors and into the grey noise of traffic on wet ashpalt and silvered glare. The damp reached through to his skin. He zipped his jacket; she didn't, flanking him to the non-valet garage's pedestrian entrance, chill as a summer stroll behind her shades. He stopped at his car's passenger door; she stepped to the wrong side of the blue Bimmer parked beside it. She looked it over.

—An M-three? Not bad.

—Yeah, that's not mine.

He opened and held the door of his '70 911S, original Bahia Red. Little had bridged his father's perplexed distance better than the McQueen movies they'd watched en famille sometimes on DVD and ratty old VHS. The vintage Porsche had fulfilled their once-shared *Le Mans* fantasy – one of few bright and shining memories.

—O nice, she said.

Finn would've had to stand en pointe to match her height in heels, but watching Chloë walk up to his car in cinematic motion, setting her tote inside, sitting, then stepping in, he shut the door on the surreal moment, and her phone trilled alarum through the glass. Dreaming awake, the greasy road feel was all that grounded him; his tail sliding on every turn, he drove towards the light breaking over midtown, a swank girl buckled in shotgun, arguing in German – of all things – on her cell. Like you'd hear in the movies. Pissed off German.

The argument continued onto cracked pavement, damp and dotted with black moles of gum. She locked the violet tote in his car; then she filched a stubby white cigarette from her black clutch and lit up with a frillless drugstore Zippo. Her smoke whorled while they walked in the warming sun; a Turcic scent tickled his memory: the fragrant still life of his grandfather's small reading room, steeped in the faded florality of Balkan and briar pipes, tarred and noseöily, the drapes drawn against Derry's divide and Troubles past but unforgiven.

Finn held the restaurant door. Chloë thumbed her phone screen.

—Sorry. International call.

—Figured as much.

—This fucking job at my uncle's. What's the point of calling in sick?

They were taken to a table for two by the window. New gallant, he helped Chloë out of her trim motorcycle leather, surprisingly heavy and luggage stiff – more than simulacre. He caught the warmth of her close scent, a vernal accord of rosed iris beneath the smoke and savour of acenaphthylene; then he shed his jacket for the new scene: her cocktail dress and red-soled stiletto heels, his not-a-Fugazi t-shirt and red plimsolls. She glanced at his tattooed arm but didn't comment, intrigue in the cant of one sculpted brow. She perused the menu; he ran his fingertips over it

IL CUORE VUOLE
TRATTORIA E CICCHETTERIA

... elcuore uuole cibo digratia ſpirituale
ꝗ altriment nō e mai cōtento.
F. DOMENICO CAVALCA

but already knew what he wanted. He sat back, shivelight playing across her face. She excused herself, and the Lambrusco arrived in her absence, pedestrians passing outside – a moment of bough-flecked contentment.

She opened up after two glasses, glowing through the cracks in her armour. She was a bully – a delighted, unrepentant bully – but insider charming since he wasn't in her crosshairs. He'd known the type too many times like he drew them: Logan, Senpai, & al., then dragging him into their quixotic shit – he, their Sancho Zancas.

Finn was a bourbon guy but warmed over the wine, at the centre of Chloë's attention, entranced by her wide, twisty grin and the funny way her upper lip turned in; a part of him leant in to kiss that grin and lingered. Amadán… He shook his head and ordered another bottle, born this way. The words, the sounds, the light in her hair; it slipped through his fingers, sands run out.

They retrieved her tote, and he walked in the dusk of her ebullience, hands in his pockets till she flagged a cab. He opened the door for her one last time, but he was shoved in from behind, knocking his ballcap to the curb.

—Chloë!

She laughed.

—It's a kidnapping.

He righted himself on the slick vinyl seat as Chloë sat and grabbed his cap. The cab launched on her "Go!" and took the jammed way round the Occupy'd financial district's grasping high-rises to a nighted downtown bar, the staff Abercrombie models in uniform black. Four-point-five stars on Yelp but dead at two-something in the afternoon. A row of flatscreens hung above the bar top, split between the latest Gaga playing to the empty room and the muted soundbite news, close-captioned on-screen, exploiting the death of Apple's CEO last week: "Who should play Steve Jobs in the movie?"

Chloë's dark eyes scanned every corner.

—I wonder what it's like here at night.

Finn imagined a lot of fake people crammed together. She checked her face in a compact, double C ideogram on the lid.

—You're not wearing much make-up, are you?

—None.

—BB cream?

—No.

—And your skin just looks like that? So not fair.

She snapped it shut and leant in, whispering,
—Bartender is hot.

Finn glanced but didn't comment: tall, dark, whatever. Chloë shifted closer, lips parted. Her mien had softened with the wine, but there was no flush warming her hint of peachy blush.
—Or is it girls?

He met her gaze.
—Just girls.

She didn't look away.
—Do you have a girl, Cris?
—No.

Chloë raised a finger, but Patrón shots interrupted. She touched her glass to his and dropped it like so much water, no grimace, flagging the pretty boy bartender for round two. Finn slammed the double plunge – bang! bang! – but stopped her from ordering a third; her raised hand capped by his, he pressed it gently to the bar top.
—No, no. Not yet. I need a minute.

She turned back to him, a smile playing about her lips, and swept her glam caramel highlights behind one ear with her free hand, away from the delicate angularity of her face, revealing a sparkling stud and the smooth scape of her neck. He pulled his hand back and stood, leaving his folded jacket on the next barstool.
—Gonna use the restroom.

Chloë caught the crook of his ink.
—I'm coming with.

She yanked him to a squeaky-tire stop before the Ladies' bling wall-to-wall mirror. She turned his blacked-out road cap around and hooked his bobbed hair behind pierced but jewelless ears, exposing his heart-shaped face to the bright fluorescent light.
—Jesus. You are a doll.

Chloë called his double eyelashes unreal, his rosebud mouth perfect. She assayed every facet, and looking up at her, warmth spread down from his chest. She knew – she'd made that clear – but she had no idea.
—Want to try my lipstick? Add some colour to your skater tomboy look?

The same old hoidenist BS; it killed his buzz on the spot. He pulled away.

—I'm not a tomboy. Make-up isn't my thing.

She raised a hand but didn't touch his face.

—But you must be doing something to get this honey skin.

—Used to have skin problems till a friend back in Japan showed me how to double-cleanse and moisturise overnight. Some stuff I get at a Korean mart, midtown. That's it.

—That's it? I hate you.

Chloë moved closer, turning him to face the mirror with a light touch across his shoulders.

—What dress size do you wear? These clothes are enormous on you like your glasses.

A men's extra-small tee and blue jeans hung with a baggy sort of fit, which her reflexion tugged at with two fingers. His irezumi sleeve reached down past one elbow, etched for evermore into an inborn tan: a vivid nine-tailed fox courant over field, flower, and cloud. Heavy horn rims were prominent with Finn's nape-length chestnut curtains pulled back; so too his button nose, unnecessarily bee-stung lips, and narrow chin. His mirrored pout annoyed him.

Kuromaku – a fixer – was faceless. No éminence grise, like Ane-san, but a black curtain, without reflexion.

—No idea. Haven't worn a dress since Catholic school.

—Then let's go shopping! There's a big department store down here… Pygmalion, I haven't been to yet.

—Chloë, I'm not putting on a dress or…

She traced a fingertip over his ink, raising goosebumps everywhere.

—Shopping for me. Then you can show me around downtown, and we can have another drink or dinner, maybe, by then?

He blinked. Sometimes the city's strata collided, but.

H E WAS WRONG – about everything.
Headlights stalked him home. He'd offered compromises but no go. Parking was iffy after dinner time; he met Chloë on Shady. Her car was sick. Sick.

The rain had stopped, but there was no one else outside. He walked her back towards his place on Walden, leant into his shoulder – a giggling fit for an hour-old joke petering out. He played it blasé, tapping his damp umbrella on the sidewalk, ballcap flipped back. "Show me that dollface," she'd say; "turn it around or take it off." She'd met him for dim sum in Chinatown on Sunday and dinner at a froufrou fusion place tonight. A hot pursuit or what? – one eye on his new Galaxy Note like a rearview.

He told her to hurry up and finish her cigarette; this is it. She'd turned down after-dinner drinks at a pub, a nightcap at a hôtel bar or her place, and insisted on coming here. On coming in. Skin softer than a golden peach, her surface was harder than diamond, and no dissuasion penetrated: not "my place is a mess", not "How about tomorrow?" Not by his hairless chinny chin chin.

Chloë peering overshoulder, he unlocked the red door to his 1840s rowhouse. Redbrick – not sandstone – with white trim, the modest façade ran half the sloping length of the block. A ONE WAY street sign pointed down towards the beachless commercial bay that you couldn't see from here, his car shit on by pigeons and seagulls alike. If the wind blew right, you would smell the ocean, but less often than you'd think.

The quiet enclave had gentrified with the decline-and-fall of a Flaubertian « bourgeois en blouse », but he'd bought at the van of a new wave of mainland Chinese; he'd watched them price out the soi-disant upper-middle-class precariat and their underemployed hipster kids. Cash was flowing in, lots of laundry – houses left empty – in the mix. He'd gotten offers. Silly money.

He opened the door, braced for his unprepared disarray, the silver chinchilla Persian miauling beyond the swing; she darted

forward. He nudged the pedigreed freeloader back, her wide
kohl eyes in need of cleaning again.

—Hidenka, shoo ¶. Careful. Koko Naishin'nō might try to run
out and trip you.

—What a name. And so fluffy.

He heel-toed out of his sneakers and squatted to make room
on the shoe shelf next to his umbrella stand. He had missed
this: the dozens of texts every day, the regular hangouts. Seeing
Trace & al. at the tavern just wasn't the same. He'd been too busy
between work and Chloë to drop in, though she'd said she wanted
to see it; to meet everyone he knew in the city. But she looked
the idiomatic million bucks, standing in his entryway amid her
air of iris-and-cigarette. A college bar wouldn't be her thing.

He shelved her steep black sandals. She studied his red-and-
white kitsune kyōgen mask, which hung facing the stairs to his
second floor. Helping her out of her dark camel cape-coat with
smooth gallanture, he hung hers and his in the entry closet, then
turned – an inch short of eye-to-eye with her, barefoot on the
slate-grey carpet in her navy minidress, cubist roses like RGB
butterflies. He was lost in tenebris and the staring abysm. She
traced an electric line down his arm with one finger and placed
her hand in his.

—Show me this mythic stereo of yours.

—It's upstairs.

Chloë considered the carpeted stairwell and the shale-grey
hallway behind him.

—H'm. Show me around first.

He drew her through an abashed tour of his garçonnière's
expansive library, trailing the silvern dust mop; he rearranged
as they went, myriad books and manga on the floor-to-ceiling
shelving and piled on the floor. Chloë ran her fingers along the
spines and turned back to him, shy of his intel and espionage
nonfic.

—Shades of grey, black 'n' chrome; it's a little masculine – don't
you think? – like a study in one of those period movies but modern. Don't you like plants?

—Nah, not my thing.

He'd ensconced the satellite-linked flatscreen in its own Hanshin Tigers–bannered solo-viewer nook. Last night's post-game

rubbish was everywhere; a win against the Carp, 2–0. But his wet bar posed a problem. No Patrón. She was incredulous.

—How can you not have any Patrón?

—Sorry, it's…

—How far is the nearest liquor store?

—Ten minutes? Long as there's parking.

—Guess I'll wait over here, then.

Chloë stretched out on the Corbu chaise and crossed her slender legs. That carefree presumption was amusing to a point. She placed her crisp-edged black Kelly on the side table – a handbag his mother would kill for, then enshrine unused. Chloë leafed through the book he'd been reading, then set it aside for her iPhone.

—Which wireless is yours?

—Those are my neighbours'. I don't have home internet.

—What.

—I spend all day staring at my laptop at work. I prefer to relax at home. Offline. Well, except for the four-G on my Note. Be right back.

—Don't forget, it's the Silver!

He returned with two lime-green boxes forty minutes later. She was where he'd left her, handbag in her lap, texting or whatever on her phone. Koko stalked the intruder, perched hawklike on the lightly clawed Goetz sofa, eyes closed. Chloë glanced up but remained seated.

—You're all wet.

—Started raining again on my way back.

—I'll have mine over ice. With lime, if you have it.

He texted her "Lol" and repocketed his phone. He left the boxed tequila, hung his jacket, and dried off; then he fetched two Galway-crystal double old-fashioneds, ice, and an acceptable wedge carved from a withered lime. She rose, leaving her bag on the chaise. He prepped hers and poured bourbon on the rocks for himself. She glared at his glass.

—What's that?

—Whiskey.

—You know the rule, Baby Doll: Patrón only.

She pulled his full glass away, hers to his protesting lips, tilting. He had to swallow or let it spill, but some went down the wrong way. She sipped while he coughed a few times; then she poured the remainder into his mouth and closed it with her lips and the tip of her tongue, shivering him all the way down. Part of him stood outside the cascading sparks and watched himself with her in the mise-en-abîme of his mind's eye. Was it her or the tequila? Too much lay beyond the veil.

Chloë followed her pattern: ambush, then break contact. She nuzzled him.

—So soft. Show me upstairs.

But she turned down a refill and retrieved her Kelly as if ready, instead, to depart. Something was off.

Concerned moue, he lifted the second lime-ribboned bottle from its box, then led her up to his aërie. He tried to guide her past his Japanese-style room, but the walnut shōji door caught her eye and fingertips; she slid it open: At six tatamis, it was larger than his first place in Kyōto but spare, the single chest of drawers topped with a wooden dresser valet. Import tatami faded hay-gold matched beige walls and fusuma, and shōji screened the exterior windows, bathing the walnut-framed alcove and hanging scroll in softened street-light.

He'd stayed up late for the game, overslept, then rushed off to work, leaving his dishevelled futon and scattered clothes centre stage – at her feet. She gave him a sceptical look.

—You sleep on the floor.

—Well...

—You're crazy. It smells nice in here, but you're crazy.

He clicked on the Akari floor lamp and went into frantic pickup mode, explaining in a rush how the same expat artisans who'd installed part of the East Asian wing at the Museum of Art downtown had remodelled the room with traditional craft: all wood-in-wood joinery without nails or glue. She got into his open closet, and her scepticism fell headlong into sputtery disbelief: band shirts, Japanese selvedge, and sober men's yukata.

—Omigod, Cris. I can't even. Shopping! Seriously, we can't go to a club till...

It was nothing he hadn't heard before: from her, from Trace. Even Senpai. He wasn't dressed for nightlife, if not a celebrity of some sort, and he'd gotten the stink eye from the maîtresse d' at the restaurant.

Chloë touched up her hair and make-up in his hidden mirror, talking this hairstylist and that boutique. He h'mmed at her pauses and slid the fusuma shut when she was done, a step behind her when she yanked open his tansu's top drawer. She recoiled.

—You have a gun?

—Shit, well…

—Why do you have a gun?

—Well, you know how I travel around the city by myself? Most of my clients… it's all guys from overseas. Huge culture gap. Some try to take advantage.

—Fuuuck, she drawled. You know how to use it?

—I'm no Annie Oakley, but stick a muzzle in their kidney, and they keep their hands to themselves. Don't try that with an automatic, though; it'll jam.

The macho ones were the biggest cowards, but you had to be ready to shoot for real. Most of them had guns, but no one wanted a shoot-out in broad daylight. Or a dead body. Or cops on-site. Everyone wanted to make money – but not off of him. Not that way. Not in effing jest. He played it blasé.

—But I've only had to pull it twice.

—Twice! That's a little scary.

—It's fine. Come check out the listening room.

—Show me your gun first. Is it loaded?

—Yeah. One sec.

He set the bottle down and unholstered his snub-nose Rhino: 357 Magnum, loaded for bear, with grooved walnut grips for that Blade Runner look. He dropped the blued cylinder and emptied it, counting cartridges, then set them aside while she waited, arms crossed. He offered her the revolver, grip first. She leant in and inspected it hands-off.

—You should reconsider this whole one-man-army thing. Come work with me at the Corporation. You're more than qualified.

—Chloë, creeps are everywhere.

—I don't have to carry a gun in my purse at the office.

—Maybe you should.

—Cris, think about it; for me. I have pull.

He reholstered and shut the unloaded Rhino back in his sock drawer.

—OK, I'll think about it.

—OK. Show me.

Her face was set, deep currents unlumined behind her eyes – something off compounded. So much for the evening.

Muted, he led her across his listening room's threshold and stood aside on the silver maple floor. She'd hung back, distant, then stopped in her tracks. Below wavelike ceiling clouds, a plush cushion-basket armchair faced two megalithic full-range speakers. Low platforms bore blocky power amps before the two stout racks holding his turntable, preamps, and power supplies, a dental air compressor off to one side. Formations of vacuum tubes stood at attention, dark and cold.

He closed the door behind her, shutting out the curious cat, and made a spot for the Patrón on the minibar. Chloë gestured across the geometric treatments hanging on his grey walls.

—What're those? Art?

—Acoustic panels.

—And those columns? They don't look like they support anything?

—Tube traps.

—All this to listen to music?

—After music, "the reſt is ſilence."

—And a bar up here too. Guess you are Irish.

—Ha ha.

—Why only one chair?

He hadn't thought about it.

—That's how listening rooms are.

—What about guests?

—You're the first person that's ever been in here – besides delivery guys. I'll warm up the amps.

Chloë tilted his stepped Escherian ashtray.

—It's OK to smoke in here? Or is this a bowl?

—You can smoke; I had a ventilation system installed. See the vents? The old master bedroom was a better space than the living room downstairs, so I had the second floor remodelled all at once. There was one load-bearing wall we couldn't move, but...

Ping! Snap! – she was burning.

—I thought you didn't smoke.

—Not cigarettes, usually. I smoke cigars.

—No shit?

—The humidor's right there; it fits a hundred or so.

It was similar to the one on the oyabun's desk but larger – Senpai had let Finn peek inside once, at her parents' walled-and-gated house in Higashiyama. Not something you'd see in the average Cuban home; at most, a few sticks in a ziplock.

Chloë lifted the lid of his wax-polished burl case and laughed a gleeful little laugh. He joined her, and she poked him with one finger: the first o on his Doors tee.
—Ballin'. Who are you?
—Still seeking a category besides *Other*.
—H'm.

She turned to his vinyl collection, displayed on the built-in shelving on both sides of the doorcase, and ran her fingertips along the sleeves. She glanced at *Happy End* but reshelved it. She circled the black leather lc3, one arm folded and supporting her smoking hand. A musing drag in faraway thought, and she stubbed out her cigarette.
—Thanks for showing me your place, but I should start heading home.

He glanced at his lambent altar.
—O. Didn't you want to hear it?
—Not tonight. Some other time.
—Another drink?

Chloë checked her phone, then put it away.
—No; it's a Tuesday, and we both have work tomorrow. But I want you to think about what I said –this isn't the Wild West. Call me anytime you want to come in, have a tour, and talk to someone. We can do something fun this weekend. Let me know when you can go shopping during the week; I'm ok with uptown or downtown. We can try getting your hair done too, but it's hard to get someone good on short notice.

She was pulling too hard on fresh strings. Pulling his chain. He crossed one arm, mirroring her, his disappointment settling in and deflating the strain of expectation. Like he'd been holding his breath.
—I'm not actually a doll, you know.

Chloë smirked, turning towards the door.
—Come walk me to my car. My umbrella's in the trunk.
—Why didn't you bring it in case?
—Baby Doll. So you'd walk me to my car.

C·P·SERRET,
DIE THE VILLAIN.

THE FALL,
III.

★

HEY SIGNED OFF with his favourite salute: —Yes sir.
T   He was the odd man out in the small Taiwanese café,
       surrounded by backlit apples, faded jeans, and fam-
ilies, a flatscreen set to CTi news. A transposed slice of Taipei.
He didn't understand a word, but wherever he was, the stranger.

He closed the off-the-record channel. Encrypted from end-
to-end, deniable; it didn't exist and never would, tunnelled via a
shrouding realm parallel to the Clearnet's flickering Flash and
tawdry scripts. Darknets were legion, and in the dark, he could
be anyone – even himself – like the dog days of dial-up. Accepted,
not tolerated, and judged by his actions, he didn't mind *dude* or
even *bro*; it was Miss and Mizz that set his teeth on edge.

Work was piling up. This fifth job was pushing it but too
lucrative to let go. It had taken months to build a stable revenue
stream after those initial odd jobs for Ane-san; months to elevate
the rep of Aphid Grin and his other handles, but now work came
to him. Aphid Grin was the man.

IP his métier, he turned down anything that might draw direct
action from Langley, Yasenevo, and kind. The trade in corporate
secrets was a grey industry – one that walked a questionable
line – but private intel firms hid in plain sight. Like that cubicled
office building on the other side of the boulevard. Centimani.
Edwardian suited 'n' tied, leathern souled, ex-spooks information
gathered and social-engineered from behind the façade – open
source intel and *Mission Impossible* pretexting the in-things.

His was the Knockturn Alley of information; they, too,
came knocking when they needed darker-than-grey ops, and
he'd turned to them at times through one of his shell corps.
Information leaked, even from black holes, or you pried it out by
any means; then what was gathered or lifted from the world's top
thousand corporations was sold to the competition – or their
stakeholders. A few mil U. S. offered for the microarchitecture

of an autonomous driving CPU? The international list of suspects fit on one hand.

However IP-hungry, China didn't pay – not on the dark markets. Much of it was hedge funds and private equity duking it out. Eating each other. Companies, even conglomerates, were small potatoes. Chips on the board. And they played for keeps. MNPI. Trade secrets. Blackmail. Nothing was off the table, or so you'd hear, and some of the work might've come your way.

That's the game Ane-san was playing, too; the game the gokudō were shifting into: the game of cosmocrats. He'd overheard the Ōkumo C-suite once, talking vulture funds in their gravelly voices. He'd stopped to check out the oyabun's glass-cased whiskey collection, and they'd arrived in formation. A smoke-lensed bulldoggish face had turned his way, and a dark-suited askari with a squashed nose had ushered Finn back to Senpai's side. His fellow undergrad had taken him to her mom, the ane-san, for his apology. She was the Promethean voice at the oyabun's ear, mother to the head family, and shadow hierarch of a sub-syndicate of gokudō wives and daughters. Ane-san still called him a fox, and back then, she'd reminded him to act like one: cling to the shadows, and hide in the walls unseen.

He took an empty sip from his paper cup and considered another caffè americano but passed; it was nearing happy hour and time for a real drink or three. See Trace if she was working. Chloë kept pestering him to go shopping and their plans for tomorrow remained indefinite. He'd ignored the last few texts; he had his limits.

A reminder popped on-screen. He opened a new OTR channel in his chat client but started at a familiar female voice close by:
—You have the prettiest hands, but you're in desperate need of a manicure and some polish. And stop chewing your thumb.
—Chloë? What are you doing here?

He rose from the comfortless café chair; his heart leapt, then palpitated, caught red-handed… in a language she couldn't read. She went for a kiss, short and sweet, Friday casual in a navy pea jacket, flared indigo jeans, and driving mocs, her Kelly worn cross-body on a canvas strap, bar sinister. She kissed him again and rotated his ballcap sidewise.
—Hey you. Kind of a halfish day at work, and I thought I saw your car when I was driving by – not too many classic nine-elevens

parked by cafés midtown. I texted you from my car, but you
didn't text me back.

—O, sorry, I was in the middle of something.

She checked his laptop screen.

—That's in Russian?

—Yeah. I, uh, told you that most of my clients are foreign, right?
I started with a couple contracts out of Ōsaka – had a connexion
there – but I discovered that supply-chain support for Russian
and Baltic subsidiaries operating in the U. S. was underserved.
I took a crash course, and so far, it's paid off.

A lie like those he'd prepared for the confessional, Russian
was the second language of the darknets, after English, and
he'd been studying up since starting operations out of Kōbe.
The élite invite-only Russian fora were frequently essential to
his work, frequented by native Russian virtuosi and Russian
literates worldwide, with prospectives from Estonia to Ukraine.
He didn't use scanners or skiddies, whatever their tongues, and
picking up additional clients in the import/export grey market –
Russophones that asked no questions and wanted no questions
asked – was a bonus. He would've carried a gun anyways. Creeps
were everywhere.

Chloë's expression didn't flicker.

—That's cool. Almost done?

—Not quite. Still need to follow up on a few things. Half an
hour? Hour tops.

—Bring it to my place, and use my wireless to finish up. Then
we can hang out unless you have other plans.

Her sudden appearance was curious and disconcerting – found
like that in a city of millions – but it wasn't totally improbable:
MLK was a major thoroughfare, networking the city centres,
and the vintage Porsche was anything but low profile. But he
baulked at working from her home IP address, even with his
layered proxies. Even once. But the idea of her place, somewhere
near that coffee bar uptown. And the code hang out…

Chloë poked him in the ribs.

—Then let's go.

—'K. One sec.

He powered down, asking if he should follow in his car, the
face of his uncertainty, faced with too many buts. She jangled
her keys against a leather-cased keyless key fob–thing.

when a shower started somewhere down that uncharted passage, visions of her naked and wet rising in his mind like steam.

He was leading his past-schedule group chat when Chloë came back, dewy skin fresh and fair, her damp hair a bold slick of jet, threaded gold. She was sipping a drink twin to his own, wearing undercheek shorts and a grey tee – no bra – which proclaimed "J'AIME RODARTE".

—How's it going?

—Not done yet. Ten, fifteen minutes.

She turned back around, the bipolar "JE DÉTESTE RODARTE" behind. She refreshed his drink, then ferried in a comb, hair-brush, &c. all set down in a clatter next to his laptop.

—I'm going to fix your Professor Snape hair. It's been driving me nuts.

—Um, OK.

The chat was in English; Finn typed faster. She stepped onto the sofa, knelt beside him, and removed his ballcap, then she began combing the tangles from his chestnut-brown hair with forceful hands and less-than-infinite care.

—It's coming in nicely, but you need to condition. How long are you letting it grow out?

Far shorter than his longtime mother-enforced length, it was the longest his hair had been since he'd shaved his head the night of his unsweetened sixteenth: the day she'd gifted him a "first pair of heels!" But he'd found that a loose chin-length bob and ballcap were the best nondescript way to obscure his features in public, both from skulking CCTV and most of the greezy attentions that had followed his mother everywhere. A hoodie, worn up, invited scrutiny and suspicion, but a ballcap was everyman camo, long as you curved the bill.

—Uh, well, I meant to get it cut last week; it's getting a bit too…

He paused, trying to find a different word, but caught up in parallel conversations, he let it go:

—Girly. I've been drowning in work, but I'll go an' get it trimmed tomorrow before we go an' do whatever.

—Veto.

Chloë poked him in a ticklish spot.

—It needs to come down to here, at least.

—Chloë.

She resumed combing.

—Sorry, Baby Doll, but I used my veto power. Matter closed.

He tried and failed to respond, the shake of his head stilled as she pulled his hair back, tight, though too short for much of a ponytail or chignon – there went the bobby pins. He glanced back when her weight shifted behind him, her fingers guiding his chin.

—That profile, she said, that neck. You ought to be a ballerina.

He pulled his head away without comment and frowned back at his screen. Something he didn't want to talk about or even acknowledge. She reached around him for her drink, the ice clinking between clauses:

—You never talk about your exes. There must've been a special someone in Japan. You were there for years.

—Well...

Deserted by Senpai for her then-new fiancé, Finn had descended to the soiled street level of the gokudō underworld; far from the black cars and tailored suits of a head family, but nothing shameful among the Ōkumo-kai, their bovarist chivalry born in anomic crime. He couldn't have said then, watching the lights fly by on the half-hour express shinkansen to Ōsaka, whether he'd sought a surrogate for her; or if, as Camus proposed, he too had gone against the grain « par nostalgie d'un bien impossible. »

A cab had left him on the slummy fringe of Nishinari at a stairwell down to the notorious Tobita Shinchi. He'd wandered alone, ballcap pulled low, to a faded outpost of the floating world with its scarlet stairway-to-heaven and a young-old girl with a Genji name and dead eyes, her hime-cut hair an undyed, unrelieved black. He'd traded a fistful of yen for sham tea service and brokered consent, capping the night in a women-only capsule hôtel, passed out on a pink pillow with a half-bottle of Scotch, cold Turgenevean tears, and a trophæal lollipop; «slezy' xolodny'e» – cold tears – the only kind he knew.

—There was a girl I met in Ōsaka. Kaoru. We hooked up, but it didn't go anywhere.

—No one else? Nothing long distance?

—No.

Chloë traded her drained glass for his full one. He didn't

object. She put it back a moment later, down to ice, and placed her chilled fingers, damp with condensation, on his forearm – an insistent pressure. He looked back overshoulder.

—Chloë, I'm not…

Done was taken from the flush glisten of his lips, her arms closing about him; there was nothing else. Naught but the press and softness of her, the clean scent of her hair, her hands everywhere, devouring him, peeling and pushing away his defenses. He had nothing of her, as she had of him, locked between his and her crypticisms, corps à corps, and conjoined silences. It was a no-limit game of the unspoken, everything on the line.

Chloë drew him in like smoke, her fathomless eyes full of his enigma, lips in abeyance, mingling breath – an open-eyed kiss. She adjusted his Clark Kent glasses. Finn caught her hand and held it, interlacing his fingers with hers.

She led him down the long passage to her bedroom. He closed the door.

THE FALL,
IV.

★

I T WAS LIKE FLOATING, that moment of peace. Drifting together, he clung to her, linens up to his chin in the battle to stay under covers. Chloë rested her head on his shoulder, her fingers tracing aimless runes of intimacy on his skin, his inked arm benumbed by the pressure.

—I'm hungry. You?

—A little.

—I'll call the Chinese place. I think they're still open.

She shifted beside him, and the bedside lamp flared alight against his cattish blink. He allowed himself to enjoy the sight of her, mid-revelation, her théâtric semi-nude yawn oil portrait– worthy. She made an irritated sound.

—Where'd I leave my phone?

—Coffee table?

—How about yours?

—No effing idea.

Chloë coughed with a dry and raspy heave, and he envisioned her coal miner's lungs with an internal wince. She pulled a fresh stud from an old-fashioned soft pack – a relic of the Belle Époque's war-shaded gloam. Two sighful puffs, then she wrapped herself in the dressing gown that hung over her vanity seat: green florals on imperial-gold silk in a faux kimono cut, a sliver of white trim feigned an under-kimono's layered touch. She stepped into the en suite bath. He sat up, clutching the covers to himself.

—Do you have another robe?

—Nope. I guess you'll have to stay naked.

—That's not fair.

—It's always fair if I win.

Chloë reëntered the bedroom sans cigarette and, speaking in a captious tone that reminded him of his mother, picked up his boxers from the taupe area rug:

—And we're having a talk about these, Missy – after I get my phone. You can shower first. I'll be back.

She shuffled out en pantoufles, taking the boxers with her. He bolted for her garish bathroom, heavy on the pink quartz, then locked and tested the door. He fiddled with esoteric shower knobs till one side of the ceiling-inset double-rainfall began to pour, catching a sidelong glimpse of the misting mirror, of estranged eyes and the neotenous face that would never feel the razor's edge, of the faded cutting scars along the curve of one hip. He'd left anomic suicide to Mme Bovary – he'd gotten through it.

He pulled bobby pins from below the ballet bun Chloë had faked with a hair donut. Those days were over. A quick shower and he wrapped himself within a plush terry towel, damp hair clinging to his face. It took him a moment to locate his glasses, folded on the vanity among her designer cosmetics, his clothes gone missing in the brief interim. He found her tucked away in her corner home-office, seated behind a large, apple-prominent monitor, smoking a stud with her usual élan and Ginevra de' Benci's resting bitch-face.

—Hey you, she said. The food'll be here in thirty. I'm finishing up something for work. They left like ten messages on my voicemail.

—Ah, Saitō-han, where did…

—Omigod, I hate it when guys do that; it's so tacky.

—Chloë-han, what'd you do with my clothes?

Chloë responded in obstupefying German; it was all but Greek.

—That reminds me, he said to her boutade, is it s'posed to be Chloë or Kuroe?

—Chlo-e. E-e-e.

—So about my clothes…

More German. He h'mfed.

—I need to check my laptop. Think I left it on.

He turned to depart, but the glint of something golden caught his eye. He crouched, hugging his towel.

—Missing any jewellery?

—Not as far as I know. Did you find an earring?

Something small and cold met his fingertips underneath her barren bookstand and its precious floaty shelves, bringing forth a new mystery that also, oddly enough, reminded him of his mother.

—Not an earring. Did you take my advice and buy a gun?

—What?

The typing stuttered to a stop. Chloë came over, trailing smoke, and peered at the cartridge in the palm of his hand.

—What the fuck! Is that yours? Where's your little movie gun?

—It's in my bag. This isn't mine; this is completely different. Strange.

It was the same overall length as a 357 Magnum cartridge, the case head stamped "4.6×30", and tapered like a rifle round scaled down for Rats of NIMH–sized rifles, but it wasn't something from a children's tale. Chloë's sneer mingled contempt and disgust.

—It must've been left behind by the previous resident. Throw it in the trash.

—Don't think we can, since it's kind of an explosive, but don't worry, I'll google how to dispose of it safely.

The living room was as they'd left and forgotten it, except for his ballcap, missing in action. H'mf. He'd bought it – in person – at Kōshien.

He dropped the spoon-tip cartridge into the pencil pocket of his messenger bag, then sat before his idling laptop. On-screen, the OTR channel had evacuated as expected, with days of ground-work lost by the board, but his VPN client was offline against the unencrypted clear of Chloë's guest Wi-Fi, his darknet tunnels still connected like black pipes exposed to daylight. He ughed but went ahead and searched "4.6 mm", and the bottlenecked cartridge led him to the MP7: a little black sub-machine gun with bits that folded, extended, and screwed on like a trans-formable and accessorised toy. He shut down and folded – no reason to tell her.

☆

AND who's Vik?

—Friend of Trace's. Vik's a fan of my sleeve, but I live on the wrong side of the bridge for that set. Old money, new money, legacies… You know more about that than I do. I've met a few of them since they stop and say hi to Trace at the tavern sometimes while she's working. She's down to earth most of the time, but her boyfriend's a big-deal football player for the university; it all ties back to him. Get involved with one, and you're in a different world, I guess. She's a completely different person around him.

Finn had turned away the first time he'd seen them together at the tavern, talking but close, overcome by a feeling he could only call *murder*. Chloë offered him his bleeping Galaxy.

—Here; take your ginormous phone. You have a text.

Not Vik but Trace.

—O, she's bartending. Says it's totally dead, and that I should come hang out.

—Tell her we'll stop by. Then come shower.

—I'll need to stop at my place again and feed my cat.

Chloë walked to the bathroom au natural – a come-hithery look overshoulder – giving him the full backside view of her skiing scar, the front welled like a second navel. She was down one kidney, through-smitten by a broken ski pole after a high-speed crash; it might've resembled a through-and-through gunshot wound, though her caste served nowhere near the front lines of war. He replied to Trace, beside the detritus of break-fast-in-bed, then hesitated before the billowing steam. Chloë was impossible. He'd let her go too far too fast, and holding the covers to himself now was a reflex, vain in the aftermath. He could've fought back harder, but she'd seen it all. He could've, but he took a gulp of air and stood in his natal guise, struggle fissuring his brow, and entered.

Blotting her dark hair dry, she led him back out, then sat him at her vanity, towel-rapt up to his new armpits, his ravisht skin tingling, newborn. No blaming the tequila this time.

She was shaving her legs when he'd stepped in but had placed the razor in his hand, guiding it over her; then, again in her grasp, she'd turned the tables. He hadn't pushed back – in the moment, didn't think to. Plenty of guys shaved or waxed below the neck, because reasons, but it was one of those things. He'd worn tights beneath his uniform skirts rather than get bullied into shaving his legs during high school. She plucked his nevers like petals.

Chloë took him Spanish doll after the blow-dry, his hair centre-parted and slicked back into a stub ponytail, lacking a doll's proper length. She reminded him to let it grow and began talking make-up:

—You'd be so Adriana with smoky eye shadow and…

For once, his refusal brooked no further argument, bullying, or brute force; so too the softer offer of hoop earrings. He reclaimed his eyeglasses and sat at the edge of her low-slung platform bed,

his clothes yet unaccounted for – he'd stopped asking. She took his place, her voice dropping in-and-out with the blow dryer:
—But seriously, you should come to the gym even though you have zero cellulite. Sure, you might keep that ballerina figure forever, eating cheeseburgers, but then you might not. My ᴋᴍ instructor isn't taking on newbies right now, but you'd need CrossFit first to get ready; it's full contact. So in six months…

Chloë lit a cigarette after finishing her half-up, half-down hair and her make-up; then, she fished through her dresser and proffered something red and lacy. He stated the obvious:
—Panties.
—Unless you'd rather go commando. That might feel strange if this is…
—Anything plain white?
—Nope.

He gulped air.
—Fine.
—And you need a real bra. We're about the same size, but…
—What happened to my sports bra? It wasn't cheap, you know, like the rest of my clothes?
—And like the rest of your clothes, it wasn't doing you any favours. Here. Yours are perkier, and a bralette will highlight your natural talents. Try it on, and let me see.

He frowned at the limp, filmy fabric.
—Hell no.
—Would you rather bounce your chin off them in a push-up and chicken cutlets? Either way, I'll tickle you till you give in.
—Chloë, that's cheating.
—It's not cheating if I win.
—Noticing a trend here.

Chloë pulled him and the de facto red bikini into her capacious walk-in closet. She handed him "Phantoms" in the form of skinny jeans, and he bounced his way in with ample curses and aggravation when his behind hung, then rolled cuffs from the excess length. "It's what you always wear," she'd claimed a few different ways, but the white tee resembled a handkerchief – label size xs, women's – in hand. She promised the red bra wouldn't show through; she was right, but there was shape everywhere. Everything. He lifted her black café racer's jacket and zipped himself in. She made a face but let it pass, smirking. Why not?

She'd won. She went preppy casual, light on the bling, in a striped marinière, chinos, double G loafers – and on their way out, his varsity jacket – her perfume walkthrough lofted from a blue glass bottle, signature brand.

Fresh off of her matutinal caffeine stack, she drove him home, then mid-town, with peak intensity. He relaxed into it, watching someone else play a video game, till she parked the Aston Martin like an F1 pilot hitting her marks in the pits, the G-forces little different from a car crash. On the other side of a wrought iron fence, the storied 19th-century university campus lay Sunday dormant, but the breezy November day felt more Eastertide than autumnal ebb, the wind scented with beginnings. She slipped her hand into his.

—So where is it exactly?

—There: on that corner across the street. Sometimes I sit on the patio on the other side. This might be the last good day for that this year, but my cigar case is in my glove box.

He held the door for Chloë, per usual. Lifting her sunglasses, she stopped short in front of him, her hushed voice overshoulder:

—Heol, hold on. That's Trace?

—The tall one, yeah. Let me introduce...

—How's she not doing Victoria's Secret?

—She's pre-med. A senior. Don't mention modelling; she's sick of people telling her that.

Leant back against the ice bin in her bejeaned lean, Trace was Vermeer-lit by the passthrough patio window, head bowed and double thumbing her phone, her wavy blonde hair tied back. One regular sat at the bar, bar-code comb-over, half a beer. The dark wood tables and booths were bleary with a few late-woken hangovers, the pea-green walls and dark Georgian cabinetry defaced by scaly banks of flatscreens, ESPN muted for the standard nineties 'n' noughties rock playlist – "Iris" for the hundredth time. A lone waitress, red of hair, called out a good morning; Finn was semi-surprised to see Alex again. Most new girls didn't last between the fuckboys and the pickup-book clowns.

Trace cheerleader-waved and came out from behind the bar in bounding strides, Alice-blue hoody unzipped. She was all warmth in her air of strawberry sorbet: big hug, big smile, big crystal-blue eyes. She shook hands with Chloë on naming and explained her bootleg "Lijntje" tee of Miffy doing lines. Trace sat them at the bar, well away from the silvering not-a-fox, then set branded coasters before them, on script in her postcolonial girls' school English:

—What can I get started for you two? Four Roses and?

Chloë shook her head, holding two fingers up in literal victory.

—Patrón shots.

Trace looked to Finn, and he consented with a canted shrug. She prepped the pour.

—This new look, Poppie. I almost didn't recognise you. How long have I been trying to give you a makeover?

—I didn't agree. She stole my clothes.

Chloë raised a finger, but Trace slid the shot glasses over. Chloë lifted hers.

—I helped her out a little.

He touched his to hers and swallowed.

—Everything I'm wearing is hers. Jacket too.

—Not anymore. Those are yours now.

—Chloë, the jacket, at least, is…

—No; it looks better on you, and leather is in right now.

—You just want to keep my Acronym jacket, don't you?

She motioned for a second round.

—It looks better on me, and varsity is in right now.

Trace filled fresh shot glasses and caught his hand when he reached for his.

—And you did your nails.

—She got me drunk and took advantage of me.

Trace's full mouth quirked, but she excused herself and attended to the empty beer glass at the other end of the bar. Shots down, Chloë lowered her sunglasses.

—I need a smoke. Let's go outside.

The sidewalk patio and side-street sidewalk were empty. She lit a hard-man cig and handed it to him, then lit another for herself and checked her phone. The first hit was a rib-creaking punch in the sternum – from the inside out – and fire-safe acrid; a fragrant far cry from the memory of Senpai's silken Seven's. A habit he'd picked up then dropped for Cuban puros. No BS embargo in Japan. Chloë exhaled her first puff, cool as a wartime cigarette ad.

—Did you hook up?

—Trace and me? No.

Chloë spat a bit of tobacco flake with the heedless swag of an Old Hollywood gunslinger.

—It's OK to tell me. I'm not jealous like that, and it's obvious there's something. Or was.

—Not with me.

—But she likes girls?

—She had a girlfriend a couple years ago, but I already told you about the guy she's with now. They've been together since before I started coming here.

—But you've hung out.

—Sometimes, she drinks with me after her shift. Not like you mean.

—Ever been to her place?

—Once, but she got wasted, and I had to get her home safe.

—H'm.

Trace swung back to them, a dramatic eyebrow for him.

—Cigarettes now?

—I have so many bad habits they have to take turns.

Chloë squeezed his leg and asked her,

—How long have you been engaged?

Trace folded her arms on the patio bar-top, thumbing the ring in question.

—Yeah, no; it's fake. I only wear it tending bar.

He turned an impatient shade of green as twenty questions doubled, then redoubled, rehashing all he'd heard about life in and around Pietermaritzburg, plus appendices – followed by the full lowdown on Brad, the exclusive nightlife of the university's jeunesse dorée, and old snaps of Trace's ex. She'd humblebragged about Hayley now and again, lingering over selfies with her Bardotesque reflexion, but Trace had left her phone with him one of those times – twice called to pour drinks – and the duckfaced slide show had turned NSFW with a flick of his thumb. He'd set her phone down after a few flushed and uneasy minutes, unsure if he should feel guilty or not.

—But we can get a group together, Chloë was saying, and go shopping uptown. Her closet is all saggy skater boy, so the intervention isn't over by any means. You mentioned Vik and Sam, anyone else?

He came to at "skater boy". A red alert.

—Shopping? What for? I'm not gonna replace my whole wardrobe like you keep talking.

Her visored smile was unperturbed.

—Let's discuss it at home, Baby Doll.

She returned to her conversation, a reining hand at rest on his thigh; it recalled his shaved skin and her denim. Irreversible.

C·P·SERRET,
DIE THE VILLAIN.

THE FALL,
V.
★

T WAS A MASSACRE – a silent horror film.
He'd spent the last few days in randomised impresario's
chairs, directing the players on his virtualised stage:
from the initial wave of spear-phishing ploys to the decisive twist
of a stiffly priced, if non-exclusive, zero-day golden key. He'd
pulled it together after losing his hand-picked first string to that
dead chat. Everyone was skittish in the dark – skittish, stupid, or
agents – but it had queered a high-return play on a hard target.

Chloë had cancelled their Thanksgiving Day plans on short
notice last week and winged her way across the Atlantic, warning
she'd be too busy to stay in touch. The Hawks had wrapped up
the Japan Series that Sunday as well, leaving him to face another
turkey day at a table-for-one in the post-season lull. He'd regathered himself, closing out two other jobs without a hitch, then
picked a second string from the available talent, with more hands
to compensate, at a higher cost, but he'd pulled them together.
He would get the effing chip.

She got back yesterday, but he wouldn't see her till tomorrow;
and then, he foresaw and dreaded, they wouldn't be alone. In with
Vik's set – through Trace – Chloë had new connexions in the club
scene; she dangled it in front of him: lots of carrot, a little stick.
He was right where she wanted – would be, tomorrow – caught
in a sequence of forced moves; she was five steps ahead. Next,
her club scene and then? Learn more German?

He'd slouched behind the stochastic proxy-chain that dis-
placed his IP address to Pyatigórsk rather than this pretentious
American coffee house, his hair slicked back, wet-look, pending
the promised return of his ballcap "Soon." One jaded eye on the
OTR channel, the afternoon dragged into overtime and out of
current articles at Intelligence Online, till, —SUM1Z breaking in!!!

He jolted upright, the tedious scrawl of prickly banter, ASCII
goatse.cx, and kaomoji fragmenting into messages of alarm and a
flight of disconnects from the backdoored server. His fingertips

play pwned too or tipped to the Feds? – Whitey Bulger did it best. Eff it; let 'em founder. It wouldn't affect his pseudonymous stakes in Bitcoin-mining ASIC farms, nor the black money accrued in gnomish vaults offshore. "Yanagi ni kaze" – a willow in the wind.

He had but to say yes to what Chloë wanted, and she'd take him away from it all. Step across the threshold of her waiting corporation, and it was done. This would all be a bad dream. But he could never forget the cortisol-poisoned stress of his tieless dark-suit days amid the rigid and counterproductive ossan rules of corporate Japan – or the mandatory kitten heels. The proffered rôle of on-call executive handmaiden, uniformed for the Zamyátinian cubicles of corporate USA, was everything he'd already walked away from. No; he would only go straight on his terms, but even that savoured of defeat, too bitter to swallow. His life would never be the same. His life. His sir.

He circled through the genericised city's universal Gothamic bleak in Ulyssean avoidance of home, of responsibility, of con-sequence, his senses bludgeoned by brutalist concrete and Koolhaas's lamentated "triumph of glue". Finn cycled through the gears, listening to engine revs rise and fall, until muscle memory parked him at his habitual purlieu, unpremeditated. "Kaizoku wa nakanai" – Senpai's parting phrase; he cut the engine and dried his face, a mote in his eye.

NFL 2011 in full swing, the tavern thundered with shouty voices and talking heads in the prelude to Thursday night's face-off. He spotted a free seat at the bar but had to squeeze past a cluster of juiced guys in their post-jock faded glory, douchey tattoo tees visible beneath open jackets, wraparound sunglasses behind bullish necks – "Dyke" muttered at his back. Proud mutilés of the real man's Procrustean bed; in lost promise, become Caliban.

Finn unzipped leather, an itch between his shoulder blades – a new target stuck to his back. He didn't bother sitting. He'd no desire to endure their sorts' tag-teamed get some! validation, should they catch him alone. One deoch an dorais, then out; the gun was purse-holstered in his messenger bag. It would have to be his last call, here, decloaked of shapeless clothes and ballcap.

He'd spent an afternoon in front of the mirror, switching between Chloë's vapour-thin low-rise jeans and the hefty pile of men's selvedge he'd brought from Japan, cursing himself for an amadán; but then, cherchez la femme. Koko had observed but declined to comment, and he'd reached a foregone decision without her aid. He'd found it strange and uncomfortable at first: shopping to the shape and size of his Balanchine build for more Phantoms and a suite of fitted band tees, "like you always wear" in Chloë's mental tones. But she'd scalded him with approval for days after – and spent the weekend at his place before departure. Now it was all warm fuzzies when he squeezed in; besides, it's what he always wore, as she'd said. Sort of. And the bodycon refit had raised a sea of blue eyes, immersing him in female gazes.

Ashley – small, dark, and sweltry – was behind the bar, pouring drinks with a fury. No Trace. Ashley spared him a half-second glance.

—Four Roses?

He shook his head, uncoiling the vicuña he'd rewound around his throat. He held up four fingers.

—Shots. Jack.

She lined up a quatrain of shot glasses, poured them all in one motion, and slid them over, amber stacks of casino chips. Finn put them down rapid-fire, like smashing charcoal-filtered Molotov cocktails over his head, and started at a familiar female shout near by:

—Poppietjie!

Long arms closed about him, clasping him in puffy-sleeved strawberry 'n' spice. Trace released and stood over him, so tall, red-zippered mint-cream jacket open, fant'sy City Bag shouldered; she'd clocked out. He pushed the empty glasses back across the bar like a bet: all in. He split four more with her, the D-branes of spacetime smearing under a flood of solvent, superstrings uncurled. She squeezed his arm.

—Let's go someplace else. Kom, kom.

A fistful of sheaved bills. She held his hand through the crowd. He said something, lost in the din; it slipped away from him, "there's something."

A pub somewhere – the blush and bluey neon hues of beer signage. Trace smiling, laughing into him.

More shots. City lights. Inane, drunkworld giggles.

The dark back seat of a cab, holding hands in his lap.

Her plush lips, hot breath.

THE FALL,
VI.

★

OLDFOILED NIGHT rattled thundrous, black 'n' blue from
G the milk-misted basin below to the transmontane shore. A
fox stood aloof in the storm's path, seven tails fluttering behind him like sashimono, his splendent eyes cast upward – searching,
seeking – his red fur fluffed against the cold.

The rain marched forward: a shower of icy spears driven sideways
by the fierce gale, and the air became as sea: a vortex of bitter currents.
The fox retreated one step, certain but struggling to see.

There – at the highest reaches – swimming among the splashes of
light, a dragon. It's serpentine form rippled, coiled, and flowed, a myriad
scales of beaten silver, one with the chaos.

The storm-battered fox flew faster than wind or rain. A shadow fell
across him – washed away in a blinding flare. A girl stumbled beneath
the growing darkness, black hair and bright kimono sodden; she cried
out, seven tails covering her face.

☆

TRACE was out: steady breath, cheeks rouged, her lipstick eraser-
smudgy: from Lichtenstein's *Seductive Girl* to *Sleeping Girl*, the
morning after. Finn sat up, and a wave of light-headedness
quaked the room and dusty streams of curtained sun. He perched
at the edge of the mattress, fallen Smurf plushies at his feet, surprised to find his glasses folded at bedside – "there's something"
recalled again to the castaway, marooned amid IKEA furniture, a
wrack of books and clothes on the floor, desk, and bookshelves.
The room was a little warm, even for him – even naked.

He looked back at the drowsing girl from a sleepy hollow; of
the founding, self-romanticised Voortrekkers from once-upon-
a-time, nostalgic for "die lekker lewe, the good life," she'd explained. Her family had survived scorched earth and the British
concentration camps a handful of years after Spain created the
first campos de «reconcentración» in Cuba – Marqués Weyler's

final solution to insurgency adopted by all colonial powers, even against other colonials. Her family had survived, but tens of thousands of women and children had not. She'd shown him photos of their sizeable small-holding, sun-worn quaintness offset by a Stålenhagian farm machine menacing some stray sheep. An abbreviated knock preceded the bedroom door's abrupt swing and a familiar female voice:

—Hey, Trace…

He yanked a bedsheet across his twice-pwned skin a moment late. Make that thrice. Megan stopped at the threshold but didn't shut the door.

—Oops, sorry, Finn. Thought it was… Nevermind.

He'd grilled her once, her tanless golden-brown skin darker than his, but she'd proved a Euromutt with no particular explanation. Coltish slim, she was au courant in yoga leggings and a stretch hoody, half-zipped, her dark brown hair bound up. One of three or four girls from the college bar scene that rented this house together with Trace.

—But let her know it's like eleven? She might need to go.

Megan closed the door, which crept ajar. Straight ones on Trace's alarm clock, he reversed course and shook her till she stirred, groaning in sleepy protest, then brushed loose blonde locks from her face, her eyes half-lidded, an instant smile. One hand moved around his waist.

—Hoesit, Poppie?

—It's past eleven. Do you… ?

—Ja, no; it's my day off and no class till one. Kom back to bed.

Trace pulled him beneath the eiderdown, into the raw intimacy of morning breath and suaveolent skin, her eyes, up close, belladonna wide and the vivid hue of the highveld's noontide sky – but a little puffy, with a few tired lines. They passed a snuggly hour, her hands fluent in the language his were learning, and it was past noon when they made it there and back again from the shower. He followed the Venusian dimples above her towel's bumster sag, then shut the bedroom door against furtive peeks and snickers from down the hall; the lock clicked in hand.

She checked her phone and fired up her blow dryer. He searched for and recovered his jeans and boxers; his new black Zeppelin tee, fallen Apollo, faked distress; and his compression bra, churned with the bedsheet. She began applying her make-up, her dry hair twisted up into two peculiar knots. He checked his texts; there was nothing new, and that was troubling, but he wasn't sure why. Nor was there a pageant of FBI or other police arrests on the newswires. No

APHID GRIN STILL AT LARGE.

Whatever had happened hadn't officially happened, as expected. Local murders and abductions weren't international news – even if they used breaching charges to get to you.

He could hire someone to follow the digital money, to trace the connexions around ████████Mgt, but that would leave a new trail of breadcrumbs for their counterintel, and it wasn't hard to google the pasty billionaire fund manager's bulging eyes and shit-eating grin.

A warning grin. This – this – was the most dangerous moment, with the highest risk of a critical mistake: Panic. Start moving money. Start crossing borders.

Predators watched for movement, and camo only worked when you didn't give yourself away. If they'd had Finn's position, if they'd pierced the black curtain, he'd've been taken. Killed.

Grit your teeth and hold still. Fade into the background; fall off their active threats list. PMCs and counterintel weren't cheap, and even deep pockets weren't bottomless.

He joined Trace at the dresser mirror, Smurf figurines cavorting among her cosmetics and a bottle of Miss Dior Chérie. She glanced at his wildblown reflexion.

—You have Heathcliff hair.

—You should read something besides the Brontës someday.

—Gaan kak. Did you want to put your face on now, or does Chloë have something special planned?

—My face?

—Ja, ja; for when we meet uptown. Four, né? I'm going straight there after class.

—O shit.

—You forgot.

—Yeah. That is today. Damn.

He'd slipped the noose – and his moment to die the villain – to fall right back into Chloë's design. But he wouldn't sit at home another night, knowing she was out with Trace, Vik, &

al., clubbing, &c. surrounded by drinking Chads. The girls had showered Finn with drunkworld selfies, and he couldn't read – couldn't relax – or listen to music; his stomach churned sour. He was cornered. Trace turned at his silence.

—You can use anything of mine. I've got a metric ton of MAC and…

—I'm no good at putting it on. Could you, after you finish yours? Unless you'll be late.

Her big smile and hand wavery were no comfort.

—Whatever, whatever; I can be late for that.

She wheeled over the desk chair. He sat, less than thrilled but moisturised on command. Soldiers painted their faces to blend in. Was it cosplay or war? What lengths.

Trace finished drying his hair and clipped it back. She put on the secret-identity glasses she rarely wore in public, set his aside, then placed him under the visagiste's microscope. "'What big eyes you have.' Can I steal your eyelashes?"

"Please do." Girls always swooned – or turned green – over his doubled rows.

She traced the contours of his brow, cheekbones, and jawline with her fingers.

—Eyebrows threaded?

He was unsure what that entailed, but envisioning something horrifically surgical, he replied negative. She lifted his chin.

—Never let anyone touch them, Poppie. Like ever.

An easy promise to make after the trauma of his mother's ruthless tweezing. He twitched at the memory, and it was difficult to relax while Trace brushed, dabbed, and blended. His phone rang – Chloë. He jumped the explanation before she finished asking where he was.

—Getting my face done at a make-up counter.

—O, OK. I was going to…

She confirmed it was on, that everyone was in for his humiliation – if not in those words. He made ambivalent sounds of consent at her pauses, then hit End: she was leaving early to help him "get ready" and would meet him at his place within the hour. Trace waited till he dropped the phone to his lap, lip brush poised like a conductor's baton.

—Is everything alright?

—It's fine.

She drew a cool line along his upper lip.

—This rosebud mouth. You should've been a movie star in the twenties like Clara Bow – ô, I took an elective on silent film and social class last spring semester. I should have one of the books around here somewhere.

Trace capped the lipstick tube with an illusionist's flourish and told him to take a look. She moved behind him, framing his reflexion.

—I'd give you flapper's hair, but I haven't 'n iron in the right size. They used quite narrow ones back then, but if you went with a boyish cut, you wouldn't even need to curl it. Or a Dutch bob with a fringe like Louise Brooks. See, if you trim it here and…

He expected a shock but felt nothing, seeing not with his own eyes, for others looked through his; a Baxtínian phoropter for Chloë, Trace, and his mother: flip-flip-flip. He grasped, at last, his mother's distress, for the mirror held the face of an-other: the daughter she'd always believed in – a catechism of her faith – and for whom she still waited in vain. A sadness settled deep in his chest, heavy as iron. Trace squeezed his shoulder.

—You don't like it?

—No, I do. Just thought of something.

—Then all you need now is contacts.

—Says the girl wearing glasses.

—I slept in my contacts. Your fault, by the way.

—That's why I don't like contacts. They're a pain.

—They'd be better for your new look.

—I don't have a look.

—You will after tonight.

Trace unknotted her hair and shook it free into tousled perfection. A magic trick.

—Are you gonna dress? he asked. Or is it terry-cloth chic for today?

She swore something in Afrikaans he hadn't heard before and told him to ask Megan or someone else for a lift "now, now" if still around, both cars abandoned along their pub crawl. Trace pivoted to her closet, ignoring the carpet of clothing beneath her feet. He shrugged into his café racer but didn't find the scarf. She pulled out a pair of jeans, then put it back.

—I don't know how you wear that thin jacket; dis bitter koud buite.

—I have something warmer, but it's bulky. I'll find Megan.

He knocked on all the doors and called a cab, no sign of Megan or anyone else downstairs but for the modest flatscreen playing *the Kardashians* to a spare living room bolstered with lawn chairs. He sank into the sofa – cut to "Kim's House"; and caught up in a parallel reality, he snapped to at a *honk!* from outside. A call of "Coming!" from upstairs, he opened the front door on the residential gloom, south side: gaunt trees; a sidewalk light with litter and fallen leaves; and an ostensively hybrid neon-lime cab, double-parked. Double *honk!*

Finn waved, footfalls heavy behind him – a hummingbird darted from the shaggy hedge on blurred wings. H'mf. Kind of nosy.

THE FALL,
VII.

★

CHLOË SPREAD FIVE BUNDLES of 500-euro notes – a purple poker hand – poker-faced.
—Five straps of Bin Ladens. Why's there a quarter-million euros stashed under your Asian-girl porn?

She'd arrived, not Friday casual but dolled to the nines: a little black dress and choker of black pearls beneath her grey officer's cape coat, updo mussed with precision, glam gradient lip. He'd been distracted. She'd moved with purpose, straight to her target: his ishō-tansu emptied onto the tatami, and his closet spilt out, back to that short box – the one he'd meant to do something about. Disembodied by palpitations, he heard himself say,
—They made me exchange my jar of punts.
—Cris.
—It's money I set aside for business trips.
—Uh-huh.
—Well, um, you know American banks won't deposit foreign currencies the way EU banks will, and you lose something on every exchange; so I, uh, keep some euros in the closet. In case.

Chloe set the cash aside atop old copies of *Bejean* and other contraband she'd leafed through and stacked beside a 500-gram bar of CCCP-stamped gold – microfissures of doubt around her eyes and mouth the visible strain in her façade. That fractional slump of her shoulder line, the downward modulation of her tone; she knew every word was a lie.
—We'll need to work on your caching skills. Thieves go straight for the bedroom closet.
—So I noticed.

He was sitting on a dead man's hand of two fake passports he'd stowed beneath his socks. His most recent purchases hung above the heaping Goodwill mound of his recently disused clothes: those judged and found wanting. His feelings roiled over the jumbled pile, "Utsusemi no | Mi o kaetekeru ...", but he drew a blank on the rest of the Heian verse, his tumbler beading dew on the tatami, down to limy ice. Koko nosed about near his gutted closet, then paused for an urgent bath. Chloë brushed her hands together with overt symbolism.

—Let's get some garbage bags and put everything in my trunk. I want to wrap this up before I fix your hair.

A prepaid candy bar phone in the dresser valet gave a dated chirrup beside his cigar guillotine, lighter, and loose change. Shit – worst possible timing. He lunged to his feet, his already laboured heart athrob, and, saying he had to take this, rushed the landing.

—Hai?

Foxes couldn't say *moshi* after all. Chloë followed him out but descended the stairs. He stood on the ledge, gripping the old black walnut balustrade that curved down along the stairwell; caught between two worlds, he listened to a go-between convey urgent word from Ane-san – he'd been offline all day. Shit. Aphid Grin was flaming out.

Chloë returned, creased garbage bags in hand. She stuffed one with gusto, and he turned away from her, from Ane-san, from the dying of his light. The long call ended with a deep sigh, and he pulled the battery and SIM without powering down. He started: Chloë was waiting in the bedroom doorway a few feet away, one hand behind her back. The façade shattered.

—What the fuck is going on?

—What? That was a friend from Japan.

—You're a shitty liar, Baby Doll.

Chloë dropped the fake passports at his feet.

—What are you mixed up in, drugs? Don't! fucking! lie to me!

Her vehemence pushed him back against the railing, and two days tumults washed over him: shipwreck 'n' storm and stranger shores. He found himself standing in sand without words; awash a wave of tiredness, he wavered under the strain and floundered.

—You can't shrug everything away, she said. We don't have a relationship if you aren't willing to talk to me.

He hesitated. He'd sidestepped her after-dinner-drinks questions about work for weeks – if with less finesse than she did his – and squeaked through her attempts at sleep interrogation. All to stave off this moment, but now she suspected the worst. Checkmate.

—It's a long story.

—Then start now.

He led her back down and battered a week of dust and cat hair from the sofa. They sat at either end, parted by a 3-D print of Redon's drowned Ophélie. He focused on his slim hands for a long moment. Hands that never let him forget himself.

—Not sure where to start.

—The cash and the gold?

—Retainers from a couple of my logistics clients.

Laundering money into the U. S. was much easier than getting it out, so he'd stuck it all in the box, deferring a solution till later. A time bomb. Chloë's tone remained flinty:

—Those Russians? Bin Ladens and looted Soviet gold look dirty.

—Every business is dirty.

—Not that dirty. What about your friends? Who else is involved: Vik? Her father is…

—No one. Like I said: one-man show.

—Taylor asked about you.

—Taylor?

—A little taller than me, deep tan, blue eyes, a little plasticky.

He recalled a fearful symmetry.

—O, right. Dunno. She stopped in at the tavern a couple times to see Trace. For some reason, I get her name mixed up. I thought it was…

—Go back then. Start at the beginning.

—Well, h'm, I met my friend Miyuki in freshman year at Shindai, and…

—Shindai?

—Kōbe University. My alma mater. I mentioned it before.

—Back up: why'd you go all the way to Japan in the first place?

—That's an extra-long story, but I started taking Japanese after school during junior high. I was into anime and manga since forever. It was all I had outside school and…

The shōnen lives in manga had been his getaway, the only escape other than running or death, and running led to things worse than death. Manga, then the books beyond schoolbooks, then music. He'd gotten through it.

—Guess I was kind of a weeb, if you know what that is, but once I was in high school and started thinking about college, it occurred to me that I should start over someplace else. On my own. That's when I started prepping for the foreign student exams. There was extra red tape 'cause I was too young for a student visa, and my parents argued about it for months while the special exception BS processed, but my mother couldn't accept me the way I was – the way that I am. They footed most of the bill to send me to Shindai, scholarships aside, so I'm not gonna complain now. It took some time, but in the end, they let me leave.

A sepia-shaded scene: the mother hadn't gotten angry at the boy when he'd insisted on going away. Nor did the mother strike the boy when he'd refused his confirmation. She would stare at him and his regrowing Sinéad hair, then walk out of his room, those last few months on loop. Chloë broke into his recollections:
—If it all started in Japan, then it had to be the yakuza, right? But how'd that happen? You're not Japanese or Korean.
—Well, I'd registered a Japanese alias on my gaijin card – my alien's ID – from day one, and the other international students thought that was weird. I didn't gel with them at all, but I think that's why Miyuki, my friend, noticed me; why she took me under her wing even though she and her friends were older than I was. She's the one that got me into baseball; she's a Tigers fanatic. We'd all hang out in the "kawaii" shops and cafés in Motomachi and on holidays in Ōsaka and Kyōto. That's when I met her family; when I realised who – and what – they were.
—Yakuza. So you joined them.
—First, they don't call themselves that – least not the ones I knew in Kansai – and I couldn't join. Not even if that's what I'd wanted; it's men only. To really get into it…

He gave Chloë the cram-school intro to the gokudō – each word savouring of unlightened bitterness – and she listened with rapt attention, asking few clarifying questions: a Dantean descent into his underworld. He laid it out like an SEC filing:
—The harsh reality, he was saying, is that double-X chromosomes make you a commodity like a cow or pig. A lot of their wives and girlfriends were – or are – prostitutes or hostesses or run fronts for the syndicate. Sure, some are average everyday women that happened to get involved with gokudō, but Miyuki-sempai kept me out of sight all the same. Her mother was geiko-han but retired to marry…
—Geiko-han?
—The geisha of Kyōto. She's the one that pulled me in on the sly before I graduated from Shindai, but she encouraged me to

go on to B-school as I'd planned. You can't just live off of the syndicate. Everyone has to have a legitimate position: a public face. I bet she thought it would be useful to have an insider at some big Japanese corporation. I enrolled at Kyōdai and moved to Kyōto.

The ane-san had been curt with him, calling him *bōya* – for the selfsame clothes now stuffed in garbage bags – or *kitsune*, offhand, all while chiding him into the most proper Kyōtoïte usage; reformed Ōsakan yanki roots deep below her flower-and-willow-world cultivation. Not that there'd been any point in him speaking like maiko; the affectation had stuck.

A woman living art, ever impeccable in her Lanvin or Balenciaga, she'd drawn him behind the black curtain and into the sordid inner workings of the syndicate, his academe-think recalibrating to the new paradigm. Extortion and carding were two principal revenue streams, and he'd liaised between her and offshore coders of fortune: those with the illicit tools and flimflam confidence needed to crack the corporate shadownet within the unsounded deep. She'd had a broader vision for the Ōkumo-kai, driving their outsource trend amid falling membership and increased legal pressures.

She'd allowed him to address her as *Ane-han*, out of the men's hearing, but she wouldn't drink sake with him, even in his watershed moment; his coming forth by day: arm ensleeved, sakazuki dry. *Ihōjin* – the stranger – among Japan's outsiders, it was his faceless online cohort that had accepted him as a man, by default, for the first time in his life. That crushing pressure easing ever so slightly, he could breathe as *Aphid Grin*.

—When she first met me, Miyu-sempai's mother told her a fox had followed her home. I still don't get why. Miyu had the kitsune-gao – one of those foxy faces, like you have – not me.

But the irezumi artist had seen it, too; that lean, grizzled man with the sinewed forearms of a Shaolin monk and Daruma's stare. He'd had the inks ritually purified at the temple of Inari in Fushimi, just for Finn's sleeve.

—It's in the eyes, answered Chloë. Did they send you back here for some reason? I thought you'd planned to emigrate.

—I got fed up pretty quickly with my day job at Yoshinori so I left after Miyu got married. The work visa rules there are restrictive, and I couldn't do what I'm doing here, independently, so…

mouth; the spitting image of a certain celebrated actress, which he'd noted aloud to her visible chagrin the first time he'd met her, fresh off her summer internship at L'Officiel. They hadn't spoken again till the day she'd spotted his sleeve – and then he couldn't pry her off.

The gathered party dispersed, with Trace a step ahead at the shoe display. He turned to Chloë.

—And my rôle in this scene?

—You can't be trusted. Get thee to a dressing room.

He sat, cornered within an overbright stall and deep within his mother's shadow, the part-English "Cry Cry" stuck in his head. She'd tried to bind them in her massclusive fast-fashion chains: his father pushed and pulled, mulish; his younger brother, Pablo Mánús, caring for naught in this world, sackcloth or silk. Finn had retreated behind the regulation skirts of Catholic school – Black Watch his prison orange. Posed thus for a time, a petit-bourgeois portrait within her have-it-all frame, blind to the craquelure of the canvas crumbling before her till the upwardly mobile illusion came full stop: her secondborn son to the Church; the abjected other fleeing, forever lost. Finn had disembarked at Kansai International, still shod in Mary Janes and tights, his mother's epiphanies left behind, hanging unworn with tags attached, alongside the Sunday Best she'd forced him into for Easter duty – a wooden spoon across the palm for any cheek.

Chloë stepped into his musings, her arms draped with layers of fabric, a subdued rainbow in shades of black. Where his mother and Senpai had failed, this girl… But it was a limited concession and temporary at that: only for the club scene and Chloë should leave it behind sooner than later – real-life already forcing her hand. Whether cosplay or war, it would be over ere long. He clung to that. She spared him a glance, sorting outfits.

—Why are you still dressed? Everything off, we're starting with a whole new foundation.

He'd numbed himself with an extra drink before they'd departed – she'd driven – and felt nothing within the first proposed look; she was looking at someone else. She guided him out to where the girls compared, contrasted, and opined, but Kristi was wide-eyed at the sight of his irezumi.

—Shit; that looks like a real yakuza tattoo, except that you have all of your fingers.

He cringed at her American pronunciation of *yakuza*.

—Well, you could call it gokudō-style, but it's a traditional tebori sleeve. Done by an artist in Kyōto.

—Gokudō?

—O, sorry. Local term for yakuza in the region of Japan where I went to college.

—Yeah, I know Chinese, but I didn't pick up much Japanese as a kid. My mom is still after me to learn more.

—I know how that is.

Two more outfits left him a doll quarrelled over at a girls' playdate, caught in a tug-of-war between Chloë and Vik – the latter filibustering anything that covered his ink. He surrendered his charge card, signing on command, then his captors escorted him outside and into another uptown fane, rich-mantled mannequins like headless idols. The scene repeated itself.

Trace found a red beaded dress at the third boutique; she held it up like the golden fleece: a midi sheath with a deep V-neck. Spanish doll again. He was nonplussed.

—What the hell is that? I'm not Jessica Rabbit.

Chloë took up the banner.

—Please? It's an Elie Saab. You have to try it on.

He huffed but claimed it with a resigned scowl; if not this, then some other. He expelled them both from the dressing room stall and bared himself down to the new foundation. He slipped in and zipped up, then strode out in his untied Visvims through an opaque labyrinth of electronically frosted glass. The girls were talking and texting among themselves, and he presented himself before a tripartite window of appearances for one heart's beat, facing the painted mask in Trace's mirror – from that very morn, so long ago. Vik went ô! and then the dogpile.

The party dwindled as the afternoon faded into city-lit evening, rope-handled shopping bags hanging from both of his hands: Trace preceded Vik and her retinue, off to prepare for their Friday night plans. A first-quarter moon unveiled above the jagged skyline, sliced in half by a pizza cutter, he sagged a moment and dropped his bags outside their final stop. It was all kind of surreal – and kind of funny – in a hit-the-iceberg sort of way, next quarter's operating funds overrun and plundered. Chloë was rechecking her phone and lit a stud while Kristi fished out a pack of Skylines and offered him one. Chloë explained his refusal:

—She's a baller; she actually smokes cigars.

Kristi gave him an X-ray vision squint and lit her cigarette in a flash of red and gold, Dupont ping!

—That's very gangster too. We'll have to hang out again, but don't tell my mom. She's terrified of the yakuza – gokudō, sorry – but she loves those movies.

—I can always wear long sleeves. The gokudō usually do, and I had to when I got this done. Till I came back anyway.

Chloë finished her stud while they exchanged numbers. Kristi bid her a hugless farewell and told him,

—Later, gokudō girl.

He picked up his bags and joined Chloë at the portal of her Parisian sanctum sanctorum, the night humours of haute parfumerie gathering without. She hooked her arm around one of his helpless limbs – a gesture from day one. Hooked ever since. She opened the door.

—Are you ready? This is the good part.

THE FALL,
IX.

★

E XPLOSION; IT FLASHED before his eyes in questionable light, and he lifted the bill of his ballcap for the
pub-dim, blinking it away. She'd tossed it at him the
morning before her latest business trip. "Not sure when I'll be
back," she'd said; "it's complicated, but I'll see you soon."

The Victorian boxty house Sionnachuighim, downtown, was
a flatscreen-free oäsis of holiday-lite dark woods, time-worn but
well kept, the piped music a mix of Irish trad and eighties' 'n'
nineties' Irish rock. He waited, withdrawn, on one of the few free
stools, near the beer tower of the horseshoe-shaped bar – like
coming home and not being recognised. Above his resting pint
of cascading beige foam, the taps pulled imports from the Czech
Republic to the Irish one, and an encyclopædic collection of
distillates filled the central cabinets. Absent the football clamour
otherwheres, happy hour rang in with a mild buzz somewise out
of time. He started at a familiar female voice close by:
—Waiting for me long, GG?

Kristi enveloped him in her evergreen chill, red duffel coat
ajar and another new handbag in the crook of one arm. She took
the next stool over, revealing the grey cardigan half-buttoned
over her red dress, but her hem ended above the knee, with grey
pumps below and bare skin in between. His look was quizzical.
—You're not cold, Kristi, walking around like that? I'd be freez-
ing, but I did read somewhere no girl that liked her outfit has
ever caught cold.
—Nietzsche? Now I'm not sure whether you're a gangster or a
terrorist. How was work?
—Meh. New client. Pickup-book slimy, but it pays. You going
home for Christmas?
—No. You?
—No.

The bartender brought his Guinness-marked glass, cloverless
foam; an extra-slim girl in black, her cheeks like cliffs hollowed

by the Celtic Sea, sleeves rolled back over alabaster skin, a liquid fall of straight black hair down to her mid-back. She spoke with the dulcet lilt of the motherland, root and Red Branch: a melody as bittersweet as a heather-scented dream of Éire, which on ruesome waking faded unremembered:

—Are you OK?

—I'll have a sidecar, Kristi replied. Cointreau et, euh, Rémy, please, with fresh lemon juice and a sugarless rim.

Her French rang sound – too sound, to the *euh*. He blinked behind stout frames.

—I've never seen you order one of those before.

She gave him a cool look through hers.

—You haven't known me for that long, GG. Did you order anything to eat?

—No; that would interfere with my drinking.

He frowned at the coupe glass placed in front of her, shaken and served with no ID asked, then lifted his imperial pint. "Sláinte na bhfear… "

Kristi raised hers a beat late, but he finished the traditional toast and took his first creamy sip of nitrogen-bubbled stout. One eyebrow cocked over eyes the colour of brushed steel, the bartender asked, "You speak Irish?"

"Some. My mam's a militant Gaeilgeoir; she made us speak it at home for years, but I've forgotten a lot."

Kristi asked her, "Do you?"

"Not since I sat the Leaving Cert," the bartender said and left.

Kristi asked him, "What did you say?"

"'Good health… and may the women live forever.'"

"I can drink to that. Ganbei!" She clinked her glass against his; but contrary to her counter-toast, she took a slow and considering sip, then checked the chunky steel bracelet watch clasped around her wrist like a tank-treaded bangle.

He tipped his glass.

—What's the point of a wristwatch these days?

—It's a GMT. I have to keep an eye on Hong Kong Time, and this tracks multiple time zones at a glance.

He leant closer for a better look at the black dial and matching bezel, its polished facets aglitter.

—Ah, Rolex.

—I'm surprised a dangerous gokudō girl like you doesn't have one. I'm sure they're big with those types.

—They are, but I can't see dropping five large on a steel wristwatch.
—Seven, but it's part of the business uniform, especially in East Asia. A Rolex signifies completeness in an otherwise perfect presentation: think a dotted i or crossed t. It instils confidence in the wearer with clients and co-workers, like a badge of reliability, and that symbolic value sets the price.
—So this is a lesson in the semiotics of corporate jewellery?
—Cute. Whenever you make idiosyncratic choices in business, it raises questions, like arriving for a meeting in your bright red Porsche versus, say, a subdued Mercedes or BMW. Armani and Rolex may be clichés but with good reason. I shouldn't have to explain that to a fellow MBA.
—O I understand Veblen goods. No doubt you look the part. You even smell like money.

An iron-greyed plutocrat's aftershave of piny woods alembicked into diaphanous clerte, hers was a virid accord of alpine air evocative of Shelley's *Lines Written in the Vale*, but he failed to recall a choice line or two short of googling.
—What's it called?
—Éloge du Traitre.
—You're kidding.
—Not at all.

His Galaxy buzzed atop the bar. A text from Trace:—My place tonight.

Kristi asked if it was from Saitō. He set it down, then shook his head, "Ok" replied.
—No, one of the girls. But where does she fit into your mascarade with her timeless wrist and haute boutique?
—Well…

Kristi paused over the sidecar and drummed her fingers. "She likes to break rules and ignore convention – a lot like you, I guess. She's flamboyant but in the wrong ways for our respective lines of work; she squanders a lot of money she hasn't earned and gotten away with it so far. I won't use the e-word, but she's living well beyond her substantial means. When you go to work for the Corporation, I recommend following my example rather than hers."

"H'mf. Not sure what's going on with her. From the beginning, I've felt like she's had this double life. Like she wasn't telling me everything. Now, I can't ignore it."

"What's up?"

"Don't know for sure," Finn said, then drained his glass, "but I think she has someone else, somewhere else. Something serious. When we met, she said she'd just gotten out of a heavy relationship, but she keeps disappearing with little warning and no communication. This time it's been more than a week, and nothing.

"She's already ruled out Christmas here like it's routine to work through the holidays in Frankfurt or something – I'm pretty sure banks close for Christmas there too. She blew off Thanksgiving the same way but with even less warning. It's not like she's going home for the holidays and isn't ready to introduce me yet. Shit, that would be a better lie than, 'I have to work, and no calls, emails, or texts till I get back.' She said she's not seeing anyone else, but am I crazy? Saitō; I don't even know her."

There was Centimani and their licensed ex-spooks. They could dig, but that rubbed him the wrong way.

—Welll, Kristi drawled, we do travel a lot and are always on call, but no contact is tough to explain. She might have someone over there, I suppose, or here, but she hasn't confided in me about anything like that. Saitō's a friend, but we're not besties ¶. You should consider your options; I have other friends you haven't met, places you haven't been. Nothing against Viktoriya's tuhao clique – they don't live in the real world yet – but…

His chin resting on one hand, he listened to Kristi expound on her set, their social circuit and supercar club. A route that somehow led back to Saitō's oft-repeated but nebulous job offer for her conglomerated kraken: "You're an operations manager," she'd say; "you'll manage operations" – nothing beyond the reach of its transnational tentacles. An offer to be swallowed whole:

—But you wouldn't work directly with her, Kristi was saying; so as far as the job is concerned, it doesn't hinge on whether you two work out or not. You can leave her out of the decision.

—The job. Can't say I'm inclined to play dress-up for work again. Nightclub cosplay has been bad enough.

—You seem to be having fun. A lot of fun, at the centre of all that attention. What was that dance move? The cat daddy?

The spotlight was edifying, and that itself was uncomfortable.

—That's the tequila, Kristi. I don't remember half of it. And I only made it a few months as a salaryman in Japan. Months.

—Look, I get it. You've been playing the rebel for a while with your jeans and your messenger bag, winging it out there on your own, but the culture here is completely different. You have a bigger future than small-biz supply chain. It's time to graduate from café terrasses: we've prepared a place for you.

Sounded ominous.

Besides, he could go back any time. Don another handle, alert Ane-san. Step over the bodies, sweep up the ash. The cost of doing business – the risk of doing business, but next time, he could be the one caught in the explosion. Saitō was a question mark, but next time, he could be the one. Caught. He stalled again:

—I've been thinking about working up a new business plan for next quarter. Expand? A real office, employees, all that? But I've been kind of distracted with Saitō, Vik, and everything else. Let me give it some more thought.

—We can hold the position for a little while but not forever: weather changes quickly at the summit. I can promise you the interviews will be eye-opening, and – believe me – there'll be no going back afterwards. But you need to come in voluntarily; it won't be the same if I have to twist your arm.

Kristi joined him for a second drink: her sidecar, his Four Roses 2011 single barrel. She turned down a third and signalled the bartender for the cheque.

—I'm going to do some shoe shopping at Pygmalion. You should come along; it's time you learned to walk in heels.

He hadn't minded the inch and a half of lift but didn't set her straight on his office experience with heels, shrugging back into his b-3 bomber jacket. A meticulous Japanese reproduction, it had survived Saitō's massacrous purge even though she'd declared, "Shearling is so last year."

—Foot-binding isn't my kink, he said. Sure, it'd be nice to be taller – a lot taller – but I'm fine with flats.

Kristi crinkled her nose in distaste.

—Ballerina shoes have their place, but.

—Taylor always compliments them.

—And Saitō is gaga over anything Hermès, so why'd I pretend to give you a choice?

Kristi's chilled fingers found his.

—Let's go, GG. It's time. ✶

SPRING GALE,
I.

★

H E SPRAWLED onto the precise pillow arrangement on Taylor's blue chesterfield, his bag a distant thump on the floor. Nothing left. Vik sat beside him at cushion's edge and picked up his limp hand. A sharp sniff and a wistful sigh.

—I love this little ring. Too bad it's fake.

He offered no objection when she slipped the solitaire from his finger, his eyelids drawn down by the sofa's gravitational pull. A few moments later, she exclaimed,

—Wait, it's not!

Taylor's voice came from farther away, curtained stage left:

—What's not?

—Gigi's ring. It's not fake, like she said. The band is platinum; the diamond is real.

A religious reverence reverbed within Vik's pronouncement, chorals of angels implied. Paige's voice rang out stage right, her unique transatlantic accent hybridised between Englands, New and ole:

—What's not what?

—Gigi's ring, reanswered Vik. It's not fake. She's been wearing a real diamond engagement ring all this time.

The sofa shifted, a hip pressing into his thigh, but Taylor's voice was no nearer than before:

—Finn, are you and Chloë… ?

—I bought it, he interrupted; keeps the boys away. Some of them.

He opened his eyes halfway – sage-green pools deepened olive under the girls' encroaching shadows. Paige waved the ring under his button nose.

—You've said that before, love, but you wouldn't need an actual diamond for…

A unicorn-rare scion of the oft dispossessed mercantile buccaneer Old Money and insolent raconteuse of Gogolian marginalia, her Titian hair was down in a mirage of most delicate feminacy; the tauréador's cape before a hidden sword.

—Although, the fakes are always multicarat, now that I think on it. We should have realised sooner.

Finn shook his head, dark Marcel waves breaking on rouged cheekbones. He spoke softly, his words hard-edged with unforgiveness:

—I hate fake things.

The girls looked at each other, and his eyes reshuttered. He drifted in and out while they discussed sleeping arrangements and made shuffling noises to rouse when Taylor brought him a duvet, limned by hallway light. She was a living work of Shirōesque transhuman art, refinished an immaculate Bahia summer–bronze, her long dark hair wound up and pinned; she was lean and long-limbed beneath her bleu-celeste mini dress and moved with the fluid confidence of a born athlete, ready to spring. She set his platforms upright by the coffee table.

—Do your feet hurt again?

—Ankles a little stiff; not as strong as they used to be.

—I'll come back after I change and give you another foot rub.

He caught her hand as she turned, and he kissed it the way Trace had kissed his once – with euphoric effect – and how he'd kissed a few others earlier this night. There was an audible catch in Taylor's breath, her eyes in tenebris, chiaroscuro two-faced. Her fingertips found his cheek; her thumb ran over the bee-stung swell of his underlip. He tugged on her other hand, and she crashed over him in a breaking wave, breathing his name, only the quilted barrier between them. Her mouth was on his, but with too much tongue too soon, and craving hands squeezed him too hard, eliciting a sharp moan.

—Taylor! Paige called from nearby. Where are the extra pillows kept?

Taylor bolted upright.

—I'll be right there; don't make a mess!

A parting glance overshoulder – wounded look – then she was gone. He drowsed again, restless, steamy breath, and in the stillness of the small hours, stumbled to the guest bathroom to throw up. He washed his face, relieved all were asleep and unstirred; then he nicked a dayglo bottle of something-ade from Taylor's fridge and chugged it before drifting again, tossed on sleepless waves.

He bounced awake when Vik dropped onto the sofa with

aplomb, a bejewelled bomb as bright and cheery as an orange juice commercial, wearing the same white bandage dress with grey crisscross straps, every blown-out hair in glamorous place. She reclaimed his club-stamped hand.

—One-and-a-half carats?

—Um, one-point-two.

He yawned, eyes dry, his ears ringing from serial nightclubs and a weak party. He blinked twice, disoriented a moment within the dreamlike sharp of 20/18 vision, about to reach for glasses no longer there. Taylor walked in, bathrobed but made-up, on the scarp of an uncanny valley by daylight. She threw a folded bath towel at his face, minor collateral damage to Vik – fast friends with Taylor since their mutual Paris début a couple years ago, or so you'd hear. He took the hint and clambered over Vik, the hardwood floor ice cold beneath his bare feet. She thwacked him on the behind.

—Hey, no boob to the face.

Taylor was unreadable when he asked for a shower cap, gazing down at him with hooded eyes, dark and fathomless as Oceanus, the world-stream. The shower provided no answers; his little black Miu Miu hung to steam out slept-in wrinkles. There was only her soapy-fresh fragrance, the sure feel of her hands, and arms that girdled him wherever they were, airbrushed tan. He stepped back into the hallway, and she yelled:

—Tracy, Brad, and Nate are meeting us for brunch.

—OK. Getting ready.

It was a running show staged for the selfie cam: from his first cosplay nights unto a théâtre of the absurd: from shipwreck to social renascence, in circumbinary orbit around Vik's and Emily's separate spheres. Again caught up in girls' tribes; since ballet school and Logan, & al. in high school – a boy en travesti viewing boys' tribes from without. He was torn between rival rites of perpetual spring-in-winter: an endless continuüm of nightclubs, roary supercars, and catered college soirées with Veuve Clicquot served in red Solo cups, then sometime stand-in as Vik's substitute plus-one to sponsored galas for the bored rich, their Savile Row black ties paired with panoply couture, and to even more exclusive after-parties.

Stage name Gigi, he riffed on Trace's neo-flapper paint-by-numbers, onnagata preparing to perform, his Betty Boop–pout aglisten with Chanel's jolie rouge, PIRATE. "You're the one that looks like a fashion model now," Trace had told him one night out, "not me. Ready for Gallíano or Dior Couture?"

"No," he'd sourpussed; "I'm not an eight-foot-tall Saffa like you."

"Ekskuus my, five-nine!"

It hadn't been easy, at times doubting himself with trembling hands and wet eyes, retracing the steps that had led him here – pushed further and further in alcohol-benumbed increments – till he'd collapse on himself, from blacked-out zenith to dry nadir. But then Vik or Kristi would call, and he'd regather himself for the next show.

Vik was texting or whatever on the sofa, amid the faux-shambolic English Country kitsch and comfort, potted plants and flowers here and there alongside trinketised Degas: La Petite Danseuse, with antiqued bodice and tulle; and the Danseuse Regardant. It was all LASER-levelled and plumbed, per Taylor's "I'm not OCD. I just like things a certain way" neuroticism.

He shook his naggin flask – empty – and dropped it back into his ardoisé Steve bag, the stealth shade of McQueen's three Porsche 911s. Finn fetched his platforms, and Paige snarked at him from her spot on the causeuse, her hair back in a ponytail, phone in hand, and mod again in a vintage Mondrian dress, black overknees, and Mary Jane saddle pumps:

—You do realise blokes will chat you up despite your ring, so long as you wear shoes like those.

—Gigi is my muse, Vik declared. She's only allowed to wear glass slippers or Louboutin.

—Vik, do you even know what muse means?

—Stuff it, Paige.

—But if you're playing faëry godmother, forget the glass slippers and magic up some accessories for her; she's got to have more than one handbag. A quirk, however delightful, can be taken too far.

Vik glared at him over her iPhone.

—Have you re-pierced your ears yet?

—Told you: not going to.

—Gigi, I told you...

He stepped into the lifted demi-pointe of a black-sailed red

heel, bold as the once Sun King. He'd been hooked on the endor-
phin high of his heightened plane ever since the heart-quailing
ô no! of surprise the fateful day Kristi bullied him into the first
pair: "Want to feel taller, for real?" It had been a breathtaking
moment of apogée, the elevation like a rail of Vik's poison-pure
coke H Cl flake; the final lip-bitten pangs washed away by Saitō's
whelming, if belated, adulation. And while the highest walkable
platform wouldn't make him six-three, nothing ever would.

Taylor reëntered the living room, dressed for the early budded
False Spring in a sleeveless white sheath and Balanchine bun, a
quilted snow-bunny jacket in hand. He shrugged into his café
racer, struck when she looked up at him for the first time, shod
in Græcian flats, her bronzed skin and upturned blue eyes bold
against the white.
—Alright, she said. Let's move out.

The suspension in her blacked-out m6 drophead dialled to
Senna, their port of call was a short but every-pebble-in-the-
road haul from the Victorian stonework façade of her hôtellike
uptown pad.

German and Italian bling packed the underground garage,
the upstairs crammed with Orwell's pigs at sterling troughs:
ranks of golden families with that Vanity Fair glow.

Brad was Superman minus the swag and bore no trace of
Brontëan brooding or even the shallowest 2-D self-reflexion.
Trace was petite beside him in heelless Uggs, her hair longer and
in a dark-rooted champagne-blonde; the fant'sy on her finger
was twisted off centre. Finn had heard, of course, but hadn't
seen her since she'd dropped out of nightlife to prep for the
MCAT – or so she'd texted before going silent. The bestial look
Brad gave him was repellent – beyond the usual crawly menace
of male gazes – but Finn managed a minimal greeting when Vik
reïntroduced him as Gigi, Taylor squeezing him from behind,
her chin on his shoulder.

Trace avoided him before taking her seat, and he sat opposite
her at their round table, clouded mien, betwixt Taylor and Vik,
his sinistral jewel sparkling with wishful flame. He allowed the
small talk to flow over and around him like a stone and waited for
something to drink. Trace's measured and cadenced trivialities
were as bland as mash without the butter, and he thought of his

mother's sausage-an'-mash – of which he'd only ever gotten the least little bit in his future-ballerina portions.

He dug through his carporal's leather satchel, heavy with the dusky odours of cosmetics and, phone held low, asked Trace what was wrong via text; she was almost within reach but more distant than the first time he'd descried her through the tavern window during a bookstore crawl. He got a clipped response:—Not here.

Taylor squeezed his bare knee beneath the table.

—Are you feeling OK?

—A little hungover.

He ordered a mimosa over Taylor's raised eyebrow and lingering hand, followed by a fruit-smothered pain perdu he only picked at while Paige took iPhone snaps for her Instagram sizzle-feed of peak experience. Nate – Taylor's fiancé – arrived late wearing a tacky pair of flash-lensed aviators, cocksure amid the high flatus of his breeding. He was the sort of pavonine brute that played tennis and polo with equal facility, or so he boasted: a narcissine puffball of egotism with cauterised emotions.

Drawn with Lempicka's fierce lines, Finn withdrew further into his silence – a weaponised Art Déco ornament outside their pedestalled bell jar, looking in; until he ordered a second mimosa:

—Hold the OJ.

He watched Trace over his second drink and the blue diamond on her left hand. She was a cameo under glass, forever looking away.

C·P·SERRET,
DIE THE VILLAIN.

E VOMITED into his computerised toilet, belly heaving
H   till he retched a thin stream of bile, then hung his head,
exhausted, his marcelled hair restrained in sculpted
waves. Kristi helped him to the sink, and after the mouthwash,
a fogged recollection. A question.

—Where's Emily?

—Passed out on the sofa with your cat.

Kristi supported his wobbly steps back to the tatami room and
lowered him to a futon, his bones jelly. She slid the door shut
and clicked off the lone Noguchi lamp. Darkness blinked into
sunlit morning, the shrill aërospace howl of budget landscaping
augmented by the V-twin purr rumbling in a ringing ear, Koko's
whiskers tickling his nose. He grumbled at her, squinting against
the paper-screened glow:

—Hidenka, get lost.

She pawed at his face, no claws. He pushed her back with one
hand, then shifted away from the warm body beside him and
sat up, awash in a dark spill of profluent hair redolent of an
alpestrine idyll with a smoking gun. The bedroom door open
cat-width, Emily peered in from the landing, greeting his reluctant movement with excessive morning cheer:

—Ni hao, Jiji!

She was the consummate baifumei, her white, jadelike skin
untouched by the sun. She could play Diao Chan on stage with
a change of wardrobe and cloudlike hair, though she knew
European luxury brands better than the Romance of the Three
Kingdoms or anything else she deemed "old fashion'." He was
unwilling to tread on the four tones in reply and croaked back
in his best Japanese morning toad:

—Emily, ohayō-han dosu.

She slid the shōji open the rest of the way and stepped in
barefoot, her mauve bandage dress, black crisscross strapped,
unrumpled by sleep but fuzzy with shed Persian. She knelt at

the edge of his duvet, set down her phone to pick up Koko, saying something in Chinese to Kristi's languorous stir-and-yawn
across abutted futons. Kristi responded in kind, which led to
a back-and-forth he didn't pretend to understand, though he
might've caught "huli jing" – meaning him.

He staggered to his feet, annoyed at *vixen*; at them talking past
him first thing, his head throbbing as he stood. He unzipped
his little black Chloé skater, let it fall to the floor, then pulled a
linen yukata from the closet. He'd never worn men's yukata in
public over there; it was a private indulgence.

Koko escaped Emily's embrace and scampered out. He trudged
down to the kitchen with a slight wobble, the handrail held
tight, then fed and watered the absent cat. Their verbal sparring
reached him all the way down here.

He downed an extra-long pour of iced rye and shook off the
shivers, his vision clearing, then held the wavering bottle over
his tumbler but stoppered it. No refill. He retreated to the first-
floor washroom and caught a puffy-eyed dipso with dry runs of
eyeliner in the mirror: Christian's Hot Mess. He washed his face
with the wrong soap, then traced the line of a prominent collarbone. He bared one jaundiced shoulder, bony points pressing
forth – the inglorious return of heroin chic via whiskey, cocaine,
and vomit. He gulped air and gripped the sink, a tremulous
worry in his chest. He'd cover with make-up, but.
—Time for a break.

One more finger of rye and, steadied, he headed back and
found them descending the stairs, Kristi in her peach-shaded
strapless midi, bespectacled vogue. He despised the othering
exotic, but she exceeded the sum of her own mixed heritage –
another cliché je-ne-sais-quoi beyond those hazel eyes. "Keiki
hanau o ka 'āina," she'd said by way of explanation: "a child born
of the land."

They were both taller than he was, of course – before putting
on their heels. Emily gestured upwards in the general direction
of his biposto listening room.
—We should have party here.

Kristi choked on a laugh.
—I doubt Gigi would like that.
—Small party, Jiji. Onegai?

He sighed in the face of her soap opera pout, though his

place was a bit low-rent for her fu'er dai set, even with tuhao –
and triads – buying up half the neighbourhood and spiking
property values.

—I'll think about it.

Emily evinced certain victory, shades of Saitō, and continued
whatever she'd been saying in Chinese. Kristi responded in kind,
then told him, aside,

—Sorry, it's rude to keep speaking in Chinese in front of you.
I'm going to drive her home. Text me later.

Didn't matter; it was nothing new. He shrugged it off and
hugged them goodbye on the threshold, their short jackets all
style and little substance. He shut the door on the late morning
chill, nose stung by the leafblowers burning oil, trafficked proles
scurrying for centavos on the quetzal.

He collapsed on his futon, but Koko scampered back in –
forgot to shut the effing door. She explored the empty bedding
beside his, curious but tentative, evoking the thorn in his paw:
Trace, a thorn since brunch. He'd go today, hash it out. But later.
He snugged down in the duvet. The cat circled like his mind.

✫

HE sat up. Trace lay faced away from him, twirling a lock of Ra-
punzel hair, a half-draped sculpture. Her bedroom was stacked
with cardboard boxes, half-filled; she was moving up.

Ashley had let him in and shouted for Trace. He'd gone upstairs to find her looking busy, an ultramarine kopdoek banded
around her updone hair. But she'd crossed her arms in a bulwark.
Walled him out.

—I don't understand, he'd repeated.

—You should, she'd insisted.

—But I don't.

—But you should.

It got heated. She'd quit the bar and was moving in with Brad
next week and acted like that explained everything. It became a
struggle: her roiled stream of Afrikaans and breaking sobs, his
entreating frustration and pounding heart. She'd turned her
back on him; it got physical. Then it got physical.

He slipped from the bed and pulled on his ironic boyshorts
and jeans. His antlered-print Jesse Sykes tour tee was at the foot

C·P·SERRET,
DIE THE VILLAIN.

SPRING GALE,
III.

★

T HE JAZZY CIGAR LOUNGE was sumptuous if conventional, overladen with Modernism's overused signature pieces – like his place. Ensconced within the sooted façade of a soi-disant luxury hôtel, it was patronised by a midlife collection of the large-but-in-charge, stout C-suite suits and Ugly American causal. Balding pates. Hoary beards. Arturo Sandoval's trumpet blazed on the embedded audio, sounding above their murmuring huffle-snuffle of capital and capital pronouns.

A surprise invitation, but Finn had taken the obvious bait and allowed himself to be drawn out of his repentine social-coke withdrawal. Gilt and red Chinese lacquer, Kristi's lighter pinged open as she lit a stubby white cigarette. "I bummed them at work," she'd explained the oblong GITANES FILTRE pack. "Hectic day." She was beside him on the Swan sofa, dressed for the office in a trim Pallas pantsuit, dove grey, her ostrich Zanotti pumps matched by a tan Struzzo tote – per their evening show 'n' tell.
—You look like someone boiled your cat. What's going on?

He blamed it on last night's loss against the Buffaloes, 4–2, but Paige smelled a rat, and he narrated Trace's "never happened" minus the happenings. The cocktail waitress interrupted Paige's branching lines of Jealous Brad–centred speculation, and Finn withdrew behind the slim *Whisky, Whiskey, & Cocktails* menu and choice cigar list. The girls ordered classic cocktails – sidecar and vesper – while he h'mmed; then he requested rye on the rocks and a Fuente lancero, "The Lost City", for himself.

Most eyes touched Paige and her lustrous hair, leant back in the paired Swan chair; a robust torpedo held correctly between blue fingertips, ASSASSIN banded midshaft in silvered black. Finn's gaze stroked the soft shimmer of silk stockings, a three-quarter-sleeved Balmain – O'Keefian florals on white – glittering above garter's peeping edge. She caught his look and, lowering her drink, said,
—Snogging other people's girlfriends at parties the way you do, it's no wonder Brad's wary of you around his fiancée – and Nate

should look out. Are you ready to come clean about whatever's between you and Taylor?

Finn froze, mid-peppery puff. It was too on the nose. Taylor herself hadn't so much as texted him once outside of Vik's group chat. Not before. Not after. Kristi rubbed out her latest cigarette; she'd declined a cigar and chain-smoked those Gitanes like a hard case.

—I don't know Taylor that well, but she's engaged, isn't she? And for that matter, she's straight. Don't…

—Care to wager on that? You've seen how Taylor hangs on her…

But Paige raised her hands in mock surrender before Kristi's unamused glare, grin undaunted.

—Very well, forget Taylor.

—Where to next? This might be a good spot for business clients from out of town, but it's too sedate for us.

Paige poised her cigar like the prop it was.

—Divya, perhaps, or that vampire theme bar? Just envisage the absolute swathe of destruction if our little Gigi walked in.

He put his platformed foot down, unwilling to take his pre-varications that one step too far, though he dared not speak Iago's "I am not what I am" aloud:

—No lesbian bars. Not my thing.

—Do you even have any gay friends, Gigi?

—Not that I know of.

The crowds ran straight and coupled through Vik and Emily's respective scenes – all cake toppers – but. "You'd think claiming to like girls is the new heteronorm," Taylor had repeated over the nightclub noise after a few girls passed him between them like a joint. "Sure," she'd amended, glaring at their antic hay; "some of them'll say it's gross or icky after they sober up and then post pics for likes on IG."

"You're nothing like them," he'd told her, tingled by the frisson of her fingers brushing his.

"Nothing at all," she'd confirmed.

—What was it? Paige replied. What do they call it when lesbians are stuck on straight girls?

She only paused for effect; she remembered everything. Always, and always overplayed her disingenuous rhetorical questions. Self-answered:

—Straight-girl syndrome.

He pushed back despite himself:

—Paige, I've never – ever – referred to myself as a *lesbian*.

—No? What is it then, *a queer girl*; something else? I haven't kept abreast of the latest jargon.

—Quare? he reframed the politeme. I s'pose that kind of fits, but I feel more like *The Man Who Fell to Earth*.

—Gigi, as much as I adore this whole tragic Virgo heroine thing you've cultivated, you're not that unique. There are plenty of girls like yourself out there, and if you feel isolated, it's because you've cut yourself off from them.

He opened his rosebud mouth, but there wasn't anything else to say – even with a rye-loosened tongue. He'd opened Pandora's box before: a cartoon boxing glove sprung out and punched you in the face. A three-week black eye. He turned away from her, underlip quivering, but she didn't relent.

—And why do you still wear the ring? – the real reason. Chloë's ghosting you. It must've been from her, but you've both lied about it because?

—No; I bought it, but…

His voice beginning to catch in warning, he dosed the remaining rye in one swallow.

—At this point, I don't know what I was thinking. Maybe I should sell it.

He placed his smouldering stick on the cigar ashtray's wide ledge, then excused himself to the Ladies'. No one joined him. He reëntered the lounge recomposed, his make-up retouched, to find Paige evangelising her quick-release rotation, brassy score by Gillespie and Pozo, her cigar tipped into the ashtray and left for dead at two-thirds.

—And best, she was saying, they all know full well they're competing for my time. Should anyone get too possessive or try to order me about, I simply drop and replace him. It's quite the best way to manage guys – or girls, I'm sure. You two should give it a go. Not together, I mean.

He shook his head, a brave mask painted on, but beneath lavish black lashes, his liquid eyes told a different tale: of the prisoner within a bronze-gilt cage and changeless transformations: a thousand-yard stare. He ashed his cooling cigar and, with cold hands, set it above a blue flame. Kristi glanced at her watch, dismissive mien.

—Men are superfluous. I have a Magic Wand and can buy my own drinks.

He tuned them out, motioning to the waitress for another rye, alone beside them with his relit cigar till a cellphone interrupted. Kristi answered, rising to her feet, and crushed her cigarette like a bug:

—Claire, what's going on?

Kristi stepped out of the lounge, stiffened gait; then Paige excused herself, leaving him alone in smoke. He sipped icemelt and signalled for his third rye, a sax moaning bright tears. His phone buzzed. A text from Saitō: —I'm back <3.

★

He checked his phone in the curtained light.

—Déjà vu.

Saitō made a sleepy noise next to him, then rolled over in bed, brushing lightened caramel-brown hair from her face.

—H'm?

—It's Sunday morning.

—So?

—Thought it was Saturday.

She chuckled low in her throat and kissed his tattooed arm.

—You're funny. Are we going to get out of here today or chill and binge Gossip Girl on the DVR?

—Brunch?

—No. Dim Sum; I want shrimp. Anyone you want to invite?

—No; I'm not sharing you.

Saitō kissed his arm again and slipped from the bed, cold air filling the vacuum of her presence, followed by a chromed brass ping! She hit and sighed on crack nicotine, the ashtray full of her victory stubs. He'd given her a gilded barleycorn Dunhill lighter, identical to Senpai's, but she'd lost it on one of her countless trips. "Which is why I buy Zippos," she'd non-apologised on return.

She stepped into the bathroom. He filched a silk dressing gown from the dresser and announced he'd make some coffee. She entered the kitchen in fumo several minutes later, robed and with a towel wrapped around her hair. He offered her the other caffè americano he'd prepared, disinclined to make another milky mess with the steam pipe of her décopunk coffee rig.

—Hope it's not cold.

—It's fine, she replied after the first sip. Thank you.

Saitō probed in the cupboard for the pill bottle he'd tucked behind a brown box of Esmeralda, pre-ground and emprisoned in plastic capsules like shotgun shells. She found it withal.

—I was thinking in the shower: Have you reconsidered quitting for good? One hundred percent all-out, including the smuggling thing?

—I went dark, as I said, and only maintained my consulting business part-time, but you've been gone so long I wasn't sure you were coming back.

—Silly.

Saitō popped a Provigil and took a slower, deeper sip from the double-walled glass mug. She smoked her studs with that same focus on her eyes: twin blackpools of glimmerous unstillness. She offered him the open bottle.

—Want one?

He declined, nibbling a bit of the Frey NOIR SATIN she'd brought back from Switzerland or wherever. She tapped one into her palm.

—C'mon; it'll make you ten times more dangerous.

—I thought you wanted me to be less dangerous.

—Not less dangerous: in less danger.

She capped the bottle and set it down with a firm rattle.

—We've kept a spot open for you, but when I talked to my uncle, he said we can't hold off any longer. Kristi already got an extension or two, and I've used up all of my favours. Your contract will be six figures to start, and you won't be doing anything that would require you to carry a gun in your handbag. Right now, you can walk in there looking like a movie star. You'll own the place.

His lips pursed sour.

—So the pay cut and office cosplay aside, when will I get to see you if you're in Europe most of the time?

—Travel's a part of the job. You'd have to go overseas sometimes too.

—Dunno. Doesn't sound like there's much of an us in this future.

Saitō shook her head while taking another drag.

—This isn't about "us", she said with smoky air quotes; it's about bringing you into the Corporation so that you'll have a future. We can worry about us after. But you have to close up shop and cut all of those ties for good: no hackers, no mobsters. This is pretty much your last chance, and I need you to stop and think about it. Your future. After this, you'll be on your own even if you change your mind. Kristi and I won't be able to help you.

His faith in a hereafter all but expended, he decided what he would let go of soon and for good.

SPRING GALE'
IV.

★

P ROMISED FINGER CROWNED with a colossus of lilac
ice flanked by clear bergs, all luminant fire, Taylor's
evening gown was an ætherian spiderwork spun of
mallow blooms – a Muchaesque purple dream. Her dark hair
was in a windswept updo, arcs of bronze-gleaming skin from her
jewelled neck to her off-shoulder décolletage and soaring slit.
He got one arm around her waist, and shouting his name, she
tried to squeeze the life from him in front of witnesses till Nate –
tall, dark, and peremptory – interposed with implicit demand:
—Brad and Tracy are here.

Nate swept Taylor away, trailing mauve, her sister Britt, and
Vik at the van of her pinch-faced myrmidons – a cortège of
would-be models in their catwalk cosplay. Finn stepped back
from his recurring guest-star rôle, in the shadow of Trace, left
behind within their sillage of calone and powdered candy. How
long till he could go home?

Bright young things strewn on the half-circle of white sofas,
engaged to their phone screens, he found a comfortless moulded
armchair set in the corner furthest from the microcelebrity DJ
in her sponsored clothes and uncreased sneakers, intermix-
ing nineties D 'n' B with contemporary progressive house, the
bass thrumming through his bones. A grim grey throne fit for
Unhappy Hipsters, it anchored the birch ply and – a feature, not
a bug – whitespacing of the Scandinavian Modernish reception
in Nate's high-rise duplex downtown.

Finn sniffed at his heavyweight tumbler. The mawkish nose
of the blended malt left him less than keen to finish it, but it
took the edge off; draped like a sabled throw, that Gigi; the to-
ken SEÑORITA on display from Vik's catalogue but out of her
spotlight. Dynastic trust funds were bedecked with other Vik-
curated social baubles, including the resident ballet troupe's
pardine première danseuse. He studied the ebony-eyed étoile
and her rakish non-Balanchine line, starting at an unfamiliar
female voice close by:

—You can only be Finn. O, my apologies. I didn't mean to startle you.

She offered a fair hand.

—Morgen. Delighted we should finally meet.

He found himself standing with her soft hand in his, looking down into the hyacinth-blue eyes which had followed his chivalrous rise. Who is this person?

—Finn, as you somehow guessed.

—It wasn't difficult. You are in Taylor's feed after all.

Morgen appeared at ease in a fitted bodice of appliqué lace, her cut-glass accent ringing sharp but effortless. A reminder in absentia that Paige was not, in fact, a Brit – not that most Brits played on the posh side of the fence. Morgen indicated with one hand.

—Do sit.

He obeyed, felled by her timbres. She brought the matching ottoman closer, her ash-brown hair falling in Romantic waterfall plaits around architect's glasses. Her sea-foam satin midi dress cut on the demure side of the knee, she'd completed her look with nude pumps, an armorial signet on sinistral pinky, and a skinny ring on dextral thumb – gold gold, not that trendy pink stuff. No bling. All modest but not quite. A twitch reached his face: a thegn-born Cantabrigian, high in Taylor's esteem and deep in her counsel, referenced here and there in parenthesis. Morgen sat leant towards him on the hewn-look plastic twist and raised her voice:

—Your platforms are divine. Too daring for me, but may I... ?

—Louboutin Mad Moi.

The two towers of his peripeteia and the price of edging six-foot-zero. Her gaze swept him.

—And the headband?

—Hermès.

—Très chic. What are you drinking?

—Scotch. Are you not drinking at all?

—I'd prefer not, but I'll likely have another glass of champagne later when Taylor opens her gifts – to be courteous.

Morgen's slender hands were folded over a taupe clutch, almost demure, her short fingernails manicured but unvarnished – unlike his cropped Déco half-moons, lacquered PIRATE-red by a girl with Giotti's freehand skills. In want of something witty to say, Finn asked which part of England she was from, but she didn't take the hint from his subsequent squint. He'd google it later.

—Did you fly over for the birthday party?

—Yes, but we were overdue for a visit. We FaceTme most days, but 'tisn't the same, is it?

Her gaze flicked to the crowd constellated about Taylor and Nate, selfie cams raised saluto romano. Morgen's eyes returned to Finn, and all else fell away, alone at an intimate setting for two—the stupid tricks with champagne bottles on an unheeded TV. His move.

—You boarded together at school, right?

—Yes; exiled to the wilds of Kent—about where you'd find your-self were you to become lost on your way to the middle of no-where. I was in fifth form when she transferred in midterm for fourth, but we were in the same House. She was out of place with the other fourth-formers, and one could say we adopted her like a stray.

He asked about the latter we. Morgen nodded.

—There were several of us: a family away from home. Not every-one made it over this year, but Elaine and Nimuë are just there. However, I do believe I'm the only one she's mentioned you to.

—Curious, what did she say?

Morgen's smile widened to a rending brightness.

—That she'd made an interesting friend.

—That's a little enigmatic.

—It's not mine to tell. If you're curious, do ask her yourself.

—Touché.

—You're younger than I'd expected. I'd've sworn she'd said you were older than she is.

—Sure, by what, two… two-and-a-half years? I'll be twenty-five this September.

Morgen studied him for a long moment, her gaze tracing the crescent of leg visible through the Chantilly lace of his long-sleeved Tom Ford gown. It came in a flash: her hands folded in restraint, not modesty—as Tantalus bound. He felt compelled to ask,

—How long will you be staying?

—In the States? A week today.

—We should hang out before you go back.

—Ah, I beg your pardon, but t'es pas mon genre.

She'd shaken her head, but something smouldered, reluctant in her refusal, in the warm flush of her skin, in her fallen gaze. He persisted with little to lose but his lace-prisoned vanity.

—No? And your type is?

—Someone who is herself and knows what she wants for herself. You'll pardon my saying it, but you seem to be playing at something. Nothing dodgy per se, but I feel I'm watching a pasquinade: a play within this play. In my experience, that's a tragédie waiting to happen.

He had to smile at her insight, and it made her all the more interesting. He tried a different tack:

—Let's hang out then, but not as a date: as friends of a friend.

—Even so, I can't.

Her folded hands tightened. A *no* or a *try harder?*

—I don't know what else Taylor told you, but I'm not that dangerous.

—Said the fox to the hen. Your look, why garçonne?

A con as cool as a bronze cast of Myrna Loy's *Hardboiled Rose*, the powdered postsuffrage face of the interbellum flapper was his ironical iron mask – one he'd locked himself into. He waved a minionette hand at the extras haunting Nate's mise-en-scène like the Ghosts of Socialites Yet-to-Become and illumined the tarnished streak of defiance within his transgressive sham without revealing anything:

—I'm a creature out of place. I'll never blend in with these, so why wear the same masks they do? Flappers were a farce, even then: coauthored by Factor and Fitzgerald. If every night is Halloween, then better that lost generation than this one.

—So, a mountain of effort in grande différance?

—It's less work than it looks, except for the marcelled hair, which is more.

Morgen cocked her head, fingers knotted below a pursed smile. She spoke, abstracted, as one solving an equation from terms to sum:

—Detached cynicism; an immaculate, ageless mask: a new *Dorian Gray.*

—If only.

SPRING GALE/
V.

★

H'D FOUND CUBAN cafés in most of Uptown America – as Havana this or Habana that – selling the mystique of a lost city to literati nostalgic for the Gatsbyesque Prohibition oäsis and Papa Hemingway. Finn's father had shown him a few 4 × 6 photos of a double-handful of relatives behind the final crumbling section of Iron Curtain, amid post-fifties decrepitude and far out of the sight of international tourists spending at state-sponsored hôtels and la Malecón. These people had no idea.

Morgen's bold-framed eyes had rarely left him on their leisured drive, small-talking about the girls' antic play; eyes the colour of evening falling into night: a wondrous heure bleue. She'd matched him, sans façon, in a Tyrian purple sweater with a peek of white collar, khakis, and rosé suede plimsolls, her hair artfully froused in a Boho braid down one shoulder.

He'd held her chair, and she'd rated the café's cliché-ridden décor quite nice – after the lovely of his 911s; and seated away from the leaf-dappled sun at windowside, l'heure bleue fell into a sapphiric eve of unstarred deep and hyacinthine spell. He removed his ballcap and finger-combed his hair, this once, unfitting. With a slight upturn of her lips, she waited for the waitress to leave the Tempranillo, then leant in.

—Who are you today?

—I don't...

—Is this the real Finn or that It-girl Gigi of whom I've heard tell? The night we met, you were this grand world-weary débauchée like one of those decadent wives married to an absentee husband: the Countess...

Morgen gestured as if announcing an eminent arrival, then canted her head, an expectant look. Some big deal Countess had graced Taylor's party at the last minute, but he'd skipped over the WhatsApp chatter. The cosmocrats and their airs... He didn't bite.

—But here you are today, Morgen continued, from garçonne to garçon manqué – sorry, the latter is in poor taste – but right now you wouldn't look out of place in the Lucy common room.

—Lucy?

—Lucy Cavendish College. Cambridge? Hasn't Taylor mentioned it?

—Maybe. Probably, but I don't remember, sorry.

—We host juniors from abroad, and she was a visiting student with us last year. She'll return as a graduate this Michaelmas.

—I only met her last summer.

—Yes, but I'm surprised she hasn't spoken of it; she's planning on a doctorate – and yes, I did notice your deft elusion of my question with a question, but perhaps it best Gigi remain a mystery. May I ask why you don't speak Spanish? The schools here offer it, I'm sure.

Their waitress had barraged him with demotic Castilian. Ugh, he hated that: the awkwardness and the embarrassment.

—They do, but there wasn't much incentive. There weren't any other Hispanic kids in our neighbourhood where we went to school, and…

—Hiberno-Hispanic?

—None of those either. And my parents – all my relatives – were way too pushy about it since I knew Irish. It was a big turn-off, so I took French instead.

Morgen tittered and lifted her glass by the stem.

—They must have been so pleased. Santé!

—À la tienne.

Her gaze fell to his slack hand. A significant look.

—Why the engagement ring?

—A prop to discourage suitors.

—Is it effective?

—Hard to say, but it's an easy excuse to make them go away.

—Taylor never mentioned it. I'd thought, at first, that it was from her in secret, but she's denied it.

He blinked, blindsided, and used Morgen's word:

—Pardon?

—Well, she rather fancies you, as I'm sure you know.

—You're not outing her, are you?

—It appears you already have – or one could say the wider speculation has begun.

—She's been engaged to Nate since before I met her, and she has a Graff engagement ring three times the size of this one.

—Even so. Lovely as it is, she never wears it. And quite frankly, the wedding date says it all.

—The wedding date? This December, right?

—The twenty-first to be precise.

Morgen paused, but Finn shrugged his incomprehension. She took a smirky sip and made him wait.

—December twenty-first, two thousand twelve: the end of the world. When I saw the silver bracelet that you'd left for...

Morgen broke off midstream, perplexed brow, and asked if she'd said something wrong.

—Nothing, he replied; not really. Only it's not silver: it's platinum.

—O, is that all?

Her look was priceless. She opened her mouth to speak, shaking her head, but it was another moment.

—So, I beg your pardon, the platinum bracelet *with diamonds* which Taylor put on in front of her assembled friends, her siblings, and her nominal fiancé.

Morgen refilled her glass, then his.

—Even were you my type, I wouldn't bloody well get mixed up in that. You've made a declaration, whether you intended to or not.

—I didn't...

He halted, reëxperiencing that first flash of anger he'd felt, uninformed of Saitō's early departure till after she'd boarded her international flight out: a text from her first-class seat. Spring had finally come for him and then left him to face the summer of his abandon alone, the bi-curious girl's party favour. He'd gone birthday shopping for Taylor two days later.

Morgen was all ears.

He looked at the wine and wished for something stronger. There'd been a few odd comments about the bracelet in Vik's group chat but no overt allegations. Nothing like this.

—It was kind of a whim, he said. They match the earrings she always wears. Nothing's going on ¶. I was seeing someone else, but she's fled to a ski resort or a beach on a tropical island for all I know. Taylor and I have hung out some, but only in groups. We've never been out together, just us – not even like this. We're not having an affair or anything like that. You're reading too much into it.

C·P·SERRET,
DIE THE VILLAIN.

Spring Gale,
VI.
★

E ANSWERED the phone after two back-to-back ignored
H   calls, his open book suspended like a sailing gull. Vik
barked into his ear without preamble:
—Why haven't you checked your fucking texts?
—Viktoriya Konstantinovna: I'm reading. Shoo.
—Stop being a little bitch and get your scrawny ass to Taylor's.
Like now.
    His heart skipped a thumpy beat.
—What's up at Taylor's?
—Check your fucking texts.
    The call ended.
    He launched WhatsApp and scrolled down over the pidgin
stream of partial sentences, abbreviations, and initialisms; key-
words: Nate, cheated, Paige.
—Shit.
    Gaylor had become a running gag, the storm after the calm.
Finn had stopped checking his messages and stayed home,
waiting for it to blow over, but the laughter had died today. Real
allegations and partisan finger-pointing. A skirmish line drawn.
He thumbed a message and sent it to Vik: —Omw.
    Wrapt in his cosy lambswool throw, he reset his bookmark,
Korsar interrupted. He stood and wavered, light-headed a moment, but stooped to restore the time-yellowed Soviet print
of Lérmontov to his prized shelf of rarissima, right below the
easeled Bulgakov samizdát displaying its cut 'n' paste inserts.
He straightened and stumbled into the sofa, whelmed by a ver-
tiginous wave, and lay a gasping fish-out-of-water, pinned till
the centrifugal spin slowed.
    He moored himself to the bar. A doubled double over ice,
downed too fast to chill. A splash, hesitate, splash refill. He gar-
gled fifty-proof mint in the bathroom, steadier on sea legs, and
rinsed the sudden sweat from his face.
    He shed his sweats for a sleeveless rosé shift dress he'd not've

worn but for most else at the dry cleaners and hid his undone frisure under a blush RL cloche, Vik-gifted new but factory-distressed. Swift-shadowed eyes, three thumbs of lipstick – dab, dab, dab – he popped into Visvim's on his way out the door, dragging laces, platform wedges and leather jacket in hand.

He drove distractedly but arrived at Taylor's condo in one piece, reshod and afraid to ring the bell, his finger poised but paused. First Trace. Now this, the twilight of Vik's idol? "'Once more vnto the Breach'," he breathed.

A long press of the button to be sure "Deare friends, once more". Vik opened the door in subdued mien, frown lines of the future in wearied relief, the rooms behind her empty and dusk-dim. She hugged him but shifted towards the open exit, her handbag in the crook of one arm.

—She's in her bedroom. I told her it was you.

—Who else is here?

—Nobody. Sam and Lily left after I said you were coming.

He frowned at that.

—And you're leaving too?

—You two need to talk. Details later.

—We haven't been doing anything behind Nate's back. If he effed up, then it's on him.

Vik walked away, saying,

—Text me later.

Finn locked the door and turned to face the waiting plunge, all shadow and silence. He dropped his jacket onto the sofa and glanced about, but there was nothing else for it; Taylor's bedroom was the only light at the end of the tunnel: beige-and-blue from the meticulous fade of a Jan Kath rug to the bedding and wallpaper, all but for the anti-freeze green of her COLOGNE, betwixt a trio of ballerina music boxes, atop her antique chiffonier. She was alone on the khaki-draped canopy bed, cross-leggèd in activewear, amid her plush Nutcracker-themed guard.

Dark hair ravelled in a careless bun, her gold-dust highlights were too artisanal for the sun, and her puffy face that of someone who'd cried, washed, then cried again, distress etched beneath her skin. A black-clad phone in her hands, the offending bracelet encircled one wrist like liquid starlight. He reached her bedside and spoke her name. She responded in kind with a wan smile, and he sat to accept the proffered hug, self-conscious within a once-routine clasp and hyperaware of the warming hand which fell to one bare leg.

—Were you out with someone, she asked, or?

—No; I was home, reading, when Vik called.

Taylor's tone flatlined:

—You dress like that when you're reading.

—Well, I didn't want to show up looking like shit, so…

—You mean, like I do right now?

He did his best to convince her otherwise and apologised.

—But it's my fault, he was saying. I didn't know anything like this would happen just 'cause…

—No. Don't make excuses for him or for what they did. I'll never forgive them for making me look like…

She let it hang, her light-lashed eyes as cold as the North Sea and dark with stormy hues. She looked away from him, jaw clenched.

—I'm sorry you got dragged into this. He's using you as an excuse.

—Anything I can do?

An inadequate thing to say, but her smile resurfaced.

—You're here; that's enough for me. Though where'd Vik go? The bathroom?

—She left.

—O.

Taylor chewed her upper lip and met his gaze again, and within repentine silence, a tightness in his chest. Morgen's words and Gaylor innuendo flashed in mind.

—You know, this is the first time we've been alone together – completely alone – like this.

—That's funny, considering everyone believes…

Her words faltered again, resubmerged within the tidal hush, and a prickling heat rose on his unconcealed skin. It was impossible to ignore her, even in leggings and a ballet-wrap cardigan, her nude lips fine without overdrawn lip liner and gloss.

—Makes me wonder how long they've been going at it, he said and regretted.

Taylor winced but agreed, recounting the output of the girls' group mind for him, defragged and complete with footnotes, appendices, and references – unpacking the tale unto a damning conclusion. He traced a fingertip over chain and skin.

—All this, and I didn't even see you open your present.

—I haven't taken it off once, but why'd you buy it for me? It must have been expensive.

—It goes with the studs you usually wear.

—O, so you noticed. A…

She hesitated on the drawled vowel, a coy hand raised behind one ear.

—Relation of mine gave them to me for my sixteenth.

Something unreadable passed behind blue eyes – something sad or in troubled memory; then she changed subjects in a squealing-rubber swerve to an off-ramp:

—So your thing with Chloë…

—I'm not going to see her again.

—O! You broke up? You didn't say…

He ducked his head.

—Not quite. I'd intended to, but she skipped out on me without warning. Haven't been able to reach her since. My closet is still full of her shit – shit, I'm still wearing it. Tempted to dump it all at Goodwill.

Taylor laughed.

—You so should. She's shady as fuck.

—I know. So done with her. Wish I'd acted sooner.

—I could wish for a lot of things.

—So what happens now: you, Nate?

—I'm going to make Vik cry and give the ring back. And then I'm moving the fuck on with my life.

—Just like that? I expected a tantrum of revenge and Paige's head on a pike.

—Well, you missed that part, but while we were talking it out, I realised I'm free from him now and of all the expectations that went with. So why drag it out? It's not like I was… I feel the same way you do: I don't want to see him, or think about him, or talk about…

—Hint taken. Forget him and tell me something else. Anything.

—Actually, I kind of miss your big glasses.

Finn huffed embarrassment.

—Wish you'd said something before I coughed up all that cash for LASIK.

—You changed a lot for you-know-who.

—Did I really or… ?

—Well, no and yes. Don't get me wrong, you always look amazing, but I'm not afraid of who you really are. You don't need to dress up for me, like with Morgen. I want you to be yourself with me always.

—Taylor, I…

The words reached his lips, then stopped, unborne by a sinking hollow. It flashed before his eyes; the in-burnt memory of fateful words in a different bedroom, almost ten years past: the beshamed wet of spittle dripping down his face after he'd fallen to the floor; Logan lost in a screaming red above the sullied tears of his fetal curl, "Disgusting!" ringing in his ears. All social ties had been shorn via an exigent midterm transfer to an out-of-parish high school and by the parting sneer of those lips that took his first kiss and frequent private "practise", as she'd said, on her laced and teddy-covered bed.

Since sealed within that eye-blackened confessional and his family's tacit omertà, his father's final wife-absent words on it had been candid, the ink-wet transfer application between them. "This is a hard road you're on, and you need to correct your expectations. It's not going to get any easier."

Mánús, in turn, had only broken his devout silence to say, "I don't envy you the weight of your cross."

Finn hung wordless within his prison-house, "Lonely and lost", with pained lips parted till Taylor shushed him, her fingers over his empty mouth.

—I know. I've known for a long time, but it wasn't till I saw the bracelet that I was sure.

She surged forward, an avalanche in tigrine motion. He sank beneath her firm physicality, yielding to the warming press – ô-so-familiar, again surreal – of her kiss and implants. He let her trace linéaments with urgent fingers and lips, listening to his breath till her hand came up between his legs, and he pulled it away, surprised she'd make that move at all. She shifted aside, her body pressed to him, her eyes a limitless blue that spanned his horizon, her whisper cascading synæsthetic tingles down his skin:

—So what now?

Taylor had no idea, and worse, she'd jumped to the popular conclusion, but he wasn't so sure. He licked his moistened lips and picked the safe trope:

—Aren't we s'posed to watch weepy movies and eat ice cream on the couch?

—No way. Champagne. We're celebrating.

H E LOOKED the part of a stray high schooler on campus tour: unmade-up, bejeaned, and band-teed, his grey satchel hung from the chairback. Across from his half-mast americano, oilyblack, the "skinny soy mocha no-whip" he'd ordered for Vik had lost its steam. Perfumed and overdressed for the masstigious Starbucks scene, the fashion editor-to-be was ready for whatever lay next on her blingshevik social calendar, her skin toasted golden-brown by a long weekend on Mustique. She sat before he could rise for a hug, heart-shaped Moschino sunglasses a cherry-red coronet atop her platin-blonde cascade.

—What's really happening? – I don't believe Taylor.

—Et tu, chouchou? Not going to say hello, either?

The teacup Morkie stared at Finn with black button eyes from the straitjacket of Vik's tabled handbag; her phone beneath one hand like a loaded gun – pointed at him – Vik's sharp retroussé nose twitched as if scenting blood.

—Whatevs. Have you two hooked up or not?

—Not that it's any of yours, but no.

Vik gaped at him.

—What the fuck have you been doing?

—We've hung out a couple times, but she's been busy. School an' stuff.

—Is she, like, seeing someone else?

—No! Well, I don't think so.

—Then why haven't…

He raised placating hands.

—I know what you're thinking – what everyone's thinking – but Taylor just got out of a long relationship, and I don't want to jump into things and be the rebound or some side piece like with Chloë.

Vik took a tepid sip and grimaced, the pain of fashionable lateness.

—It's not a rebound if you were already involved. Duh.

—We weren't…

—Having an affair? You two've been in orbit since last year, and I told her she should take you on a getaway for two before the wedding.

—What!

—Nate wouldn't've had a clue, but she kept saying she doesn't like girls. Such a liar. I saw how she reacted to that Tiffany's box before she even opened it. Everybody did, even her douchey fiancé. He put new rims on her BMW for her birthday. like, sure, her car is on fleek, but really?

The cant of Vik's head said everything.

—This is your chance. Your moment. So unless your ex is back in…

—She's not.

—Then you must be hooking up with someone else, if…

She'd misread his hesitance for a different kind of conflict, to broach or not to broach, the question. Finn denied and counter-accused:

—I'm not seeing anyone else, but who else are you talking to besides Misha?

—It's only talk, unlike all the boys trying to step to Taylor right now.

—What? Which boys? She hasn't said…

Vik interrupted, lifting her phone:

—Why would she? E'to vojna: make your move or lose by default. Most of them have been waiting for Nate to fuck up – check her FB. I'd bet there are even some girls, now that everyone knows, like that girl…

—Jesus.

—But like I told her, Taylor deserves someone special. And be-sides, you know how she is about ballet.

A deep shadow fell across Finn, seated far from the sun.

—What does ballet have to do with anything?

—She said you have "a classical line" or something. Hasn't she asked you about it?

—No.

Though texting, Vik's look was shrewd.

—But you must have.

—For a minute. My mom made me.

She hadn't spared the rod but, losing her temper once, had left visible bruises with a hairbrush. One of the other dance moms had threatened to call the police, and the ballet school had spat him out like soured milk and alerted the other dance studios in the area, severing the strings of her ballerina marionette once-and-for-all. A shock release from the inescapable routine that reached back to his earliest memories, in an exertion long emptied of all but its geometry – an abstract relation of moving lines; he'd filled his novel afternoons with manga, sixties punk, and semiweekly Japanese till Logan and the snarly dazzle of her unlicensed Jagger-gap grin. She'd prised him out from behind his books and into the teen dramatics of her all-girls claque and their inexhaustible boy-talk.

—I wasn't into it, and I'm sure it showed: I had the form but not the feeling. You have to express everything with your body, and I wasn't…

—But you are. You don't see what we see. It's a part of you.

Vik sniffled and took another sip of her mocha, eyes fixed on her phone.

—Taylor says she gave up ballet since she doesn't have a body like yours – not that she would have gone pro anyways. Not with her parents. Says she got too buff, so she switched to lacrosse.

He dug his nails into this arm. Harder.

It had always been there: the crushing pressure of his absolute prison, shrinking: already too small but closing in, squeezing the air from his lungs. Cutting had held the panic attacks back till he'd started slipping away – far away – within the bovarysme of shōnen heroes' journeys.

—What she means is it's a genetic thing. Ballet dancers are as fit as anyone competing in Olympic track an' field, but they don't bulk up no matter how hard they train – the ones that do get cut or drop out like Taylor. At least they used to, but I'm not that fit or flexible anymore. It's a residual resemblance at this point.

—Don't tell her that. She has some kind of ballerina fetish. Like, look at her: she wishes she was you, but you do look great together.

He made a face.

—A *ballerina* is a principal dancer in a ballet company – like the one at Taylor's party – not every poseuse or has-been that's done barre. Or every little kid pushed into dance by their mom; I've never been a ballerina, and a fanatic like Taylor knows the difference.

—I doubt there's enough of those ballerinas to go around. You'll have to take Nate's place and go with her to the ballet from now on – we can so go shopping if you need more formal gowns! And don't forget, she has all of those old costume ballets on disc. Pack something comfy to wear over there.

Finn grunted, expression flat. His mother had leant towards the neoclassical: Maillot, Kylián, & al. He'd found them abstruse, at eight or ten, but in light of his mother's aspirationalism, he'd seen Taylor's balletomania as an idiosyncrasy of the cosmocratic bell jar. His window wall.

—H'mf. How many times can she watch *Giselle*?

—You could wear a white tutu in the bedroom. Details after.

—Yeah, no.

—But she's home right now. Studying, she says. You should shave your legs, put on your face, and get over there. Bring an overnight bag.

—Vik, that's a bit…

—Gotta run.

Vik texted another moment, then stood and shouldered her dog-laden purse. He half-rose in confusion, hands spread on the tabletop.

—O. I'll, um, walk you to your truck.

They pushed their way through the packed coffee-bar press of backpacked kids and silvered bohos, out onto a sidewalk a-swarm with frumpy students. The brick-walled swards of the expansive campus were separate and unequal: an ivied string of capsular pearls wound across the midtown pale. She led him through a cramped, exorbitant parking lot, then fished in her handbag, somewhere beneath her shivery dog, for a keyless key fob–thing hung with a cloisonné Pinkie Pie.

—There are so many crazy rumours floating around you two. I've even heard Taylor was cheating on Nate with a model. You moonlighting on me, Gigi?

Finn leant against the B-pillar of her oligarch's-little-princess Geländewagen, an enamellike grand feu–white.

—Sounds like Nate is trying to save face by making shit up, by making me into something I'm definitely not. Sure, I've had plenty of practice being fake in front of a camera, but I'm not eight feet tall or whatever. Not even in Loubs.

Vik gave him a dark look over her Kubrick movie-poster shades; then she climbed up and up into the driver's seat, door left wide open while securing her handbagged pup. She turned back to Finn and caught a fistful of his shirt, pulling him into a chocolate kiss of the most luscious lips ever, and the tip of her pierced tongue met his with the surging heat of an electric current. She released him from her botte secrète but sighed, sounding disappointed in the end:

—Those lips. But I didn't feel anything.

Hard-boiled beneath the shell, he faked a comic shrug.

—Sorry?

—Text me later. And remember what I said. Get going.

The door shut with the steely resonance of a bank vault, and Vik queen-waved before rolling past. He signalled with two fingers. She pulled away into steady afternoon traffic, the sun aglare on its brillig balcony seat. He fanned himself with one hand.

—Wow.

SPRING GALE⸍
VIII.

★

AYLOR'S DINING ROOM table was laminose with open
T   textbooks and the latest iPad, an old school H P 12C,
and a pristine bottle of mineral water transported by
ship, rail, and truck from Amphion-les-Bains. He hung his bag
on a high-backed oaken dining chair, the seat stacked with back
issues of Bilanz. H'mf. Swiss-German.

She sauntered over to her living room and yawned with feline
flair, space-framelike capri leggings below a king-logoed Brine
tee, Le Corsaire midplay on the modest flatscreen: pas de deux. He
held a fragment of Byron's ur-Corsair close but wouldn't recite or
even think of it here. She sank into the sofa, phone beside her,
long legs ankle-crossed beneath her Arts-and-Crafts coffee table.
—Thanks for the drink. My brain was about to fry.

She sighed after another sip, eyes closed. Finn drifted nearer, a
wavering petal on a winding brook, and debated on where to sit:
right beside her on the sofa, or just within arm's reach, or away
on the easy chair – she's too busy for anything like that – or on
the causeuse like bait on a Conibear trap. He remained standing.
—No prob. I was having coffee on campus with Her Most Serene
Highness, and she mentioned you were hitting the books.
Figured it was the least I could do.
—O? What's Vik up to?
—She didn't say, but she was dressed to the nines.
—Mike, I'd guess. What's this called? It tastes like white choc-
olate fudge.

An anticipatory grin blew his punchline.
—Liquid Cocaine. I asked the barista for something strong
enough for a long study session. It has four shots.
—Four shots after Adderall and a half-tab of Dexedrine. I'll be
ready for lift-off soon.
—A D D? Had no clue.
—No. It helps my grades.
—Um, isn't that dangerous?

—A lot less dangerous than letting my GPA drop below three-eight. In my family, perfection is expected, not rewarded. You wouldn't believe what…

She spoke a little of the allowance from which her five-star well-being hung and of the myriad earmarks attached to her pending trust fund, algid with old pique and bided time.

—And my parents' wills have more clauses and subclauses than my prenup.

Taylor closed the parenthetical with a shake of her head, eyes burning colder than her drink. She took a gurgling sip as she hit bottom.

—I have Inderal, too, for nerves before tests. Altogether, I'd say it's worth half a GPA point, at least. It's like steroids in pro sports. Mandatory if you want to be in the game.

He left the heffalump under the rug, conspicuous bump, and picked up one of the glossy booklets stacked beside her coffee-table picture books.

—Rhinoplasty? What for; deviated septum?

—No, but I've thought about a nose job for a while. Graduation present to myself?

His make-up failed to conceal his doubled discomfort. He hadn't gone home to change clothes, &c.; but after one last look in the rearview, he'd paused to put on an-other face in a budding panic despite Taylor's assurance to the contrary – the taste of crow so much like rose-scented lipstick.

—Taylor, your nose is perfect.

—No; look closer: there's a dorsal bump like my mom's.

—You might've bumped your head, but there's nothing wrong with your nose.

She'd pointed with emphatic insistence, but her nose appeared to have been sculpted with Camille Claudel's obsessive passion, every contour exactly where it belonged. He crossed the MINEFIELD warning.

—I hate to be the one bringing this up, but is it plastic surgery addiction?

—I've only had my boobs done. I'm not addicted to anything.

—That's all? Really?

—Yes, really. What'd you think?

—I don't know. You seem too perfect overall.

—The way you said that, it wasn't a compliment.

—Taylor, I meant…

She sat up and set down her drained cup of cloudy ice with an assertive rattle.

—No. Listen. I take care of myself: I don't smoke. I don't do drugs. I almost never have more than…

He listened like a scolded child, head hung and cursing Vik. Taylor counted out the strictures of her hard-striven illusion and forged on undaunted, out of fingers:

—And that's half my skincare regimen, at most – and none of that is surgical either.

—Sorry, I never would've guessed it was that much maintenance. But one thing, how long does the spray tan last?

—I go once a week.

—Could you skip one? I'm curious.

She checked her phone.

—I guess, but I'm not going blonde.

He played dumb.

—Blonde?

—My natural colour. I figured you were going to ask. You'd be hot, blonde. Or ginger?

—Not my thing. No wild hair colours or body mods.

—And you haven't had any work done at all? Not even lip fillers?

—No, I've always looked like someone punched me in the mouth. I wouldn't be satisfied with anything surgery could achieve for me – and what you have to go through? I didn't even want my mom to pierce my ears.

His refusal had led to the worst belting she'd ever given him, from a snapped spoon to the wooden hairbrush that had broken his ballet chains; she'd beaten him to the ground. His ears forcibly pierced withal, he'd tossed the gold studs in an airport restroom after the final goodbye, only to wipe his eyes against unexpected tears: "'Today, Mammy is dead'," quoth sotto voce, trembly lip, failing to laugh as he'd imagined.

—Do braces count?

—No, but getting poked with needles on a stick might.

—That's different. But actual scalpel-and-stitches surgery? Not the answer for me. Nothing short of sci-fi magic.

—But it is for me. You're like a jewel, and I bet no one would be willing to work on you anyway, but it's not fair you get to look like a model after five hours of Photoshop.

—I'm not even gonna go there, but if you try getting a nose job, I'll sit on you, so you can't go.

—Go ahead. You don't weigh anything.

He stepped up with rushing abandon, but Taylor caught his wrists mid-descent – a twisting, tussling, laughing rassle; and, turned over her lap, the first slap across his bottom shocked him still. A thrill shivered through him, again and again – a new heat burned his face, then mirrored, alight from the belly down. Pulsing; it was fire.

Her voice husked:

—That's for what you said.

She pushed him down onto the sofa, eyes gleaming, billows breath. He didn't stop her. Didn't want to. An-other face pressed through her features – or a trick of the light – and the stranger's mouth found his. Again and again, familiar hands caressed, twisted, and stung, branding every inch of skin while her lips planted flags on every promontory of his surrender.

★

TAYLOR's bedroom was duskfire-lit orange-rose in passing. Her head was at rest upon a folded arm, other face submerged or never'd been, and he gazed into the Palantírian deep of her distended pupils – was it her or the amphetamines?

—Are you still feeling… ?

—Nate? No; it was never a romance novel. Our relationship was like a rôle that they made us play, him and me. They've been trying to groom Nate to be the next JFK and need me to be his Jackie – never mind what I want ¶. So much for the once-and-future Camelot, thank God. But I've known Nate a long time – way before college – and I cared about him, sometimes. Sometimes he was mean. You have no idea ¶. He had a certain appeal, I guess, and the best dimples. Not what I'd always dreamed of, but not totally awful.

—Not totally awful; that sounds like a romance novel.

—Right? That's my life: all romance novels and a linear algebra test tomorrow.

—Why the eff would you even need that?

Taylor shifted up onto one elbow.

—Quantitative economics. Linear algebra is super boring, but

worth it now that I can pursue my goals unhindered. I don't
need Nate or a hyphenated last name; they were in my way. Why
settle for a brilliant career and First Lady?

Finn squinted at her non-sarcastic ambition. Who is this person?
—So what happens now, post-Nate?
—Well, no winter wedding. I still have finals and graduation in
May. And then Cambridge in October, but I'm leaving early and…
—I meant long-term. The big picture.
—Well, first, my PhD. They wanted me to go to law school, but
fuck that noise. I have a Fellowship waiting for me at BIS, in Bâle.
And then after a few prominent positions, a seat at Davos, and a
teaching stint at a university, I'll get myself appointed Chair of
the Fed. And join the Group of Thirty at some point.

He pictured her seated among Fleming's SPECTRE.
—The G-thirty? Didn't know you were a Bond villain.

She pinched him. Hard.
—PhD economists steer the ship – you know that. Most of what
you see on C-SPAN is a sideshow to the calls made by the central
banks. Finance news is the only real news.
—I don't watch any news. I read…
—Finn, you have to, or you won't know what's going on behind
the scenes. My mom and the rest of them don't get it, but you'll
understand once I become Fed Chair, and so will they if they're
still around ¶. That's the most powerful seat on the planet, not
the ones in the White House and Bundeskanzleramt. Monetary
policy is what…

Every word of her Weltanschauüng rang with a ruling-caste
confidence embrittled by long ressentiment, her heart balanced
not with a feather but by sceptre and orb. She was – would be – the
face and white-clenched fist of her supranational „Geldadel", her
upstart money-aristocracy, of Spenglerite „economic war-man-
agement and [the] ceaseless struggle of money against law."
Nation-states were small potatoes. Chips on the board.

„And while historians will make a bigger deal of the first
woman President", she was saying, „the first woman appointed
Fed Chair will have a greater impact on world history, whether
she gets credit for it or not. That won't be me, but my time will
come – after loads of preparation and bullshit politicking."

„So not Cæsar's wife but Cæsar?"
„„Cæsar or nothing'."

C·P·SERRET,
DIE THE VILLAIN.

SPRING GALE,
IX.
★

H IS UNEASY WAIT ended with a welcome bell. He opened the door to censored siren logos – boxing Mélusine – on the twin paper cups in Vik's hands, and Taylor's ring shawl drawn about his shoulders, accepted his in a prayerwise clasp. Vik was school-lass drab: from destroyed designer jeans to cheeky twin-tail hair, a posh spoof of the matriculated norm, but her handbag was an oriflamme of rude display, waved under the noses of campus Russophobes, with a year's salty tuition in porosus crocodile. He could no longer tell *posh* from *poshly'j*, steeped in exclusivist poshlost' – or *poshlust*, per Nabókov. She closed the door.

—It sounded like you needed one. 'Mericano, right?

—My hero.

A light squeeze scented with bubblegummy tuberose and they faced off on the chesterfield, surrounded by the objets trouvés of Taylor's horror vacui, Vik's handbag set atop the coffee table with her petit chou, a pink bow in his hair. She lifted her sunglasses and took a sip of her soy sort of mocaccino, phone in her other hand.

—Alls you need is leggings; then you'll look like a couple while you lounge here together.

—I'll pass. And since when are you even a fan? Never seen you wear them.

—They make me look fat.

Fat was her favourite hate word, though her jeans were leggings-snug.

—You're not fat, Vika, and real curves are a wonderful thing.

He caught a fleeting hint of eye-roll – an unwanted touch brushed away. She set her cup aside.

—Only my relatives still call me Vika – well, and my stepmom. I don't use it here. Not anymore, and…

"Only my dad still calls me Vikusha," she'd said to his first-and-final attempt at the diminutive, but he'd heard Mixaíl call her *Vika* more than once. Stuff it, Gigi. Vik sniffled and pinched her nose.

—An anorexic size zero is in no position to say shit about curves.

Finn groaned with melodramatised effort.

—I'm not anorexic. And FYI, I've been drinking those protein shakes. I'm back up to a two now.

—Ha, please. You're like those gymnasts with delayed puberty.

—Been there, done that, got the bloodstains.

—How'd you like to get punched in that pretty mouth?

He stoppered his smirking lips with a long sip. Vik gave him an irritated look, thumbs paused above her listing phone.

—So what had to wait till I got here?

—Well, I followed your advice yesterday, and now I'm out of my depth.

—You got what you wanted, so what's the…?

—Wait. What did Taylor tell you?

—About last night? Everything, I guess. I told her she finally caught her sylphide.

He shivered, exposed before the knowing twist of Vik's smile, and held himself, bare arms spotted with coffee-stain bruises.

—Huh. You *do* know what happened to the sylphide when it got caught?

—There are worse ways to go.

She bloomed within a warming air of Woodhousian gloat. His Galaxy vibed atop the coffee table. She glanced from her phone to his.

—Everyone knows, by the way.

—I wonder how they found out.

—Gigi. You took Taylor from Nate by throwing it in his face on her birthday. You hooked up, and now you're hanging out in her place like you live here. Where's the fucking problem?

—It's… I never believed this would actually happen. I wasn't ready for it to be real, for…

His voice failed, expression crumpling. Vik leant closer, her words hushed:

—Did she, like, do something gross?

—No, not gross, but for one thing, there's no way it was her first time, though she kept pretending it was. H'mf. Still is.

—Like, not her first time with a girl?

Finn frowned, again-bit, but nodded, his fingers knotted blush and pale.

—Has she ever said?

—No, I told you yesterday: she always said she didn't like girls. She must be a bigger liar than I thought.

—She's way more experienced than me and kind of… kinky?

Pale eyebrows rose.

—What? Did she read that *Fifty Shades* thing and, like, buy some handcuffs?

—No, nothing that campy. No props.

—You need to show me on a doll where the bad girl touched you?

—No need for a doll. Everywhere.

He took a longer sip of his cooling coffee and gathered himself for the trial – the whiskey in his flask drained to the last minim first thing.

—With Chloë, at first, it was like we were trying to figure out how to – you know, you've seen porn – but…

He gave more details than his wont, aflush with wet memory of the seething frequency of breath and skin, unsure if Vik followed or was uncomfortable in her silence. He forged on.

—And now, it's even the way she looks at me. This morning I kind of hid in the bathroom till she left for school.

—So, those bruises?

—Yes.

—Should I talk to… ?

—No; that would be weird.

Not that his admonition would stop her – nothing was off-limits in their TMI girl-talk. He was no longer shocked or surprised by the frank ruthlessness of their relationship realpolitik, wishing he could scrub his mind of all he'd heard about bimmerati boyfriends and hookups with one-night Chads.

—But you can see I'm out of my depth – way out – and she's out of my league.

—Are you for real? Compared to you, Taylor's, like, a muggle, and from the sound of it, a fucking freak. She can't buy what you were born with, not even with everything she spends on her look, and who knows what else is in her closet.

—Vik.

—No, Gigi; listen to me. You're out of her league, and not only in looks. It's the way you wear Loubs like they're two-dollar flip-flops, the vintage sports car you drive every day – even to get groceries – and…

She touched his arm, her fingers gauded with wirelike rings of rose gold.

—It's the hottest ink I've ever seen. It's the way you do it all, like you just don't care: no one compares to you. I mean, shit, you even smoke cigars like a boss.

The bottom fell out, tugging on the corners of his rosebud mouth, the boundary between himself and his illusive rôle breaking or broken down, like a Venn diagram near union. He clenched red-tipped fingers no longer his. After everything, he'd become Ane-san's maiko. After so many lies.

—You know I'm right, she prompted after waiting with more than her usual decorum.

—Yes. I've painted myself into a corner.

—Gigi! Do you even want to be with her? Maybe you should walk away and…

—No, said something in his voice; I'm staying.

Vik raised a hand to his cheek.

—I told you before: I thought Taylor deserved someone special. I might be wrong about her but not about you. You don't act like you're the centre of the fucking universe the way Nate and these fuckboys do.

—Yeah, no; I despise them.

Finn took a deep breath, long decided to be nothing like the fuckboyerie, ever, no matter what. Vik dropped her hand and asked him for news of the expatriate Japanese tattoo artist whose references he was checking on her behalf. The morning waned while they discussed her slapdash ideas for a new piece of concealable ink, a once-warm coffee soyshake forgotten alongside her handbag and its silent captive till his phone buzzed with an emphatic iMessage shortcut-text from Taylor: —On my way!

Vik offered to skip her afternoon classes and hang but made herself scarce after he promised details and to split if Taylor got too weird. He lay still on the sofa and watched the whiteness of the ceiling instead of the muted TV, thinking of Trace and the oceans between them – oceans between veld and moor.

The lock rasped with an inserted key, and the front door swung open. Taylor's smile was immediate and natural below

a quizzical brow, stretch hoody unzipped
above leggings and trainers,
black 'n' blue her
colours.

★

C·P·SERRET,
DIE THE VILLAIN.

NIGHT,
I.

★

ILVERLESS CLOUD. Veiled stars. The grey grumbles of
S   evening traffic and the flashing thunder of e-lit sirens.
   Carmilla's was raised in streetlamp-shadowed relief,
black-on-black, above an opaque and featureless glass door. He
blinked in delayed recognition.
—O. I'm not sure about this.
   Taylor had used the keyword *vampy* in her message, but he'd
prinked and primped with the riddle unsolved. He wanted to
slap himself. He'd found the dress shrivelled over one of his
hangers like a black samite scarf – a fogged recall of Saitō wearing
it once; "fanservice," he'd called it. A foot of flash tape to secure
the risqué plunging neckline, his skin became tan tiger stripes
through the clawed design, in a straining stretch of webby fabric
held together by anime physics and a whiskey-dosed suspension of disbelief. Foundation tint and concealer blended away
the bruises covered by most other dresses, and plum gloss the
almost-healed split lip.
   They were two-of-a-kind before the black gate and the blood-
less horizon but for his undulant waves and her ungilt flat-ironed
hair. She was as radiant as the daystar in black eclipse, stripped
of that rich but too-even airbrushed sheen and its plastic air of
artifice. High-heeled over-the-knee boots went all the way down
from her black peplum romper in a stretchy second-skin fit, his
Daffodiles just bridging the gap in lifted heights.
   Taylor had picked him up and parked without explaining;
then, scattering gawkers by the wayside, they'd walked together
to their secret destination, midtown new busy after rush hour's
slomo surge and fall, a spate of honks and catcalls from cars
stopped at the light. She'd told him,
—I'm going to show you off.
—Show me off? he'd replied.

—You know, like if you got a new handbag from the Row. You need to take it out and show it off. Make everyone jealous.

—You compared me to a bag.

—That was a compliment, dummy.

She'd brought him to a stop before the dark edifice, but his knees went weak after his ô, and their extravagant kaiseki-ryōri dégustation sank in his belly like tumbling lead. She nudged him.

—Jesus, Finn, don't hang on me; it's just a bar. C'mon, I've never been here before, either.

—Is it even open?

—Can't you hear the music?

Taylor tugged him forward till the handleless door levered wide, and he took a deep breath, towed within: "#1 Crush" at the threshold of aural comfort, the lights turned down strip-club dark. Tavern-standard booths upholstered scarlet against blackened woods, the black-clad staff was clearing the red 'n' black chequered floor of tables and chairs. A period portrait of Mircalla, Countess Karnstein hung frameless alongside other prop art; it was always a Countess or Marquise with these things.

He shied from the full brunt of massed female gazes, clinging to Taylor's arm as they passed through a modest midevening crowd: office-wear lingering over after-hours drinks, wannabe Suicide Girls and obligatory flannel were interspersed among the neap tide of evening wear. They sat at the bar, but Taylor appeared taller, though seated, her chin raised.

—See, you didn't die.

—The night is young. I feel like a piece of meat.

—You look super-hot. I was tempted to take you straight home after dinner.

—We can still do that.

—No, not yet. Here we can let our hair down and have some fun without the usual…

She scanned the surround.

—Faces. Besides, the night is young, and this isn't our last stop.

—So, after this?

—Another surprise.

Taylor's self-assured calm rang off-note to the tune of her "new to all this" refrain; this scene below her, she looked down from a high seat. How many girls had there been? How many lies? Morgen had known something, but how much? He filed it along with Taylor's other BS, but recent days had passed in a heated whirl – if outside her many "I'm too busy" nights – his social continua sundered in an instant: Vik and her contingent siding with Gaylor, Paige everywhere else.

Caught at the boundary of Taylor's event horizon, he struggled against her – not to resist, but to incite and to yield. He was on the razor's edge without a net or safety word. It was no game but dangerous, thrilling, and real.

A bartender cut in, Goth nonpareil in cat-eye glasses and a 'toony Burtonesque style, with haphazard stitch-lines inked on butterscotch skin. She presented ornate absinthe menus, talking up the flavour of the moment. They ordered a fountain for Taylor and a cocktail for him, but the bartender questioned his choice:

—No green faëry?

—I am the green faëry.

Her teeth were white against witchy lip gloss.

—Kayla.

—Finn.

She stared at him a moment longer, then turned to pull a bottle of Frapin from the top shelf. Taylor squeezed his bare knee and leant close to his ear.

—I don't think I've ever been invisible before.

—O stop.

Kayla set a small single-spout fountain in front of Taylor, followed by an absinthe glass, a slotted spoon, and a caramel-coloured sugar cube. Then Kayla made a heavy two-handed pour into a stainless shaker filled with ice. Taylor started the drip, the droplets opalescing into the green liquor before her.

—It's pretty, like the colour of your eyes in changing light.

Kayla placed a coupe glass by his hand with the delicacy reserved for nitroglycerin, a black umbrella garnished at napkin side.

—And your atomic bomb.

He clinked his glass to Taylor's, braced for the boom! A few rounds drew them into thujone's jovian sway, and their bubble of flirtation, out on the floor, distanced from the heating press of bodies around them till Taylor pulled away with a curse. A tall woman, aloof from the sea-parting crowd, clued him in with a Norma Jeane wink.

Von Teesian retro-glam compleat, a slinky violet gown wrapped around her gracile tournure, defying all but cartoon imagination, all the way down to shoes you couldn't see. Thirtyish, with that air of peak refinement, of the optimal form; her forties' pin-up hair was the richest shade of chocolat noir, framing a face from his mother's fashion rags a decade past: from the dainful poise of her chin, lips as full as Vik's and glossed cherry red, to the wide-set eyes and the proud feline cheekbones built over a square jaw. No mere face but an eikon. Her name escaped him, but she'd been another cliché heiress turned top model. He'd soured on models after discovering the swaggery James King was, in fact, Jaime.

Taylor's hands slipped from his waist, and she drew herself up, shoulders squared. He stayed put, drawn by that heavy-lidded gaze but held back by Taylor's rigid composure. A frosty exchange of air kisses read intimates but hostiles – a duel long past first blood – and all eyes and phone cameras were on them till he was beckoned forth and engraced. Taylor made bleak-faced introductions:

—Finn, my cousin Tessa.

Tessa was taller than Trace in heels, pointing to platforms behind her hem.

—Enchantée.

—Enchanté.

She leant in, a surprise la bise for him as well: left, right, left. Her fragrance was smoky, decadent, like burning fields of jessamine.

—Second cousins. Come along. My car is waiting.

He held Taylor's hand as she followed at Tessa's gown-draped heels. A white Phantom idled in the no-parking zone, rear windows blacked out, and a white-uniformed chauffeuse opened the coach door. He slipped first into the isolation of the partitioned cabin. Taylor backed in beside him, a warding hand placed between; she faced the entrance of Tessa's violet stretch.

—How'd you find us?

He took in Tessa's photogenic angles and proportions, cut for the mirror concealed behind the DSLR lens. She wasn't wearing platforms but thin-soled heels, that tall. She lit a gilt-tipped white cigarette in methodic silence, a sadō master mid-ceremony, to answer after a meditative draw:

—Don't ask foolish questions chérie – you, of all people, should know better. But be thankful it was I who did. Word of this little spectacle might not reach the rest of the family or will be blamed on me. My position is less fragile than yours.

—How, exactly, would anyone find out?

Tessa sighed on an exhale.

—This sudden incompetence is troubling. I've paid off the life-style photographer that was shooting the crowd when I arrived – the one you somehow missed. Carmilla's is a tourist trap, after all, and it's Friday night. Think of the camera phones in every purse; there are consequences. Your petite amie appears peakèd. You've already dined?

—Yes, but...

—Something light then; tapas perhaps?

She spoke in the manner of one accustomed to obedience without argument or question. Cigarette raised in the other, she rested a long-fingered hand on the thigh bared between Taylor's boot and hemline – an unchallenged claim on absolute territory.

Tessa looked not at her but him, lucid eyes of amber-brown beneath vailed lids, asking her, aside,

—Does your lovely friend know about us, chérie?

—She doesn't know anything.

MIDSOMER,
NIGHT,
II.

★

HIS EVENING'S IMPRUDENCE aside, Tessa began
T   after the waiter withdrew, I'm aware of your little tiff
with Nate and the rumours of who's come between
you. Have you really returned the ring?

Taylor's ruddy scowl deepened, revealing shades of expression
Finn hadn't heretofore seen – short of that first snap of anger
when she'd belted him, profuse with teary contritions after;
though he'd never offer to help her cook again. He was the odd
man out at their four-seater, leant towards Taylor's end. They
faced off across a linen field, steel bared.

—If you've heard all that, she replied, then my mom…

—May have heard as well.

—Shit. She's going to summon me home again. Did Britt… ?

—No. Nor Hunter.

Tessa swirled her glass of Málaga red, Lacrimæ Christi, and
took another ruminative sip.

—When did you intend to tell them of the broken engagement?
There are great expectations centred on you and Nate.

—Sometime this summer. I was thinking… I thought if I waited
till…

—It was too late to avoid disaster? You should've come to me
immediately, but I see why you didn't; it's obvious. You're obvious. We'll prepare something, but tomorrow when your head
is clear. Try the wine; it's excellent.

She turned from Taylor's fuming silence to his watchful one,
assessing him over her wine glass in a gesture that recalled
Morgen, but talked past him again:

—And where ô where did you catch this particular vixen?

—I've been called that before, Finn interposed, but I'm not a
vixen.

Taylor placed a hand on his inkless arm.

—Let's leave her out of this. I told you: she doesn't know anything.

—But she must, said Tessa. If you'd kept her secret, kept it dis-crète, then yes, you could keep her ignorant, but now she lies at the heart of the coming storm. Our family, a family...

He sipped his wine, Jerez brandy back. Tremors of tension quavered from Taylor's clenched jaw down to the fingers squeez-ing his arm while Tessa continued her lecture unchallenged. Their prized bay-window view of the snaggletoothed downtown skyline went unwitnessed, the classical Spanish guitar unheard, three floating candle bowls between them, captive and burning lonely.

—And those like us, Tessa was saying, must live two or even three separate lives. It was too risky to parade her out in the open – even with your college friends – and while you haven't courted fame as yet, you're not exactly anonymous; the wrong image in the tabloid press or the old society pages and there will be repercussions. A high-profile theme bar like Carmilla's is too théâtrical – I've warned you about those sorts of places before. Why not Divya or... ?

—I couldn't. I didn't want...

—Your other lovers to see your prize, your prize to meet your other lovers, and for her to discover your alter egos?

Taylor looked at him, abashed puppy dog eyes a touch too wide and sea-cold. He'd known, but he'd had no idea. It was clear Tessa had manœuvered this revelation, and her poisonous words shivered over his skin with the unlight of the new moon:

« « Chercheuses d'infini, dévotes et satyres, | Tantôt pleines de cris, tantôt pleines de pleurs ... »

She recited another quatrain at length, misappropriating Baudelaire's verses like psalms illumined out of context – were a Lesbosian tragédie staged before the dimpled poise of her chin – scattering Pierian rose petals, blue as scorpion blood. No song of Bilitis, this.

—But no more business talk for tonight.

Little left but the idlest high-circuit badinage, Taylor drank with humourless efficiency through the second bottle. Tessa's wedding band caught at his curiosity, but he played his cards close, marvelling at her sinuous grace – even the smallest ges-ture choreographed around her transcendent inflexions. The flowing wine and processionade of rich yet ephemeral bites ceased when she signalled the waiter, her car awaiting them on their descent to street level. Inside the spacious cabin, he found himself wedged between them and gazed up into Tessa's amber vaults, seeking the hidden volumes of Taylor's story.

—Where now? Taylor's parked at…

—My home's nearby. Certain matters are best kept private.

She yanked his head back by the hair and kissed him like it was a foregone conclusion. His foremost objection folded beneath him when Taylor kissed his neck from behind. Then the flash tape ripped free with a sharp band-aid sting; they tore his plunging neckline asunder.

They left him naked and alone upon a vast canopied bed, hollowed amid the tousled and bloodstained fine linens: a voiceless heart in undreaming sleep, one hand on tender breast. Just a body washed ashore, shuddering breath.

He stirred at a gentle knock on the door, riven with soreness and lead-limbed, one sylphidine wrist bound with a scarf the shade of weeping plums, flamingoes rampant on rumpled silk. The air moved behind him, Taylor voicing his name with clarion sunshine – all's right in the world. She spoke again to his moveless silence in questioning tones that circled the bed:

—Finn? Are you awake? The car is ready to take us back. Sorry about your torn dress, but…

Her buoyant chatter ceased. Wreathed within reëclipsed radiance, she held a black bundle in her arms and a white card under her thumb. He was numb to his expression. She'd emerged from Tessa's shade wholly other: once-slipping mask fallen away, she'd teetered on the abhuman, his every limit breached and done, raccoon eyes watering.

He slipped nude from the sheets and unknotted silk, irrelievable shame dragging at every motion. His wrists purpled with bruising, he accepted the heavy bathrobe and pursed the business card without checking it. Taylor stood apart, ungreeted and unanswered: the troubled linéaments of a prince in rarest doubt. She faltered:

—Tessa said… She said to go to any boutique uptown. Pick out anything; it'll be taken care of. You… Call her PA.

He followed Taylor to the grand staircase in the main entry hall, the strike of her heels reëchoing museumlike off of chivalrous frescœs and cavalier bas-relief, him wrapt within the rich penury of ivory-black amid a vast Piranesian flagrance ornamented with Rayonnant flourishes and long mediæval shadows. The hybridised interior was even more grotesque by daylight: from whitewashed boiserie and gilded gesso to vast ribbed vaults, Pentelic marble, and ersatz Mannerist statuary. Abstracted from himself, it recalled Bickel's bloodied flights of era-bridging costumier's fancy for *La Reine Margot* – the Proddies speared like Taiji dolphins.

The chauffeuse left them on midtown asphalt, next to the black mass of Taylor's parked coupé. She drove, no questions asked, and unheeded scenery passed back across the bridge to the bay. She stopped outside his home. He stared out the glass. Her voice warbled with strain:

—Are you breaking up with me?

His was dull and distant: a gritty, shell-shocked sound:

—Park for now. We'll talk inside.

He showered till the water ran cold, scrubbing a paw-printlike bloodstain from his inner thigh with red-lacquered nails and a well-worn loofah. He slipped into the jacquard shell of an anil yukata, still muted, and checked his throat in the closet mirror. He'd passed out at least once, a fant'sy silk rumāl noosed about his neck.

He filled two tumblers with ice and poured himself a double rye. A deep swallow – quit drinking tomorrow – then he poured two more. Taylor waited on the sofa, shoulders hunched, Koko shedding on her lap and purring in noiseful bliss. He handed Taylor a glass but sat across from her in the relocated LC3, his legs folded beside him. She hesitated, chasing a small sip with a deep grimace, eyes downcast. He asked,

—How'd all this begin: you, Tessa?

—They were always sending me away. That time, to board in the UK. I made some new friends – you've met most of them – and ended up summering at Morgen's. We ran into Tessa, in Paris, by accident; she was still modelling then, at the peak of her career ¶. I'd known her forever, and she knew who I was – what I was – better than I did. She's irresistible when she wants something; I was fifteen.

Taylor's eyes – expectant, pleading – lifted to meet his.

—She was sophisticated. Glamourous. She'd been everywhere and seen everything. For the longest time, I wanted to be her ¶.

After that, I spent my hols in Monaco or wherever else Tessa wanted to go. My parents didn't care where I was so long as I maintained my GPA, didn't cause them any embarrassment, and showed up for Christmas in Southampton. Nothing changed after sixth form, and…

No doubt they'd crossed paths back then, unknowingly, between two summer jaunts through Paris and Nice that had left him with mixed memories of all the French girls he hadn't approached and Senpai's addiction to maki-au-Nutella.

—But, Taylor continued, we got into a big fight while I was at Cambridge, so I summered here. You remember.

—You never mentioned her. Not even once.

—I wanted to forget her. I didn't talk to her at all last semester. Not till Christmas, and not much then. I honestly didn't know she'd show for my birthday, and I don't know why she's stayed so long…

This Taylor as fake as his Gigi, her barroom aliases like his Finn, her story was full of holes. Holes that you could drive Vik's tank through, but Taylor's expression was more than suggestive of all she'd left unsaid. And those "I'm too busy" nights pressed him; he called Tessa's words to the witness stand:

—And "your other lovers"?

—They never meant anything. They were hookups. Anonymous. I told… I lied. To all of them: they've never even known my name. But I haven't hooked up with anyone else…

—Except Tessa, right? This whole time? – and now me too.

A single droplet fell into Koko's mithril coat, and Taylor's contritions ran together, evincive yet empty, in a lachrymal he couldn't match from the waterfalls frozen above his gelid abysms; for he'd yielded everything, pliant as a manikin. He'd yielded, and they'd taken.

She blubbered, wiping her face, the Cioranian mirror of his hollow: her tears, his comfortless tears; his smeared blood, her blood; Tessa's venom, their Maldororian venom. They were two of a kind amid his and her lies and livid stigmata. He crossed their divide and hung his arms about her, the olive wreaths of her Ozymandian glory. Eyes closed, he rested his head on her shaking shoulder and breathed her perfumeless air – he clung to her, a stone pulling him down into the airless deep.

C·P·SERRET'
DIE THE VILLAIN.

MIDSOMER'
NIGHT'
III.

★

A FOX PADDED lightly through dun pasture, the moon high and bright in the even sky. Frost rimed the soft earth; in blue shadows, a cricket's bell. His black nose found a sweet fragrance, delicate on the breeze ruffling his copper-blond fur.

A noble house stretched across the hill's horizon, flames flickering behind shōji screens. Before an open door, she knelt, jūnihitoe violet under gold, carnations wild. Hair darker than night waters in flowing trail, she raised a reed flute in jadelike hands. A piercing trill skipped over the tumulose vale, and the fox froze: paw raised, ears twitched, tails still.

Great clouds drifted, traced in light, sailing on the eventide. A sangen twanged, dissonant in the darkness; he knelt before her at the edge of sight: konōshi shades of blue beneath midnight's breath, weeping cherry, five tails fanned behind.

☆

FINN wobbled down a precipit stair with midafternoon maladroit, zombie grace; his nightingale soubrette turned graveyard croak:

—What effing time is it?

A chilled burn softened the bleary glare of his library, blinds ajar, where Koko lay within a spot of sun warming her Arctic coat. The second drink was slower but also without savour, the flavour of fire on an ashed burning ground, a dark goddess dancing in the afterflames of his explosion.

He ignored the basking carpet – already fed somehow, somewhen – trashed last night's emptied bottle and retreated to the bathroom upstairs, refilled tumbler in hand, unsurprised to find the soaking tub filled and waiting, the temperature set and forgotten again. He ignored the shambling gurokawaii scarecrow in the bathroom mirror, set his glass aside, and started the shower.

The water beat over him in a pulsing scour, pearly suds be-grimed by the grey wasteland. He touched his forehead to the cold tile of the narrow stall, eyes closed.

> We are the hollow men
> We are the sick men
> Leaning together
> My liver hurts. Alas!

Dostoevskij-infused Eliot reverbed within the sonorescent space. Trailing water, the third drink eased knots of tension, breathing slowed, j'accuse quelled. He blew steam and sank to the seat inside his cypress-veneered ofuro and the onsen heat, a damp washcloth folded across his throbbing head.

He wandered through another snow-capped April, beclouded an Earagail majestic above Gleann Nimhe after the long tension of a squalid border checkpoint, his mother muttering castiga-tions in their puttering rental car while camo-clad British boys with black 'n' tan rifles held the partition line: now leaving FREE DERRY. No shit.

An unwelcome chime brought him back from sheep-speckled evergreen swards and heather moorland, but he let the doorbell pass till a sharp tattarrattat! was crowned with a double ring! He rose sputtering curses, wrapped his wet skin in the yukata, then retrieved the revolver from his bedroom, summonses resound-ing. He tramped down to the front door, Koko in attendance, and yanked it open to find the so-called Tessa on his threshold, her fist raised to knock again. His rage guttered and blew out like a candle.

—View-halloo, she said. Am I in peril?

—Ah, no. Sorry. Wasn't expecting anyone.

The Countess appeared younger by daylight with neat up-done hair, her make-up light but for a bold red lip; she was slim-profiled in her fitted equestrienne nod of glen tweed and white jeans, a camellia pinned to her lapel.

—Then may I?

The cat objected, shaking a damp paw by his pooled footprints. He motioned with the Rhino and stepped aside.

—Um, sure. Come in, signora Contessa.

—Why not call me by name?

—Your title is funnier.

She grinned at that. He'd googled her old editorials, reminded that she was also the cliché American heiress married to an Italian Count – like a prewar plot point warmed over from Wharton and James. The titular Countess made her entrance with an imperious jackbooted stomp, which Koko shied from in a skittering hop and scamper. The Countess surveyed what little there was to see from here, all quaintrelle flair and a no-doubt affected peregrine air, crop-nailed pianist's hands in her front pockets, thumbs on display.

—This may be my most unique experience entering someone's home.

He found her golden eyes hard to meet, though they'd taken in his everything. Or because.

—I was relaxing in the bath. I stayed up late, watching the game. What brings you to the slums?

—My apologies for the unannounced visit. I thought to amuse myself by surprising you, but you've surprised me instead. I've made dinner reservations for us this evening, but we have...

The Countess removed her patent-black paddock boots and racked them between two pairs of his sneakers. Without them, she stood a mere five-eleven – also according to Google. She nodded at the kyōgen mask.

—And I see your affection for Japanese style extends beyond your skin.

—And I see you're cosplaying again. Sort of Horse and Hound this time?

—Fox hunting, though my vixen is bedraggled and baring fangs.

He let vixen pass and didn't challenge her presumption regarding dinner. He waved her through the library suite. She stopped and looked at the literary stuff – Taylor treated it all like wallpaper. He made no apologies for the mess this time, but he had the gun. The Countess declined a drink and followed him upstairs. She peered into the bathroom.

—Le trône?

—In its own compartment behind that door on the right. There's also a, um, powder room downstairs next to the laundry closet.

—The tub looks big enough for two.

—It is, but it's a snug fit. The washitsu – the tatami room – is over here.

He led her into the rush-matted space and popped his revolver back into its Kydex purse holster. The door slid shut behind him. The Countess circled his rumpled bedding like the cat.

—I always forget the scent of Japanese-style rooms. Somewhat like fresh-cut grass or hay?

She dropped her canvas handbag by his ishō-tansu and paged through the clothes hanging within his open closet: a collection that encapsulated the else errant Gigi. He made a perfunctory effort to straighten the bedding and folded the damp towel but needed to vacuum soon. She turned back to him with a light smile, his saddle leather belt folded in her limber hands.

—Aren't you going to ask how I found you? It wasn't Taylor.

—Why bother? I'm sure you can afford to find out anything you want, signora 'tessa.

—Phfft. Taylor's been stuck on *Tessa* since she was, what, twelve? Thirteen? And still…

He had a few dark speculations on why that was, whispering to him from the holes in Taylor's story, but he didn't interrupt the Countess's monologue. She segued to him:

—Quite the mystery, she was saying. You live rather freely, almost as one independent: your work little more than a part-time hobby. But your assets reported to date don't appear sufficient to support all this – nor your income, your assets. I can only conclude you are a criminal of some sort, but that trail, too, is cold; so a good criminal – except that you patriated funds from Bermuda to pay for shoes and party dresses. And your offshore credit card is a bit two thousand two. Better get with the times and…

He let her speak without comment and his best poker face, though his heart raced, well aware that the cost of keeping up appearances with Vik & al. placed him at increased risk of just this kind of discovery – and with a few notable missteps. The Countess gauged his non-reaction in turn.

—I don't suppose Taylor knows about you, not that she needs to: « Tout est vol » after all. And now that she's home, facing up to her responsibilities, I think it best for her that you slip away and have a fresh start of your own.

She came off like an actress laying it on a little thick, her dramatic pause an obvious cue. He leant on the tansu and played it cool.

—Taylor's s'posed to be back in the next day or two, but I'll bite. You've made me curious.

—I mean to bring you back to Monte-Carlo with me, on a permanent basis.

—Permanent? Why would I move all the way to Monaco?

She smiled then but read *serious* around her languid eyes, his folded belt over one arm.

—I can offer you a pied-à-terre in La Rousse – or Saint-Jean if you prefer, not that you would stay there often – an allowance, the usual. We'll ship over your cute little car or stow it at my property here.

—Your celebrity draws too much attention for someone like me, Contessa. Too many questions. Even some of these events with Taylor's friends, the paparazzi are…

—Bah oui. You'll have to wash your hands of anything you're involved in – I won't ask what – but I'll take care of everything afterwards ¶. You belong with me in Monte-Carlo, with the best of France and Italy at our feet. It will be a new chapter for you.

As her dependent, the unspoken angle. He would retire by thirty, but his net worth, off the books, was little more than a rounding error besides the high-profile conspicuous waste of the richest and most celebrated crooks.

The Countess untied his obi's hasty knot and pushed the yukata off his shoulders, cavalier despite his shaken head, but he made no stimulative show of resistance as for Taylor. No; leonine eyes shone with what the Countess wanted, the anticipation a voltaic tang on the tip of his tongue. She smelt of eau de Cologne, overripe with bitter oranges, but too few cigarettes to reek. She tapped him with the folded belt.

—Now. On all fours, damoiselle.

MIDSOMER,
NIGHT,
IV.

★

HEY LAY SKIN-TO-SKIN in a cornflower blue mead,
T   but afternoon road noise rose to the sound of their
breathing. Taylor slid one hand over him from neck
to navel, a sculptor smoothing golden clay. She propped herself
up on one elbow, and shadeless sun caught the ash highlights
in her flaxen hair.
—Either you missed me, or you really like my natural colour.
—I didn't expect you to be gone for so long.
—It was four days. I texted you.
    He fingered a wavy lock of her faux-natural fair. The bronzeless
'n' blonde boarding-school Taylor of Morgen and friends. The
exile and her ur-mask.
—Yes, he replied; but at first, I thought it was a day trip.
—I wish, but I didn't get off that easy. Thank God finals are
coming up, or it might've been a few weeks. So funny that you
walked right past me at the airport.
—It's weird. I noticed you, but I didn't recognise that you were
you at first.
—But you do like it.
—It's totally hot. You look like Supergirl now.
—Supergirl? You're such a nerd.
—You'd prefer Barbie?
—Now I'm going to kill you.
    She was joking, sure. But the micro-inflexions around her
eyes gave little warning before a snap, and she'd snapped for
no discernable reason. Sometimes she made contrite sounds.
Sometimes not. Her fingers found his waist.
—Better yet, we'll dye your hair blonde too.
—O no, he said through a giggle as she tickled him.
—O yes. I'll make an appointment with Charles. He's been dying
to do your hair ever since he laid eyes on you.
—Both of us blonde? Too *Garden of Eden*.
    Taylor relented.

—Garden of Eden?

—Unfinished Hemingway novel. A couple goes blonde on their honeymoon and gets mixed up in a threesome. Things get complicated.

A shadow passed over her features in the cloudless light.

—No, no more threeways. I made… I told Tessa it was off the table.

—H'mf. She asked me to go back to Europe with her.

Taylor bolted upright, her face turning red.

—What! When?

He propped himself up on both elbows.

—She came by my place while you were gone. Uninvited.

—What did you say?

—No. Duh. Why would I move to Monaco?

—That bitch! I knew she wouldn't leave you alone. I fucking knew it! I finally get you to myself, and now she wants to take you away from me, and after what she did to Morgen.

Taylor stared off into space; this, the face of Morgen's "tragédie." He didn't react to the reveal, and Taylor asked if he'd already known: if Morgen or the Countess had told.

—No, but I'm not surprised. If they met in Paris, as you said, then I had to wonder if you weren't the only one – Tessa's kind of a predator. So all of this has happened before: the three of you.

—No; not like this. Morgen and I are friends. We never, and I didn't find out about them till later. Until too late, until she'd thrown Morgen aside like trash.

A single tear slipped down her cheek, and he followed its trail, impassive, wary of the crocodiline shadows that lurked below her glistening blue surfaces, and unsure, this time if he'd caught her in a lie. She wiped it away.

—I wouldn't have invited Morgen to my birthday if I'd known Tessa would crash my party. At least nothing bad happened to her this time.

—Why haven't you told Tessa to go hang?

—I tried. I did. After I found out about her and Morgen, I told her it was over. I already told you about that, just not the reason why. Nate was being a jerk after I opened my presents, so I went home after the party, and Tessa was there, waiting for me. I forgot she had the key. She was forceful. I caved.

—But Morgen knows about you and her, now, right?

—No. No one does. No one but you. And when Tessa revealed it in the car that night, I knew what she wanted. What she was thinking.

Nate – or someone else on his side – had seeded the off-chat rumours about Taylor, and the unnamed model Vik's contingent had somewhy conflated with Gigi. Finn let it lie but didn't permit the deflection of responsibility.
—What you'd wanted too.

Taylor hadn't hesitated; at times, she'd made it hurt, hitting every ROUGH SEX and related genre porn checkbox there on the Countess's canopied stage. Taylor grimaced, eyes dry.
—I'd thought about it. What it would be like, but after...

She stopped short, looking down and away. He prodded:
—Not what you'd expected?
—It wasn't worth the risk of losing you, and now she's trying to take you away from me. Sometimes I hate her!
—Maybe we should run away together.
—Omigod, that would be...

A wistful smile and a shaken head.
—But I would so get disowned.

He sat up, on second thought, taking his own bait.
—We can actually do it soon as you graduate. We can go. Anywhere. Forget Tessa and her games; forget your parents and their control issues. Just go.
—You're so cute. I wish I could.
—What would Rimbaud do? « L'hiver, nous irons dans ... »
—Don't! You sound like her with all of that quotey bullshit.

He huffed.
—Taylor, sometimes leaving is the only way. I did.
—Are you serious?
—I'm no billionaire, but we'd be OK.
—Finn, I'd lose everything.
—I don't care about your money. C'mon, I'll even buy you a Subaru and a flannel shirt.

She gave him a firm pinch.
—I'm so going to kill you, but actually, what we should do is summer away together. Get out of here and away from all this: from her.
—Like where?
—We have a place on the Vineyard. My parents won't go near it

during tourist season, and everyone else will be in Southampton or overseas somewhere. I have my own set of keys, and we'd have the place to ourselves.

—Sort of a trial elopement?

—You. But no one would bother us. Tessa hates any place small and quaint – anything out of the limelight; she'll go back to Monte-Carlo or wherever. My parents will put in an appearance here for commencement, but we can leave right after.

—You're sure?

—A whole month. Two if you want. I'll leave for England mid-September and stay with Morgen's family for a couple of weeks before we move into the college for the semester. But can you take that much time off of work, or could you telecommute?

—That wouldn't be a problem, he lied. I can do what I need by email, but what would you tell your parents and everyone else?

—Everyone's going their separate ways – there's no need to say anything specific. But I'll have to come up with a good story for my parents. Not that they care.

—They cared enough to haul you back to River Oaks and dress you down over the big breakup.

Taylor groaned and fell back, covering her face.

—Don't remind me. If I hear the word *duty* one more time, I'll shoot myself.

—That bad?

Details had been scant, but she put him off again:

—You don't want to know. We just need to be discreet from now on, but I'm stuck as a blonde for the next couple of months. Damn Tessa and her... Nevermind. Guess I'll leave it this way for the summer since I won't have Charles to maintain it.

He blinked at her use of the Countess's mot d'ordre.

—And what about today? Do we... ?

—No; I need to catch up on schoolwork. For reals.

—And tonight?

The Countess had Taylor lined up, and he waited to see how she'd frame her reply. She held his gaze – a twitch of her left eyelid – then looked away.

—Busy.

He'd zeroed on her tell but didn't call her on it: an intermezzo trio or three-way duel? He made disheartened noises and gave her a parting peck.

—Guess I'll get out of your new blonde hair for now, but to-morrow, lunch!
—You should make me Cuban food sometime.
—Took it for granted when I lived at home. Never learned how.

He pulled his clothes on over weals, fresh and fading, and left her amid gilding lambence and rumpled sheets, the rest of her condo curtained-dim. He ran slim fingers through bedroom hair, then snugged down his ballcap. The steel-reënforced front door locked itself behind him.

☆

THE Finnish electromechanical lock snapped open like a rifle bolt and a humid rush of air washed over him. Taylor peered through the gap, a few harried flyaways about her pinned-up hair.
—Finn? You're really early.
—O, the concierge let me come up.
—It's fine, came the Countess's voice from behind her. I was just leaving.

He'd squandered the morning pirating the latest anime and manga raws, coppery-auburn finger waves peeking from beneath his ballcap; he'd given Charles free reign on the colour, but it had come out a hair too close to his mother's shade – though she was freckled fair.

A little spot run by silver-haired Neapolitan anticonformistas,

Caffè | La Volpe
e il Gatto

had the fastest Wi-Fi within walking distance of his place and a soundtrack of hissy mix-tape cassettes – catching up on this week's One Piece, &c. was nothing covert after all; a secret hide-away for conformistas too hip for chain coffee bars: scruffy boys and beatnikish girls in lumberjack colours and stout-rimmed statement glasses: a close-mouthed transfixion of iPhones. A torpedo-nosed marionette was propped against the antique me-chanical register – dead bones reaching towards transfiguration.

The cute barista had talked him into the buzzy novelty of a "flat white" alongside his decadent once-a-week breakfast slice of imported Sacher-Torte, but it sat half-full afterwards – more

Saitō's speed – till replaced with a meticulous pour-over of Sidama Guji. He'd strolled home after, navigating the sidewalk hazard of a PBR-poseur gang and their stupid tricks on fixed-gears, and dumped his messenger bag for a prepacked trolley case and his satchel, ready for the promised homemade lunch and "whatever" after.

Taylor swore underbreath but stepped aside and pulled her door open the rest of the way. The illustrissima and ci-devant supermodel was seated on the sofa, legs crossed, as if she weren't going anywhere. Elegant in an ivory crêpe dress with a black bow at the waist, the Countess's glacé-black ankle boots belied the restraint elsewise implied, her hair swept up in a chignon crêpé, almost Gibson Girl.

He pushed his wheeled valise aside, green eyes and tone cool.
—Signora Contessa. You're looking pretty today.
—Alice, she replied as she rose to her feet with ostentous grace and feigned coy; you're too kind – bed-head 'n' all.

The Countess picked up her deep purple Nano and hung it from inside one wrist, her amber eyes clear in the late morning light. Yet for all their precious shade and her hidden realms, she wasn't Balzac's tragic La Fille aux yeux d'or – if anyone found the dagger's point between them, it would be him. An obligatory la bise, then she plucked his shoulder strap.
—That handbag doesn't work with a ballcap: too paperboy. You need something sharper to offset your casual look.

The Countess brushed him aside for Taylor, who stood rigid by the open doorway. Taylor said something indistinct, and the Countess thrust her up against the door, which banged hard against the stop. Taylor's resistance collapsed like a house of cards, and he turned away from an odd prickling discomfort. He dropped his bag on the coffee table and himself into the Countess's spot, arms crossed. She finished marking her territory.
—Until next time, Alice. J'me sauve.

She departed swiftly in all of her unhurried state, his eyes following till Taylor shut the door and threw the extra deadbolt, her fine mouth twisted, sour.
—Sorry, I should've made her leave sooner. I noticed your hair, but I didn't want to let on in front of her. Who did… ?
—Your guy. I went straight to your salon from here.

He set his ballcap on the sofa and checked his coppered

coiffure in a mirror compact: shaped into two sweeping finger-waves that broke into a foaming mass of pin curls, per Charles' cold method – enter the thirties. Taylor asked,

—But how'd you get an appointment that fast? Even if I'd called for you, it would've taken a couple of weeks, at least, to get you a spot.

—I walked in and asked for him. He took care of me, but the receptionists there hate my guts.

The salon had emptied around them while Charles worked, as exacting as Dürer painting his Venetian blonde. Taylor broke into a bewildered smile as Finn told the tale, the cliché ray of sunshine breaking procellous cloud, centre frame. She shook her head.

—I don't know how you do it.

—It cost me a selfie.

—Um, what?

—After it was finished, he asked me to take a selfie with him. I'm on his Tumblr now.

—You look like a fox. But let me check on the food. C'mon.

Polished copper pots were steaming on the bespoke Italian stove, and stainless bowls filled with chopped vegetables of sundry sorts awaited, cut the way she expected: perfect. He wouldn't touch her left-handed single-bevel knife ever again, nor anything else within her kitchen. Hers was the most genteel of masks, for this staging not of Butterfly but M. Hyde. She took up the blade.

—Why'd she call you Alice? I didn't want her to know I didn't know.

He leant against the central counter of her large eat-in kitchen.

—My first name was Ailís before I changed it. She mispronounced it. Badly.

—Why change it? It's pretty.

—I was named after my grandmother, mother's side, but it got me teased at school – and everyone says it wrong anyway – so I went by Cris till I moved to Japan. I used a Japanese name there, then changed it when I got back.

Hearing it butchered at U. S. Customs had jarred him into action. First and last disavowed, he'd written Chris on the paperwork, then shredded it, anxious and exposed. No one would find out about that slip, but Taylor struck near the mark:

—And Cris came from?

—My old middle name, after my grandmother, father's side – and Saint Cristina.

—So Alish Cristina?

—Ailís Cristina on my birth certificate; Ailís Críostíona if my mom was in a mood, which was often.

Taylor got it on the third try.

—It suits you ,though.

—No, it's too girly.

—You're good at being posh and feminine when you want to be – you're like Morgen that way. Did you keep your last name, or did you change that too? I know you don't talk to…

—Fionn is my grandfather's name, mother's side, so it's kind of like a patronymic minus the prefix. Would've been Ó Finn with, but.

He shrugged. She pointed with the knife.

—Why not a Hispanic one?

—'Cause then people would expect me to speak Spanish, and that's annoying.

—You've never been to Cuba?

—No; the embargo makes it hard even if you have family there. I visited some of my relatives in Puerto Rico when I was little; that's the closest I've ever been.

He crossed his arms and left it there. Taylor smiled to herself, and he braced for her to drill down to the surname he hadn't spoken aloud in over a year. She emptied two bowls into one pot.

—You're full of little mysteries, aren't you, Ailís?

—Taylor, I'd prefer it if…

—I'm kidding. I told you: I accept you the way you are. I've never even called you Gigi, have I?

—No, but Tessa's not going to let it go, is she?

—No. Probably not.

C·P·SERRET,
DIE THE VILLAIN.

H E PASSED BELOW the Gothic tympanum, absurd San-graal in relief, and closed the heavy outer doors behind himself, unmet. Discrétion was the Countess's creed, her NDA'd domestics undetectable but for the spotlessness of his path through her post-feudal palazzo. He found her upstairs within the sprawling salon-cum-office, far below the chande-lier-hung Baroquian ceiling one wasn't supposed to gawk at, seated amid a faint haze of smoke, her dark oak desk centred on an Aubusson rug and backdropped by a Gobelinish tapestry of courtly idyll – probably fake. She fit the tableau the way anything, anywhere, fit her, yet dépaysé somehow. Gasping for Græcist airs? He paused at the doorway.

—Did you buy this place furnished?

—Interesting question. Why do you ask?

—It doesn't seem like you.

—My idiot husband purchased it this way and for far too much. It's rather garish throughout, but the real estate market remains too depressed to make it worth disposing of, for the time being, at least. Myself, I would as soon stay in a hôtel.

A large crystal ashtray was half-filled with gilded stubs, a slim guilloché lighter and a flat pack of White Russians beside it. A nocturne hung lightsomely between blue particles, emanating from an unseen source. The Countess glanced up at him, tucking her dark hair behind one ear.

—You look like a danseuse étoile, posed there like that – such poise – but I expected a garçon manqué this evening, Ailís.

Finn had rejected the hoidenish failed boy niche and dressed to his deepest no; a black swan, sinuous and sleek of plume, in a short – "You'll like this one; it's vintage!" – Molinari cocktail dress, the bodice tapered above its layered tulle flare. And no platforms, this once, but the most ætherian pumps in his possession: an optical illusion in floral dentelle – more suggestion than shoe.

—Si tu veux un garçon, then shouldn't you call me Finn? Or Cris?

—Cris is far too plain for you, and Gigi too frivolous.

He took an indirect approach, swanning among objets de curiosité and morceaux de musée, both authenticated and spurious. A painting in an ornate frame caught his eye but didn't register for a moment, a strange inkblot staining the ormolu continuüm. He faced the display easel on which it sat.

—This didn't come with the house.

—No.

—Is this the real one?

—Phfft. With Picassos, who can say? You're in the habit of arriving too early; I have things to finish. You may as well return home and change.

He set his bag on her desk.

—No.

—Darling, said the Countess without evident sarcasm, I'm overseeing a small empire; my husband has no head for these things. He's too busy playing in the city to pay heed to the accounts – he and his latest favourite. He told me, only this morning, to increase the hedge funds as the griselinias are looking shaggy.

Finn lowered himself into her lap, forcing her to stop typing and sit back. It was one of few positions that let him match her, eye-to-eye, bound for a spell within lionesque limbal rings; the same hooded eyes but of a different shade and unapologetic in their predation. He prodded the „blonde Biest", new frost nigh invisible beneath her signature shade: „Your roots are showing."

„I don't know what you're talking about."

A smile hovered around her lips despite the obvious strain not to. She relented: „Give me fifteen minutes to finish up something important and to make one or two calls. Go pour yourself a drink, and I'll be right there."

„Eff this garbage."

A surging swing of Odile's wing swept all within reach off her desk: papers scattering, her laptop made a colossal death rattle, and the crystal goblet popped like an incandescent bulb.

—You can finish this trivial shit after I'm done with you.

The Countess raised an unruffled eyebrow.

—O, really?

He slapped her once, back-of-hand, hard enough to jolt and

raise a high colour. Fingers to her face, she gaped, drowsy lids snapped to wakefulness.

—The bedroom. Now.

★

THE Countess yielded to his every whim from evening to small hours, the concubine point-vise – savoured in accord with her Sadian délicatesse, a pose she'd expounded at overlyrical length within the tedious opulence of her master bedroom: a hodgepot of dead Louis, XIII through XV, and only one of many curtained stages in a palais fit for a sojourn of 120 Journées.

He patted her face dry with a white towel, a blindfold down around her neck. Her chest rose and fell in easing billows, stretched out before him like Venere dormiente, bound not by dream but to the bombproof headboard. How far below the fame and peerage lay the real woman or her hollow? – her multëity of selves layered like a matryoshka doll. She asked what he was thinking: the last question he'd ever expected of her. He forced a smirk, false as a trophal rictus, unbuckling the borrowed harness.

—That if this was real, you'd be pregnant by now.

—If you had a real one, I'd never let you touch me with it. I can't fathom the appeal of dainty boys, and you would make for an impossibly pretty boy.

—But it's OK if I wear a prosthesis?

—Prosthesis? It would only be prosthetic if something were missing.

He froze, bewrayed by his own words, his cleft manhood an open wound before her mocking gaze. He dissembled:

—Potayto–potahto. You didn't answer the question.

The Countess took a measured breath, her smile irreprest, and in metred tones recited a couplet in Latin, followed by a significant look that didn't translate. An indefatigable précieuse despite her pedigree and position, her grace and gracility excused most of her airs and graces but spotlit the self-doubt at the core of her display: the gnawing uncertainty of an autodidact, of a high-school dropout with a celebrated career, fame, and riches, overcompensating for her stunted CV.

—Sounds profound. What does it mean?

—No Latin in parochial school?

—Some, but I was more focused on preparing for the EJU –
the Japanese entrance exam for international students. The
Nietzsche bit rings a bell, but that's it.

—Not Nietzsche. Ovid, by way of Gautier de Châtillon: "*Travellers
on a reckless path,* | *We strive for what is forbidden to us.*"

—Forbidden? I doubt you've ever been forbidden anything.

—Yes, forbidden. Did you choose to love women?

—Well, no.

—Neither did I. For us, the pleasures of men – of manlike things –
are forbidden ones, such as they are. À rebours. But pleasure is
still pleasure.

It was a needless rationalisation – spice for her libertinage
and the pleasure in power. She gave a thoughtful shrug against
her restraints.

—Even you were curious. After all, you allowed…

—The thought makes me ill. I told you…

—That you don't want to be penetrated again. Yes, so you've
said. I've known women like that before. Still, you came when…

—That's not the point! I never wanted to be… that.

He tossed the tumescent artifice onto the wide bed, haunted
by ghost pain and disinclined to revisit what he'd allowed, the
black pearl rising, bilious, to his throat – a horrorous cycle of
disgorge, gag, reswallow. He pulled around a lion-footed tapestry
armchair at the bedside, refilled his glass with her overoaked
millionaire's cognac, then sat back, simmering in re-torn feel-
ings, on the Inquisitor's seat.

—You and Taylor: how did it happen? It's not particularly discreet
to start sleeping with your little cos.

—Second cousin. It's less discrète than is my wont, but more so
than someone whom I recall broke up a high-profile engagement
for the selfsame girl.

—Shit happens. Go on.

—I never saw her that often while she was growing up. I'd mod-
elled since I was fifteen, and for years she was one of a half-dozen
strangers that I called *cousin*. She was young – eleven or twelve –
when I first guessed her inclinations. A pretty little thing then
but nothing extraordinary. Yet there was something in the way
she spoke – the way she gestured with her hands – it was clear
which way she would lean later.

—So you whisked her back to your castle in La Sila.

—Rien si bête. But another Christmas, a couple of years later, my husband and I – newly wed – put in an appearance at the clan gathering on East End. Taylor had sprouted up, and there was nothing subtle in the way she looked at me then. Don't look at me like that. Nothing happened.

He didn't expect her to tell all, but her expression belied the tale.

—Is that when you started calling her *chérie*?

—I've always called her *chérie*; it's hardly rude.

—Forget it. What happened next?

—We ran into each other in Paris somehow – she was with her little friend Morgen. I'm unsure if it was an accident or if she'd sought me out. What she wanted was obvious; she found her way to my *hôtel*.

—A fifteen-year-old girl.

—She told me sixteen.

—Taylor said fifteen.

—If she didn't lie to you, then she must have lied to me.

—Add *seduced by a fifteen-year-old* to your list of life failings. Go on.

—Why, if you've heard all of this from her?

—'Cause you're the one who's tied up. I can come back in a few hours – after you pee yourself – if you want.

Her eyes narrowed at him, weighing something.

—She was persistent. Her mother called me some months later and told me that Taylor wished to visit with me during school breaks instead of returning home. It caught me off guard, but I didn't object.

—And after that?

—That's enough. That's how it began, but she's the past of our future; she understands that – even if she's not forthright with you; she can't offer you anything. Playtime's almost over, and soon we'll pack our things and go.

Naked. Cuffed. The Countess was in the driver's seat. He squeezed the walnut armrests in annoyance.

—I haven't agreed.

—You came to me tonight, Ailís. There's a gallery opening down-town tomorrow that we'll attend after shopping and a light lunch; it will be a small taste of the life that awaits you. Our life.

—You can't spring shit like…

—You'll need something appropriate to wear. And a new hand-bag. My treat, of course.

He h'mfed.

—You're way too sure of yourself.

—You're far too sure of Taylor; the knife is already in your back.

—H'mf. You admit you're trying to split us up.

—Of course. That doesn't make it a lie.

C·P·SERRET,
DIE THE VILLAIN.

A LOW-LYING BLANKET of cloud, blue-slate silver-lit by matutinal glare, hung over the sleepy green of the Countess's bijou midtown estate. Overwatched by dated Modern mid-rises and the drab philharmonic, it was part of Generic City but not, behind her hermetic single-storey walls. A murdered-out Bentley GT coupé was parked between his Porsche and the marble-fountained parterre, heady with carnation pinks and all the flowerage of Grasse. He slipped into the cush passenger seat, and a hummingbird flitted past with a soft but voracious drone. The automated iron gates opened at the end of the driveway.

—Taking me shopping uptown is hardly discreet. Especially not in this.

—The boys took the Rolls and, no disrespect to your little car, but I prefer twenty-first-century climate control. You'll be my assistant for the day, or so I'll say if asked.

—And you think anyone will go for that the way I'm dressed?

Her eclectic wardrobe of tailored couture and obsolete sample-size fours closed to him, he'd reëndued the villain, a Lutens' stopper trailed from navel to jugular notch – all lavender treacle and bottled smoke. He'd switched to the ballerina flats in his car, sceptical of walking any real distance in those gossamer heels, his hair brushed but humid curly and clipped with an antique Bakelite bow barrette.

Her smirk smiled in response. Suited, scarved, shades of blue, she started the twin-turbo W12 engine, which idled with a low pantherine growl.

—They may conclude I pay you too well, though you do look the model, mid-editorial – a very short model. Taylor claims you were a hipster tomboy – her words, not mine – until your ex remade you in her image; though I can't imagine. Tell me of the legendary Chloë.

—I've never been a tomboy, hipster or otherwise. But Chloë? Wilful. Impetuous. All "blow Winde, come wracke", but mysterious in a way: de cape et d'épée. Her life's some kind of soap opera, I guess.

Their gentle launch paused at the gateway, the matte black-on-black Bentley merged into trundling stop-and-go traffic. The Countess spared him a sidewise glance.

—And rather fashionable, I take it?

—The Terminator wears Prada. Most of what I wear, like this, is really hers.

—But if you still have them, then…

—She comes and goes as she pleases while jet-setting around the world – kind of like you and Taylor.

—Touchée. Was it she who taught you to strut in heels like Vlada?

—No; that was YouTube.

The Countess pulled over into valet parking, tires still cold given the horse-and-buggy pace of traffic. She handed the keys to a boy in vermilion, then paused on the pressure-washed uptown pavement, surveying the façades that stretched before them: the transnational luxury chains that had broken his bank balance more than once; rarefied, yet replicated in generic cities, per the triumph of scarcity marketing and commoditised identity. A playdate promenade for the likes of Emily and Vik, a support group of eight-to-twelve-cylinder penis augmentations crawled by in a Pathétique of overrevolutions, their faddish matte-black wraps more suggestive than stealth. The Countess drew him back from their strident confessions of inadequacy.

—It occurs to me that we can play with the idea of the fifties' gamine: a middle path between your revision of twenties' garçonne and your pouty paperboy chic.

She thought it out aloud as she drew him into the first boutique, florid with hoidenist euphemisms and melodious adjectives, which amounted, all told, to nothing. She lifted a long-sleeved purple button-up from one rack of tops, and he stiffened, dollface blanched by another Gautier's lines when she recited from a dangerous book:

« « Trois choses me plaisent : L'or, le marbre et la pourpre … »
She stopped short, ever smirky, and asked him : — Something wrong, ma chère damoiselle ?

—No. I'm fine.

—We'll start by getting you into something more suitable for your rôle, then move on to something more appropriate for the gallery opening and whatever else inspires us.»

She built her gamine thesis, selecting notable pieces with a dandiacal eye. It proved an exhausting circuit up, down, and around, interspersed with dozens of fitting room fouettés and interrupted by the occasional fangirl for autographs or self-ies with the "Countess!" They ducked into a one-star for the aforementioned "light lunch", ditching a hangdog paparazzo to encounter two of her society acquaintances – once-debbies of Paige's Mayflower-branded ancien régime, Office Lady drab in their finery – who insisted she join them.

He'd regarbed in that purple button-up; a white pair of Seven's ironic – for him – Boyfriend jeans, rolled cuffs pixie-high above glossy saddle shoes; and a jaunty Chanel canotier. Sancho effing Zancas. Finn set his rope-handled shopping bags aside, out of the waitstaff's way.

The grande dame had been machined into zero-grav ageless-ness, her tone smoother than her too-shiny forehead and lofty with condescension; she spoke from far above him, per her ungracious mien – a botoxed-and-filled Grace Kelly replicated into microëxpressionless life.

—And who's this? she asked the Countess. A protégée?

—No; Ailís is my assistant. My chief-of-staff.

The expressionful younger nodded, eyes narrowed at him under mobile eyebrows, her face puckered by bitter snobisme.

—Yes; she has the look but not the stature.

—What a wonderful opportunity for you, said the elder, then down her chiselled nose: —And a pretty name. Irish, from the sound of it.

—Yes, he affirmed without tossing his drink in her face; on my mother's side.

The sour younger arched a pluckless brow.

—And are there qualifications for a personal secretary these days? – or is it just a pretty face?

He laid out his operations and logistics CV in a dry, matter-of-fact tone, and surprise scrawled chagrin across her hauteur. She puffed up from a backup supply of hot air secreted somewhere on her person.

—You look too young for that.

—Yes, he said.

It became a game, the signora Contessa at her most urbane; he, the stilted Dottoressa. After lunch concluded and they'd escaped the clutching Ghosts of Socialites Past and Present, her long fingers smoothed his crisp collar without need and brushed away a stray red thread.

—Now I need to buy you something special as a reward.

—No, you don't.

She chuckled.

—Such a delicate and sulky boy you make, Dottore. Yet you seem so much more at ease now. Perhaps I will make you my live-in assistante personnelle, take you with me everywhere, and call you Cristiano. Let's confound them all.

He turned on inferable erotemes like a spit, roasting under her golden lens, and, lips parted, his heart palpitated against the close bars of his ribs.

—You can't afford me.

—You haven't heard my offer.

—Which is?

—Room and board.

C·P·SERRET,
DIE THE VILLAIN.

HAT, THIS OLD THING?

W   This old thing was an opalescent sea-foam gown that brought out the turquoise hue of Vik's eyes and the conspicuous tan beneath her pharaonian bijouterie; she was anything but colourless, but he was wise to complimenting her Manolo's first. The restaurant had that poshly'J pick-your-shade-of-Bauhaus interior shared by every upmarket contempo joint in Generic City and his place, but the maîtresse d'hôtel had made them her discrepant centrepiece, soft-limned by a linear chandelier at a linened table for two within easy view of the austere anteroom – exhibited amid murmuring voices and eyes covetous of the doppelgänger of

THE ACTRESS THAT SHALL NOT BE NAMED.

Vik had invited him to a celebratory Maghrebi dégustation – her long-awaited irezumi tomorrow – with naught for them to select except the wine, and the silver-haired sommelier approached, at last, with their first bottle. Lips pursed in a permanent fugu pucker, he presented the bottle to Vik, the label rendered like judgement or prophecy:

—O'four Sine Qua Non, INTO THE DARK.

The elaborate tableside ritual of sampling, decanting, and pouring evoked a Eucharistic sensation: a Magian liminality, closed, beyond reach. Finn commented after the guéridon wheeled away, pews-hushed:

—Sounds – I dunno – not-French.

—It's not. Stop avoiding the question. I know you. What's Taylor so busy with? Finals are over. Misha has business tonight, but?

Finn flipped through the pack of lies Taylor had foisted on him like well-worn playing cards but cast them aside for a Brutusian blade.

—Tonight she's out with someone else.

—Wait; what? You don't mean…

—A date. Yes.

—But I thought you were exclusive. Taylor said…

—No; I doubt she's been exclusive with anyone. Ever. She's a Chad.

—O God, who? Do you know?

—I know, but I can't. You'll have to ask…

—Gigi, it's me.

—Well, I will say it's someone she's been seeing for a long time. Years.

He left Taylor's faceless roster of pseudonymous hookups in her closet, unmentioned but unforgotten, along with his suspicions about a Morgen-Taylor-Countess triad. Vik's eyes were as round as Koko's.

—Wait, years?

—Many years.

—I bet it's a girl, isn't it? That lying suka blyat'. Um, Tracy? She met Brad through Taylor and Nate, and I'm pretty sure Taylor knew her first; I saw them talking on campus right after I met Taylor at the ball. Anyone would think Tracy's a model.

—O, I had no idea; thought it was the other way round. But no, it's not Tracy.

A time-faded image of Taylor and Trace at the tavern needled him: the two of them leant close last summer, conferring too low for anyone else to hear. There was something. He took his first considering sip of the aërated SQN, afraid it was wasted on him; it tasted like wine. Vik followed the breadcrumbs, glass forgotten.

—OK, someone else from since before I knew her; looks like a model or a real model: the Countess? But they're cousins, and she's married, right? And didn't she leave a long time ago? She should be skanking it up in Cannes with the other celebrities.

He shook his head, swishing his glass in imitation of the guests seated at the other tables.

—No; she's here in the city. It's clear Nate or whoever was outing them with that rumour, but everyone fixated on me. I'm seeing her now, too, and at this point, I'm not sure which to call the other woman.

—Gigi, no; I can't stand her! She's such a stuck-up bitch. The way she showed up for Taylor's birthday at the last minute, and…

—I missed all that, but – believe me – I know. She wanted me to ditch Taylor and go back to Monaco with her, pretty much first thing.

—O Jesus. You said no?

—Of course. I'm not moving to another country to be the play-thing of some libertine.

—You should get the hell away from both of them. Taylor's been lying to me from day one – about everything.

Finn contemplated his distorted reflexion in the wine glass.

—Everyone is lying to everybody.

Vik drained her glass, lifted it for a refill, and asked him how it all had happened, "the fuck" punctuating every few words. He unfolded the tale in fits and starts between small decorative courses, warming as they finished the SQN; then she called for a bottle of '02 Schrader RBS – a brave new initialismed world. She intercut her retconned suspicions at opportune moments till his narration stalled at the threeway. She sniffled and shook her head.

—E'to pizdec! Taylor was into it?

—Taylor was all over it.

—Walk the fuck away.

He h'mmed, then showed his hand:

—She's asked me to spend the summer away with her.

—That was my idea, but three's a crowd, a fucked-up crowd.

—I meant Taylor an' me. She thinks the Countess will eff off and go back to Europe.

—So Taylor's into threeways but didn't want to share you with the Countess afterwards? What a fucking mess.

He refilled his glass.

—Taylor preferred us not knowing about each other, having it both ways and turning the tables on the Countess. You know, we're not going to be able to drive at this rate.

—Whatevs. We can get a cab.

He huffed a toxic laugh.

—Let's use the Countess's car instead.

—O, like her limo, you mean? She lets you use it? Does she buy you presents too?

He started dialling.

—One sec.

—Ha. You're like her mistress.

—Yeah, no, he rejoined two minutes later. It'll be here in twenty.

—Does she let Taylor borrow it?

—She needs to be discreet with Taylor. Less so with me.

Vik cocked her head in a sad show.

—After all that, you're still a dumb-ass.

Dessert was equally minute, and he concluded that he was far more full of wine than food. She paid with a matte-black AMEX.

—I hope I got that right. I can't do math right now.

They exited arm in buzzy arm, into the uptown night, the Phantom prominent by the valet stand. The chauffeuse climbed out in tailored white and opened a coach door for them. Vik slid in first.

—OK, this is pretty nice.

She suffered from an onset of dizzies on the way to her place and rested her head in his lap, rambling about her irezumi appointment till nearer their destination, she said,

—Misha will be home soon – let's do a hôtel instead. That new one downtown.

—What will he think of you alone in a hôtel room with an infamous home-wrecking tramp?

—Misha's a pig. He'll tell me to make a vid.

Finn laughed a little too hard, a little too forced, then directed the driver to change course over the intercom. Vik was looking up at him with saucer eyes when she asked about the three-way, and his floaty buzz wavered, turbulent, the black pearl pressing on his heart. He raised one hand to the pressure and took a slow breath, generic city lights sweeping by.

—It was too much. The two of them all over me, it was like… it was like being thrown to the lions in the old days: the more they pull you apart, the more worked up they get till nothing's left but a few drops of blood.

—O Gospodi.

—They let me sleep by myself, at least.

His cheek twitched. Vik reached up and touched his face.

—Did they hurt you? It's like…

—No, he lied; not really. More…

The black pearl swelled. It was hard to breathe, sweat beading, stuffy; the cabin closing in, he shivered with a chill.

—But the Countess has a lot of… a lot of accessories, he was saying. Not the sort of thing I ever expected to be on the receiving end of. I thought, it'll be OK, I just have to get through it.

He glanced down at Vik, then away.

—I did... I did whatever they wanted. I couldn't say no to either of them.

—But you wanted to say no, didn't you, Gigi?

C·P·SERRET,
DIE THE VILLAIN.

★

T HE HÔTEL'S MOGUL SUITE was staged like a movie set with ample room for crew and cameras: broad as an imperial corner office, glass all the way around, and custom furnished by a celebrity designer – per the brochures in the foyer – in a lurid postmodern-vomit style. A bit much. The brighter-than-daylight city square shone from below them and the starless empyrean, pale shades of Dōtonbori. Vik sat, removing her rolled-strap sandals.

—Let's hide out here till my ink is done.

—What? Through the weekend and… ?

—You already promised to go to the tattoo parlour with me tomorrow, and this way, I can protect you from those two. They could show up at your place tonight and…

—Vik, they didn't force me.

A tremor rippled along her jaw.

—Your eyes say otherwise.

—Forget it. Why'd you get a penthouse suite with one bed? Were they out of doubles?

—No; I can't sleep by myself. I need to cuddle.

—What am I, a teddy bear?

—Why else would I keep you around?

—H'mf. Get some drinks. I'm gonna take a quick shower.

He retreated to the opulent bathroom, the vivid shimmer of coppered auburn caught in reflexion: the Picture of Ailís M——, the girl that had never been born. He unzipped his little black Dior, stepped into the walk-in whirlpool tub, and took up the handshower.

The river of memory eddied around an endless moment: caught between Taylor and the Countess, a new pain sawing him in half. "It's not my fault," says a voice surfacing some-whiles, somewheres, only to sink again, leaded with doubt, into the nacreous dark. He stepped from the bathroom wrapt in a hôtel robe, damp hair curled about his cheeks in the deepened tinges of sunset.

Vik was abed, bathrobed, and not watching the TV, a flute of bubbling rosé in one hand and her phone raised in the other, an ice bucket with her usual pink-labelled bottle of Dom within easy reach.

—Can you believe room service doesn't have tracksuits? What a shitty hôtel.

She thrust his waiting glass at him.

—Come 'n' get some.

He clambered onto the extra-wide bed, but above the duvet, and she hissed at him not to spill the tipping platter of chocolate-dipped strawberries. Fresh fizz went up his nose.

—What're you watching?

—One of those comic book things. You like?

Compared to shōnen manga, there was little appeal to the broken circle of recyclic superheroögnies; to the frozen forever-champions of returnless inconclusion. He passed. Vik flipped channels, with a squee for The Notebook, already in progress. He gave her a look.

—What did Misha say about us staying here till next week?

—He asked for a selfie. Smush in.

Finn used to ego-search, ensuring there was nothing to find other than by design: his staid LinkedIn profile; and the Finn Strategic Supply & Operations website in three languages. Enough to blend in, but Gigi's painted pouting face was everywhere now; a nanocelebrity within the inadvertent burgeon of a Westerfeldian reputation economy-to-be, along with all of that unexpurgated EXIF data; from the virtual underworld to virtualised front-page news, doxxed in the fine print.

Vik's Instagrammable moment was produced over an arduous hour, after lighting, make-up, and hair, with dozens of photos taken, post-processed, and discarded. Vik tugged her bra straps back up and showed him the racy final product, which showed nothing below the collarbone and bare skin above.

—See? No boob.

He finished another flute of champagne, one hand supporting his shoulderless bathrobe décolletage.

—Terry Richardson would be proud.

They stayed up till they ran out of coke, flipping channels and repeating their stock lines on life, the universe, and ink. They popped more champagne – smash cut to black. Finn awoke, overwarm and smothered, one arm pins-and-needles beneath Vik's ribs, the other raised defensively amid the fading fragments of a four-armed black deiform: clutching, biting, savaging; sublime. He extricated himself without waking Vik, then blinked into a suffocating sirocco of sugar, spice, and everything soft; she was nuzzled against his neck, one leg across his, her heart thrumming against him. He rotated himself out from under her, and she made a murmuring sound of sleepy protest but remained still till he drowsed between her breaths.

They traversed the entire width of the bed by cockcrow, and on the precipice, he groaned within her clutches: sweaty, aching, and bone-tired. He rose, wobbling with alcohol, and steadied himself against absurdist furnishings on his way to the bathroom. He showered again, filled the walrus-scale tub, then dozed within, soaking till shaken awake to the dawning pressure of his usual morning headache. His gorge rose at the scent of fresh coffee and buttery baked things; he needed a whiskey first.

Vik's eyes were shadowed with dark circles, but she looked ten times better than he felt. She cursed, pointing at the raised crescents that marked his toothsome skin.
—Gigi, did one of them bite you?
—Taylor gets overenthusiastic at times. The heat turns them red.
—Break the fuck up with her.
He gave a wan chuckle.
—You're the one that told me to go for it.
—I didn't know she was a psycho.
Vik dipped a finger, then sniffed a few complimentary bottles of luxe bubble bath, upending one into his clear hot water.
—The spa downstairs is shit, but you should have come with. Banyas are the best for hangovers, even without venik.
—So that's why you don't look half-dead.
—I called for you like five times, but you didn't respond.
—I didn't hear.
She untied her robe as she turned, Pinkie Pie tagged passant across her ribs. He closed his eyes, tracing her footfalls by ear: she padded back and lowered herself into the tub. He asked,
—What are we going to do for clothes? We didn't pack anything.
—We'll go shopping after my ink, then change hôtels – my dad's paying. I don't want to go home and pick shit up; it would mess up my honeymoon vibe.

He dared reopen his eyes. Vik was neck deep, her heroic embonpoints obscured by shimmering distortion and the soap suds crossing their divide. He shrugged assent, his shaking hands folded underwater. The flask was in his bag, on the console table.
—Well, I need to feed my cat, at least.

She yawned, crossing her open mouth.
—Make Taylor do it. Lying pizda.
—She doesn't have the key. Guess I'll ask Kristi if she doesn't mind; she still has my spare.
—O, her? You guys still hang out?
—Not for a minute. She got too pushy trying to recruit me for her big corporation a while back. I hate headhunting, but they've forgotten about me by now.

★

He sat up, slowly, slowly, to stave off the white flashes and dizziness, but the tide of nausea washed back in. He stood with care and pulled on a black yukata. The doorbell rang again; he left the gun.

He checked the peep, then opened the front door, speaking Taylor's name with a weakness that surprised him. She saw his face and clenched paling fists.
—I'll fucking kill her! Did she...
—Come in.

He stepped aside to let her through, and Koko stretched on the library threshold. Taylor reached out to his bruised and taped face but stopped short.
—You don't answer your phone; Vik cussed me out and then booted me from her chat, and no one will tell me what's going on.
—I fell.

He locked the door. Withen and wheat blonde, she crossed her arms and said his name in single-word demand – a Britomart of the proudest preppy „Blut und Boden". He led her into the library and lowered himself, slowly, slowly, one hand on the sofa arm. She sat across from him in the armchair, radiating barely checked anger.
—You don't get a black eye from falling. She hit you.
—No. It was bad luck; I fell off the hôtel bed and hit my face on the nightstand. My fault.

—How, exactly, did you fall?

He sighed, the train wreck ahead but smashed before impact. It was already over.

—Well, she pushed me.

—If she pushed you, then…

—It was still my fault.

Taylor recrossed her arms.

—How, exactly?

He stalled, eyes downcast.

—What'd she tell you?

—I don't believe her; that fake bitch is covering her own ass. She's played at being bi off-and-on since I met her; she's messed with a bunch of girls and ghosted them afterwards. Every! single! fucking! time! She's full of shit.

—But what did she say?

—She said you tried to force yourself on her. And then she told me to go fuck myself – ô, after calling me an evil lying cunt.

He closed his eyes at the accusation, spoken aloud, his gut twisting again but not from the concussion; the fall a fragmented memory: euphonious pleasure in his ears, a bale-fire in his brain.

—I don't remember it that way, but I can't… I can't contradict her. I don't remember everything.

—Tell me all of it.

He began his head-ducked confession, and Taylor's face darkened, the edges of her mask peeling away like smoke.

—Finished the shading, he was saying, so we went back to the hôtel again and got wasted. I don't remember everything, only pieces. We were talking and laughing. I was on the right side of the bed, and then I was on the left side, and we were kissing. I don't know who started it.

—Coke?

—And Molly.

—Jesus, Finn. Did she say no?

—That's what I keep thinking about. She didn't. Not that I can remember. I didn't know anything was wrong till I hit my head. I was confused.

For a moment, then horrified. He took a deep, shudder-fraught breath.

—I always thought… I always thought I'd never be like those guys that take advantage of drunk girls. I was kind of proud of it, even. I had no idea I could be like that, that I would do anything like that if I was drunk too. I thought I was in control. Now, I'm just like them.

He hadn't seen Vik's face then. She'd turned her back on him, her silent judgement final.

—Vik took her things and rushed out without saying another word to me.

—And then?

—When I tried to stand, I got dizzy and threw up. I called an ambulance and spent the night at the hospital for observation.

—Why didn't you call me?

—Taylor, I couldn't. I wasn't ready.

For everything to end. Not all at once. Taylor puffed like a pressure valve edging the limit and glanced up at the sky beyond his ceiling.

—What did the doctors say?

—Concussion. They did a CAT scan: no fractures. The black eye should go away in a couple weeks; the tape should fall off by itself.

—Christ, Finn. Does she know?

—No; she won't talk to me.

The severance hurt more than all his injuries combined, like the shock of repentine death, an ache without remedy or relief, his sin irremissible. Sin – a word he hadn't heard or thought of in years and one now beyond the boundary of church and Confiteor. Taylor stated the obvious, hinting nothing:

—Everything is so fucked up.

—I know.

—What did they say about the concussion?

—Seven to ten days to start feeling better. Tylenol for the pain.

She sat back with a shoulder-hunched sigh, steaming, and her left eye twitched a few times, or he might've imagined it. Still a pillhead like much of her caste, a single vein was prominent along one side of her forehead, delicate as Pietà.

—You can't be here by yourself, not like this. You'll have to stay at my place till you feel better, and by then, we'll be leaving for the Vineyard.

He spoke her name again, confused by the calm in her voice, in its resolve or resignation. He licked his lips and hazarded,

—So you're OK?

The floor leapt straight for his face.

C·P·SERRET,
DIE THE VILLAIN.

MIDSOMER,
NIGHT,
IX.

★

H E LAY IN A SPRAWLING curl on Taylor's bed, her tablet faced down beside him – a pavonian boy in swannish guise, felled by Leda's blow. A looped soundbite of Rick James had replaced his high-brow lines: "Cocaine's a hell of a drug."

After the scathing fires, after the black rain, Taylor had knelt beside him, profuse with every contrition he'd heard before, pummelled to his floor with arms clutched overhead. He'd lain here, coddled since within her shade-drawn blues, the last few days in the listless anguish of his cyclic *Saint Sebastian*, arrow-pierced and weltered in blood.

He malingered beyond his malaise, sick of bed but too drained to stir, till something prodded his leg. He reached down, seeking Koko, but cool fingers brushed his hand – he jolted upright but wavered in palpitating vertigo, his oft-bruised wrist in the Countess's grasp. She pulled him straight up, almost to his knees, and spoke a dead name. He tried to twist free, recalled again to that narrative climax with the Marquise de San-Réal, but there was no poignard visible. Yet.

—Are you in disguise? I thought *prep* was a four-letter word, signora Marchesa.

The Countess held him fast and twisted his arm, her hair bobbed and fifties' swirly; chinos, polo shirt, and boat shoes a throwback to some preppy-girl default. She bent him to herself and took her first kiss, then thrust him back down roughly, in déshabillé disarray, declaiming, "'Whene[v]er the manly part of thee would plead | thou tempts us with the image of the maid'."

The effect of Behn's words was spoilt by the winking corners of her lips and the flubbed metre of the first line, an amateur production of the Sadian hero. She abandoned her pose to sit beside him, chocolate wrappers crackling under them like dry leaves; he resat up more slowly. She slid her fingers up his tattooed arm.

—I'd intended to come for you a few days ago, but Taylor complained you were *a raging bitch* – her words, not mine.

—Come for me? Are you planning to haul me away in a sack? She's at her graduation ceremony right now, but she'll be back after she sees her parents.

—Yes; I know. Playtime is over, my Cristiano, and it's past time you joined me at the grown-up's table. We can leave for France tonight, and my attorneys here can help you arrange things later – I would hate to miss the entire Cannes film festival, and you can make your début this weekend. My husband has already left for Greece; he won't be in the way. Come, get your things.

—And Taylor?

—Taylor needs to focus on her future. Once we've departed, she can summer wherever and with whomever she likes; it's none of our concern. You'll be my assistante personnelle from today on, and you'll receive the appropriate salary for appearance sake – a pittance beside your allowance. You will want for nothing, and you'll go everywhere I do.

—And you think no one will figure it out?

—Tout au contraire, I expect everyone to deduce it immediately; for "you withall ſhall make all Gallia ſhake" like du Barry, reincarnate; though like money, it won't be discussed in polite company. But I must ask, what of your other activities?

—I closed up shop some time ago, actually, but I'm spending the summer with Taylor on the Vineyard.

—The house in Oak Bluffs? You'd rather go to that mud-footed village than come to Cannes?

He turned away from her, facing nothing.

—I've already decided. This isn't one of your sordid tales, madame la comtessse.

—Obstinate in the face of what you really want or playing hard to get? Or have you succumbed to Taylor's fever dream, une folie imposée? She won't be able to offer you anything before the curtain falls. Every summer, countless French abandon the pets they no longer find convenient. She will keep you as her handbag dog for now, then leave you behind in the woods or by the side of the road. You won't be the first.

He bit down on a flash of red, turning on her.

—The same way you left Morgen?

—Morgen was a pleasant diversion, nothing more. She would

take your place, I'm sure, were I to offer it to her, but she and Taylor will settle for each other's... companionship, as before.
—You're lying!

The Countess lifted his chin with three fingers.
—Am I? Forget them and come away with me now.
—Get out!

He tried to push her off the bed, but the tide turned on him in an instant – no strength in his limbs. She pinned him close, his conflicted resistance twisted into a knot within, her lips on his, immersing him in her gilded scent. His arms fell limp; he couldn't – wouldn't – fight her for real with maiming tooth and savage nail as for a stranger. She released his wrists, and her hands traced the boundaries of her counterclaim. Then she tugged hard on his boyshorts, and a seam popped.
—You belong with me. You know that I...
—Stop.

The black pearl yawned, the abysm of his abysms, and he fell away from a body not his own: sinking, sinking –

It's not my fault...

She drove a distant, ragged breath; then she stabbed him but not with a knife. He resurfaced with an unheeded whimpering, "Don't...!"

He sweltered – just get through it! – his breathing laboured till quake and aftershocks, tears bleeding, overwashed by her purpled darkness and an insensate light. She shifted away and upright, then wiped at the wet, faded bruising beneath his eye, but he brushed off her hand and covered his turned-away face with one arm. He quavered with a sob, and a bubble of saliva burst when he told her, again, to leave.

"I could make you come with me," she asserted. "That's what you want, isn't it? For me to overcome you, over and over again, to drag you along by the scruff of your neck, but you must learn to heel when I call you. We are running low on time. Go and get your things."

"G——, no."

The Countess made a sniffy sound of disgust, and the mattress dipped, the heavy pressure of her presence lifting away. He dared not look, but her voice receded, crackling cold with anger:

"Perhaps I need to let her disappoint you first.Come to me once she's left you by the wayside. It's only a matter of time, Dottore."

Then she was gone.

He held himself within the shade-drawn blues of
Taylor's bedroom, a fetal curl, shivering.
She couldn't see, couldn't know, but
his limbs wouldn't respond.
He couldn't stop
shivering.

★

C·P·SERRET,
DIE THE VILLAIN.

H E FELL GRACELESSLY into the black leather passenger seat of Paige's bright yellow AMG Streetfighter – she lived to say "my Streetfightah", arch as could be – in the shadow of a landmarked Gilded Age corner mansion turned super-luxe condominium. Radcliffe was frosted with cherry blossoms, and Luluheads in stretch-fit macaw colours passed within their snow-white shade on the way to uptown yoga studios, BYOM – absent Kyōto's swarming tourists, school kids, and maiko cosplayers. He fastened his seatbelt.

—What's the drama?

—I've told you, Gigi dear, there can't be more than one redhead at a party. It spoils the feng shui.

—Were we going to a party?

—No; just a spin, unless you have someplace in mind. Coffee, perhaps? There's a spot…

Midis were trending on the reserve of the Lesser Depression, but Paige had eschewed Brahmin restraint for a lavender-on-white aquatic print minidress, her Titian hair up in an involute Vespucci braid, long neck bared – her upsized sunglasses even louder than the rest. Arriviste exuberance beglamoured her colonialist quarterings, far removed from Merchants Row, a prodigal bloom livening long fallow soil.

—But I do like this natural make-up look on you, she was saying. I don't recall you wearing it before.

—I'm not a tomboy. And I'm not wearing any make-up. At all.

—You're disgusting.

—You don't miss your make-up-free school days over there?

Her glossed lips twitched with derision. She respun one of her stock tales of transatlantic nomadism along the way to that spot she knew; an Anglo-American fantasia highlit with satiric aperçus. They circled, looking for parking, and she parallelled while he hand-signalled. She shut the driver-side door, and the first tremor shook him, followed by the icy trail of the first tear. He cursed, vision blurring through filled eyes, and her voice rang with alarm:

—Gigi! What's wrong?

The first sob racked him, and Paige caught him in her arms as his knees gave out, his ballcap falling to the sidewalk. She held him, stroking his auburn hair, and he cried himself out, without release but safe for the first time in a long time – and a deep sigh eased from him, cleansed by her Light Blue air. Passers-by gave them curious but disinterested glances.

He regathered himself and released her with a non-coke sniffle and a deep breath. She asked what was wrong. He wiped the last meltwater from his face.

—Nothing. I don't know. I've had these weird crying fits for days.

But his expression bewrayed him, his plump lips crushed together. He shook his head and picked up his cap. She removed her sunglasses, gunmetal-blue eyes grave.

—Very well, coffee first.

Paige guided him through the door of a narrow coffee bar, one arm around his sylphidine shoulders; a single row of tables was down one side, light with uptown poshlyachki, their branded paper cups, and purse puppies in SERVICE DOG vests. She withheld further comment or question till they were alone at windowside, pour-over coffee steaming before him in a glass mug – "for here," she'd ordered – her stark Delvaux handbag set atop their table with the imposing presence of an anvil forged by Le Corbusier. Finn forestalled her:

—You still banging Nate?

—Catch and release, but that does bring me to why I wanted to catch you before I left.

—Where're you going?

—Where won't I be going? I won't say who inboxed me, but there's a rumour Nate and Taylor are back together and that the wedding is still on. Of course, now that I've picked you up from her flat...

—There's no way. We're going away together in a couple days – for the whole summer – once her parents leave, and I've been staying at her place pretty much since she finished finals. I haven't seen a trace of Nate, and she doesn't want me even to mention his name.

—That's brilliant, but what has you so upset if everything's going so well?

His cheek twitched.

—Well, Taylor and I are exclusive now, but there was someone else. For a while. Till recently. It was an ugly breakup.

Paige perked up.

—Someone I know?

—Can't say. Well, I shouldn't, and it doesn't matter anymore; it's over.

—But you're still in tears, love.

—Too much stress with everything. I'll be fine – I am fine. You looking forward to Slytherin this fall?

—Slytherin? – ô, the law school. I'd've preferred a change of scenery, but remaining here was my third choice; I won't be shedding any tears.

He ignored the nudge.

—How's the scene been without me?

—Nought's changed.

She paused for a sip of her not-a-milkshake caffè macchiato.

—The scene's a Möbius strip: hashtag sameshite. The club names change; new kids join, old kids go. Sameshite everywhere. We'll have to try something new once I've returned and Taylor's gone her merry way to mucky ole England. Visit a jazz club? See a play? Something.

Would he turn into his father after all? He didn't contradict her and kept the plan to himself. Nothing was firm.

—That sounds mellow. Have we reached the jazz age?

—You'll need someplace to wear your Louboutin's, or is this I'm-not-a-tomboy tomboy-look your new thing?

Dogged by antiquated hoidenism, he air-quoted in exasperation and gestured down the line:

—It's not a tomboy-look. Look around. Regular people on Earth dress this way; it's unisex.

—Are you sure? Tomboy is trending.

He rolled his eyes and said her name. Paige leant closer, speaking in a hyperbolic whisper:

—Have you missed me?

—Sure. You're my best frenemy.

She grinned.

—Will you tell Taylor that we've spoken?

—Eff no. Not till I find out whether she still wants your head on a pike.

—I don't see why she would. Nate said he was lucky to get it in once a month; it was all appearances. Of course, after giving him a couple of chances, I wouldn't fuck him again, either.

—Huh. Taylor made it sound like a lot more than that back when they were together.

—At least one of them is lying. No matter; Nate was simple enough to replace.

—You still prefer this whole dating-rotation thing you've got going?

—As the childhood survivor of serial divorces, I think you'd have much less stress with a rotation of four or five expendable girls than with these all-consuming relationships of yours.

Finn crinkled his nose.

—It's not for me.

—Then your ring fits after all. You and Taylor living together, summering in the Hamptons together, picking out China patterns...

—Paige.

—O c'mon. Low-hanging fruit.

She gestured with her glass demitasse at something past his shoulder: a hummingbird hovering beyond the window wall, absent flower or foliage, then zipping up and away.

—I hate those things. One flew into me once.

C·P·SERRET/
DIE THE VILLAIN.

WINTER/
DAWN/
II.

★

HE JUNE DAY OPENED bleak and coolish for the fi-
T   nal leg of their long and winding drive: from inter-
states to the sameliness of smalltown New England,
onto a sluggish, rust-stained ship which crawled over an oily
sea daubed Payne's Grey; it spilt them out into another dismal
vill, close-huddled in the undying wind. Taylor drove with one
hand on the wheel as they passed along a bike-pathed coastal
road, into a blind turn across cycle-traffic and dense boscage;
and there, at wanderings' end, the fortress hidden on this isle of
her... content? His crying fits had eased, but her temper withal
had shortened; she didn't know anything.

"Cthulhu Sleeps" cut mid-stream with the engine. Finn stepped
from the car, awash in a damp and salty chill. He snugged down
his lifting ballcap and re-zipped his olive Baracuta. A Shingle-
style Victorian summer home far larger than the one he grew
up in – much like the Big Houses burnt during the Irish War of
Independence but dressed down in Puritan-grey – met the cir-
cular parterre driveway, the lawn and environs kept in absentia.
They brought in the groceries they'd collected in Falmouth, then
began porting the luggage. The furnishings were draped in white
against the dustish and murksome air. He avoided his thought:
—We need a fairer selection of music; that was a shit-ton of EDM.
—You said that yesterday. If you'd download some music on
your phone, then...
—No one sells what I like in lossless.

Taylor gave him a patronising look that said *nerd* without
needing to use the word, her filled lips wasp-stung. She'd gone
all-in.

They'd departed over a week later than he'd expected – not
till after the cast came off her reset nose, still swollen, her eyes
circled with fading lividity. "I'm sick of looking at my mom's
nose," she'd said on the surprise call from pre-op the morning

after her parents' flight out. "Don't try talking me out of it now. You can come and see me tomorrow." She'd undergone both procedures at the same time.

—Sorry, my car doesn't have a record player.

—I'd buy you one, but Simon Yorke doesn't do car audio.

She called him a nerd, her endless portmanteaux piling in the period-film entrance hall, beside the case of rye whiskey they'd argued over – "That's insane", she'd claimed, a case of blanc de noirs already in their shopping cart. The M-monogrammed valises, brass-and-leather-bound, were more at place than himself, at best a porter out of livery in his jeans and trainers. She led the way back to her car, and he dragged his heels behind her. Her voice sharpened:

—Seriously, what's with you? You're not…

—Like I said: nothing.

Taylor slapped him, and he folded over the fender. The second blow knocked his ballcap to the asphalt. He flinched, but she grabbed his upper arm like a child's and squeezed it hard enough to hurt.

—Then stop it, she said. Right now. We're going for a walk on the beach to clear your head. You don't know what I'm risking for us – so that we can be here together. C'mon. We'll come back and clean up after.

—OK, OK, but the cat.

—Hurry up.

He left Koko to begin her explorations among white cotton dunes, his vintage Fuso nine-speed still racked to the trunk. He walked a half-step behind Taylor, down to the driveway's hidden entry, and they crossed the highroad to a handrail that overwatched the Atlantic, briny brume roiling over the beach below them – air that prickled your tongue. The Cape had sunk beyond a sfumato horizon, the sea blending with pearl-grey cloud. She took his wrist and drew him to a concrete stairwell, down to coarse sand and dark waters, the seagulls sailing on a wind wet with vaporous spindrift.

She frowned outward, blonde hair streaming, the face of her transpacific longing. She hadn't mentioned her autumn move – or Morgen – on the entire drive, but he read it in every line. He avoided his thought:

—To look at you, I'd imagine you on some private estate, riding horses in your free time, all dolled up in a jacket and riding boots. Something like that.

Taylor's voice changed. Distant.

—I had horses, but they were… My mom made them hostages against my good behaviour. After a while, I didn't want to go home anymore; I don't like remembering. Now, with my goals, I won't have the time or place for that. Not for a long time. Tessa offered the use of her stables in Abruzzi, but.

—We're free of all that here. No parents. No Tessa; she called it a mud-footed village.

Taylor huffed.

—Right now, Hunter's surrounded by idiot girls that'll do anything to be in the Hamptons, and Britt's in Ibiza, or Saint-Tropéz, or who cares. My parents are abroad, probably in Tuscany. So thank God we're in this quote, unquote, mud-footed village. I have so much to show you: Katama Beach, the gingerbread houses…

—We have all the time in the world.

—I wish. We have time, but it's not forever.

They strolled over strewn seaweed and mussel half-shells, not quite alone along wuthering lows, steady traffic flowing by above them, but she took and held his hand more gently. He asked what had happened to discrétion, and she responded with the best of her brilliant smiles, her teeth fit and polished like pavé jewels.

—The Vineyard doesn't count. I don't really know anyone here anymore. And my mom was never nice to the neighbours – not that you can see them past the landscaping – so there's no one to tell on us. We can relax.

—It should always be that way; it's two thousand twelve.

—It's not that simple. But one day, once I'm out from under her thumb, I'll change everything.

★

THE air vibrated. Her tablet held in both hands, Taylor was face-timing on the Chippendale with first-stage rocket thrust ebullience after her matutinal amphetamine cocktail. The straight-edged nose, the out-turned swell of her full kiss-me mouth, she'd looked car-crashed the day after in her private room at the clinic, bruised, swollen – now, enstranged. He pictured her with the missing default spray tan and dark hair; that was someone else entirely: some Instagram starlet with a million adorants. She didn't respond to him, standing there in the morning room doorway. He turned and left her alone with Morgen's disembodied voice.

He soothed his nerves with a jolt of rye and stepped outside to cool down in the warming air. Koko was crouched on the veranda, thalassic wind ruffling her fur – she'd sped out earlier, once he'd unlocked the pet door, to park herself a few short feet away. He sat on the swing bench and flipped his drifting hair.

Taylor had amended her "I accept you the way you are" with a but. He'd left the party clothes and most of his make-up behind, only to be pestered into a sideswept pixie-cut bob as soon as they'd settled in, doubling down on *gamine*. She'd clasped her hands in answered prayer and said, "You look like Twiggy did in the sixties. Well, if she was Hispanic. And ginger – ô, and had your rosebud lips."

"So not at all."

He didn't need to paint on the lashes, still just a doll, swaying on a doll-house swing. Taylor came out the front door.

—ok, I'm off to Pilates.

She was in the same elastane ensemble, blonde hair ballet-bunned, her keyless key fob–thing in hand, bearing the Bayern roundel. He scratched his nose.

—I thought we were riding our bikes to Gayhead for lunch.

—I slept wrong. My neck and shoulder are sore.

Taylor made an exaggerated show of stretching it.

—I need to work out the kink. We can drive down after I get back.

—'K. Guess I'll hang here then.

—You could always come with and try it out.

—Nah, not my thing.

He watched her callipygous bounce down to the car. "Deep in …"; the door shut on him and Byron. "Lonely and lost to light …"; not a word was uttered within rearview, and the raspy snarl of her v10 withdrew, devouring the murmured fragment: "'my heart responsive swells, | Then trembles into silence as before.'"

Finn fetched a pigtailed Fernandèz lancero and his topped-up flask. The Big House had a period smoking room – antique smoking stands 'n' all – but smoking in it was unthinkable, according to Taylor. He toasted the foot of his cigar alight, slowly, slowly, to a perfect circle ember and cut the cap after – unlike those that cut first, then scorched their tobacco with extravagant puffs into flame, after toasting. Super old school. Koko sat with him for a time, clouds crawling across the faded-denim sky. Then she was gone.

The stick softened in his fingers as it warmed, and a large RC plane banked high over the driveway, then disappeared overhead – line-of-sight from who knew where. The trail of its shadow recalled Taylor's extempore assertion that escalating drone strikes overseas signalled his opportunity to invest in the drone supply chain and reap the dollars yet sewn in the killing fields, evergreen – tipped to the key military contractors and the stock tickers that controlled them. „See", she'd gloated, „like I told you: finance news is the real news." „Eisen und Blut", commoditised for export; Machtpolitik her C-SPAN sideshow; it didn't matter who burned from the Hellfires, only that quarterly production increased, year-over-year. He shook his head.

He'd woken restless and alone had witnessed the mulberry dawn amid the lost orisons of childhood, the everyday matins of gulls, and the soughing leaves of an impasto garden, muzzy with wet textures and a Hesperian symphony of fragrances more potent than the perfume galley at Pygmalion. He'd regressed to a solitary bowl of instant stirabout and a cup of café filtre, spelt in remembrance of self and story: from his fey genesis, false Eden and illusory androgyne, through irreturnable changes as cruel as Kafka's Verwandlung – all orisons overcome by an unknown karma and silenced.

His mother had replaced three alienists in quick succession; those that had failed to "make her into a normal girl" after puberty failed to "set her straight", as she'd predicted. She'd taken his blue jeans and left him with skirts, dresses, and kilted-skirt uniforms – despite his female classmates wearing jeans everywhere outside of church and school. A generation or two earlier might've found him consigned to an Irish convent laundry; so spared the asylum but not the rod.

His stick reached a synchronous end with the growling return of Taylor's car – or near enough – and he dropped the smouldering stub into the chipped Cowboys coffee mug that held his ashes. The flask lay flat beside him, underhand, where she wouldn't see it. She climbed out.

—Hey! I'll take a quick shower, and then we can go.

He followed her in but used a downstairs bathroom to wash up before trailing her to the second floor. He tossed his Black Angels tee for a faux-tartan button-up, sunglasses, and ballcap, then descended to the catless veranda to wait; Taylor was still in the shower. It was a timeless moment, in pensive ebb tide. She reappeared in barely-there shorts and thongs, a caftan shirt-dress off one sun-freckled shoulder. Her hair fell to the bared side in wheaten curls, non-Jackie-O sunglasses below her floppy straw sun hat.

—Long sleeves and jeans? Don't you want to wear something cooler?

—I'm fine. I don't want to burn. I don't tan much darker than this for some reason.

—Yes; that's why I bought sunscreen.

—Next time.

—You said that last time.

Taylor drove at a leisured pace, coasting halfway there on their inertia, but they arrived too early for lunch, so wended their way, arms linked, along the narrow beachline till time caught them and the sun beckoned them back from overhead. They sat outside at a table below a green-and-white patio umbrella, the ocean outstretched behind her. She hung the vintage Randolph aviators from her décolletage, a faint dash of freckling across her nose and jugular notch, the sunglasses lifted from her grandfather, or so she'd claimed; since they already had it all and didn't buy anything – or so feigned the self-mythologised robber baron New Money of industrialisation, aping the pirates that preceded them.

—What're you thinking?

—About a steak and probably potatoes.

   She ughed.

—I'll order for both of us since you obviously don't get seafood. I don't know how you survived in Japan for six years.

—If you're a vegetarian, then you shouldn't get seafood either. I've never seen you eat so much meat before we got here.

—It's not meat; it's fish.

—Are fish fruits or vegetables? Or legumes? – no one knows what those are.

—How 'bout this? When fish evolve big brown eyes, I won't eat them.

—And bacon?

—Doesn't count if I didn't order it.

—So you eat most of mine.

—You shouldn't order it.

He flinched when his Galaxy vibed in his back pocket, his expression transitioning from perplexity to pique when he checked the screen: not Kristi, again, nor Paige, but sanless Saitō: —I'm back <3.

Taylor evinced agitation, absent a twitching tigress tail, while he speed-typed duelling replies. Her fork rose, a threat, midair.

—It better not be that sailor girl with the tattooed fingers.

—Sailor-girl doesn't have my number, and besides, how does that even begin to compare to the landscaper's daughter – excuse me, the landscaper's hot daughter – showing up, looking for you?

Taylor flushed, eyes of deep rue.

—That doesn't count; it was a long time ago. Before Tessa even. But if it's not her, then who're you texting? It's not Tessa, is it? She never texts, but you look pissed.

—No; it's Chloë. I'm telling her to get her stuff out of my place.

—O wow. Finally.

His phone vibed again: incoming call. He swiped, sending it to voicemail, then powered down to end the siege.

—I've said all that I have to say to her. I'm done.

—But how will she get into your house? Does she have a key?

—No, but Kristi has my spare. I messaged her.

Taylor's gaze went flinty.

—That Asian girl? You still talk to her? Isn't she friends with Paige?

—Told you: she and I are just friends – and Paige had nothing to do with it. Luckily, we're out of town, and Chloë can get her things before we go back. I won't ever have to see her again.

C·P·SERRET,
DIE THE VILLAIN.

E HIT END.

H   —It's done.

—There had to be a better way, Taylor replied.

—It's just a car, he lied.

He set the Note down, unsure what his expression conveyed. The Porsche took with it the spectre of Aphid Grin and the haunted maybes of a return to his former life. His life. Nevermore sir, *dude*, or even bro; it faded, a sliver wraith, sighless.

He picked up his e-reader and slouched into the sofa, false cool, otherwise troubled by the missing Koko. Through unshuttered windows, the sky was bleeding peach into blue beyond encroaching cloud, and again she hadn't scooted in through the pet door, her pedigreed tail up. An old plasma TV hung over the cold fireplace, warming the large Regency-fitted room like a sunlamp. Taylor picked up the remote.

—You're sure you want to come.

—Thought about it for a while: you'll be living there for years, and I'm not doing the long-distance thing. I see it as an opportunity to relaunch and expand my business – I've been slacking since the fall, and it's effing July already. I've set up a shelf company out of Cork, and…

He didn't get into the specifics and hoped she wouldn't ask; the shelf a shell long in use.

—Now I have the capital to expand, he was saying. I can run this side remotely, as you've seen, but I may need to hire someone to hold things down over here once business picks up over there. I'll rent a flat near Cambridge and keep doing what I've been doing. I can work from anywhere, really; the world economy runs on container ships. Well, and oil tankers.

—What about your place in the city – ô, and a UK visa? I meant to ask you about it before.

—Don't need one; I have an Irish passport. And I'll keep my place. We'll be back someday after you finish school and your

Fellowship. If nothing else, it's a good investment. My property value is through the roof.

Taylor sat up, unused remote still in hand.

—Then why not go back to school once we're in England? You're a thesis away from a PhD of your own. There's so much more you could do besides run a small consultancy. I can even help with your CV.

She reminded him of Saitō and Kristi, of their attempts to place him on career rails of their choosing.

—You-know-who calling me *Dottoressa* in public cured me of that for good.

It wasn't a real reason, but Taylor didn't argue the point yet, unmuting the soi-disant business news instead. Above a stock ticker in perpetual motion, the Beeblebroxian two-ring election circus was soundbit in the Orwellian duckspeak of talking heads, the Vineyard to be spared a presidential motorcade this year – or so they quacked like teleprompted ducks. His e-reader sagged.

—Again? Isn't there anything other than politics?

She'd declined his offers to pay for satellite, for baseball, repeating, "No modifications to the house." She gave him a wry look.

—What's with your big aversion to politics?

—In my family, *politics* usually meant the Irish republican cause. My mom's from Ulster – the North.

—O, I didn't know. You only said Irish before. Usually, that means from Boston or New York, but it explains the passport. I was wondering.

—Yeah, dual citizen. My mom's old-country Irish, and she was something of an activist in college at Galway, but not a Volunteer or anything.

But he could see her holding an Armalite, her eyes as grey as a Derry morn, life-stained by a Bloody Sunday. She'd misheard the distant *crack! crack!* of bangers with twelve-year-old ears, then the cri du cœur of sirens; only to watch the aftermath in BBC black 'n' white, the family gathered round; and in the following days, she'd found a British shell casing in the gutter, the brass leprose with green corrosion. She'd picked it up with twelve-year-old fingers, her make-do ballet duffel in her other hand – the final year they'd sent her to dance classes.

It was a core strand with the repeating pattern of memories woven throughout her tirades on "those Orange bastards" and

generations of sectarian apartheid: of the failing cliff's edge
of the family fortune, fallen into the Gehenna of second-class
citizenship and forcibly deracinated from Waterside into the
jammed tenements outside the old Derry walls; from the sharp
retort of British rifles to the call for civil rights; to the violent
abuses that she'd seen and heard of by the militarised RUC – "No
better than na Dúchrónaigh," she'd say of them and any word
of the feral SAS.

—She came to America to find work, but you'd think she still
lived there the way she got worked up. She had her reasons; I just
got tired of hearing them. I haven't willingly watched the news
since Omagh – not that she didn't give me an earful.

—Omagh?

—An especially ugly bombing in Northern Ireland a few years
before nine-eleven. I've had my fill of horror and of the press
wallowing in it for profit like they enjoy it – and rewarding the
effers who do that shit.

They jumped at three loud knocks. Taylor got to her feet.

—Who the hell?

He set his e-reader down beside his phone, wishing he'd
brought the revolver over her objections. She walked to the
window and peered through up-angled blinds.

—It's my mom.

Taylor flinched when three more knocks echoed. She turned
to him.

—It's my mom.

He rose, but Taylor lifted one hand, turning towards the entrance hall. He reached over and re-muted the TV; a faint hor-
ror-movie groan reached him from the front door. A female
voice as hard and sharp as flaked obsidian cut through Taylor's
cowed murmurs, and a thin woman with a severe ash-blonde
bob swept into the drawing room in a winged skirt suit, ice-blue,
couture-cut from the Lagerfeldian future-present. Curveless
linéaments. Taut skin. Below frozen eyebrows, her eyes were dark,
knowing, and humourless abysms the blue-black of a bottomless
oceanic pit; she looked down Taylor's old nose at him. Taylor
followed and introduced him with the feeblest of gestures:

—Mother, this is...

—Gigi, would you be so kind as to excuse us? I need to have a
word with my daughter.

He retreated towards the central staircase, mumbling his acquiescence, Taylor's face averted from him, vailed lines. He began ascending the stairs, her mother's words following:
—I'd heard a rumour, though…

He raced, heart thumping, to the second floor and through a dormant bedroom to an unlit window. A large black Merc was paused behind Taylor's Bimmer, engine still running, a capped driver limned behind the xenon headlights' glare – it would be over soon. He returned to the landing over the main staircase, a muffled monologue resonating in the distance with the forgiveless tone of a Spartan matron's death 'n' shields declamation. He hesitated, then descended the Persian-carpeted stair, step by step, till the words came clear:
—Rotten thing, you can't disguise this as some cliché experimental college fling. I haven't the patience for any more of your scandals.
—Mother, I…

He started at the sharp sound of a slap that reverberated in the Big House like a Wimbledon serve. Her mother's words followed like hammer blows answered with the meekest flattened silence:
—Did you think I would let you track mud on the name of this family again? How many times have you embarrassed us? How many times have we paid to bury your indiscretions? We're not like those dime-store socialites that clown and parade themselves across tabloid news and reality TV – the ones you've so desperately tried to emulate ¶. Look at yourself. You're pathetic ¶. You will not jeopardise the union between his family and ours. Is that clear? Nate is aware of his responsibilities, and as you know, the wedding invitations were sent out weeks ago. Clearly, we've been too lax with you, and you've been distracted by this play-thing. Thankfully – for your sake – it hasn't reached the level of public scandal ¶. I've already chastised Hunter and Brittany for their complicity, but your grandparents are unaware, and I've not informed your father of the specifics this time. You may still be of use to the family, so enjoy this perverse little liaison with your spic, but get it out of your system before you return to college. "Cæsar's wife must be above suspicion", and if need be, you'll be set aside and cast out."

He couldn't make out Taylor's response, but her mother was clear:

—No; my helicopter is waiting. You just bear in mind what I've said – what I've inconvenienced myself to come here and say. You have a future waiting for you, child, unless you choose to squander it; don't force us to cut you off. If you choose to defy the family in this, then prepare to walk away naked because you have nothing. Do not embarrass us again.

Taylor's souteneur swept past the foot of the stair without a backwards glance, the rat-a-tat of tardy rain followed by the sound of the front door firmly reshut. He descended the rest of the way, step by step, reliving Paige's warning: the warning he'd hand-waved away.

—Taylor?

He found her weeping silently, slumped to the floor. Light-headed, stomach-churning, he knelt next to her and placed one hand on her shoulder.

—Why? Why'd she say you're going to marry him?

Taylor didn't look up, tears running smoky tracks around her double-palmed face.

—Tessa said… It was Tessa's plan. Nate came with me on that trip when I went home, and then we went to see his parents too. That's why it took so long.

—What!

Anger and dismay at war within him, he rose to his feet and away. Her hands balled into fists against her forehead.

—We denied everything. We told them we were still together, that there was nothing wrong.

—Taylor!

—Finn, we had to! Our whole futures were riding on it. Still are.

—And you've been talking to him this whole time?

—I had to so that we could keep our stories straight. So no one would suspect I was really here with you. We said…

—But now what? Are you going through with it? You can't just be a stage prop for his political career. And what about us, our future? When were you going to tell me?

—Sometime during the semester. I was thinking… I thought if I waited till…

Something went cold in him: a flame switched off.

—This whole thing was a time bomb, wasn't it? It just blew up in your face sooner than expected.

—Finn, I…

—I'm gonna go look for my cat.

He turned on his heel and followed her mother's heavy foot-steps. Behind him, an inchoate sound melted into sobs. He stepped outside, braced by the undying wind, the sharp pattering not rain but coarse hail that bounced as it fell, salting the earth.

H E HAD THE PLACE to himself but took a seat within Sionnachuighim's partitioned snug, his ballcap blown back south by southeast; some people out there were still eating breakfast. Michaela entered through a kitchen door, stage left, carrying a filled glass rack: Snow-white, herself. He leant over the bar.

—Micheáilín, what's the craic?

She set it on the bar top, responding with weather-beaten fortitude and a steely eye:

—Finn. Are you OK?

—When life gives you lemons, pour whiskey in your lemonade. Rye, please. On the rocks.

—You finished the last fifth of rye yesterday. There's more coming, but not till tomorrow.

He squinted at the cabinets behind her.

—Jameson eighteen, neat. My grandfather had a bottle. Don't think he ever opened it.

—Water back?

—If it makes you feel better.

Michaela shook her head.

—Jaysus.

A week had vanished into the bottom of a rocks glass, recallless in obluvial baptism. The Vineyard had decamped in all of a day: in an argument with one sum: for all, zero. "Whether or not I get married isn't your problem," Taylor had said back at her place. "I'm not going to live with him. All that matters is if you want to be with me or not. Come to Cambridge like you planned. Nate won't be there, and you won't even see him once. I'll only be gone two weeks for the wedding and honeymoon – we'll be fine. We just have to be more discreet. My mom can't suspect anything."

"That's no different than what Tessa wanted," he'd replied,

trolley case in hand. "For me to be your secret plaything on the side while you're married to someone else."

"The difference is that it's me."

His hand shook with a slight tremor till the first warming mouthful settled below, his left forearm itching under the clam-shell brace. He listened with uncaring ears to the Corrs while animus dissolved, sunk within bourbon-barrelled tincture of oak. It replayed with every sip, thinning, translucid. He ordered a second.

"Forget your trust fund," he'd said; "forget your piece of their estate – it's a trap. I work; I can pay for school. People do it all the time. You can still be a big-deal economist. Nothing's stopping you."

But she'd snapped back: "You really want me to be disowned by my whole family, to never get what's mine? I'm not going to let Britt and Hunter have everything!"

There'd been no way around the money, and they'd circled each other in the looming shadow of her trust fund – eight years away and chained to heavy clinking shackles – while surrounded by the comforts provided by her weekly allowance, with both car and condo, in title, her parents'. He'd hounded her, asking "How many millions?" five different ways.

"One twenty," she'd replied at the last, voice brittle, "right now, but by twenty-twenty, it will be more."

"Thanks. Nice to know the winning bid."

"O fuck you, Finn."

"You'll never shake those effing pills, Taylor. Not till you get away from them – from her. The anxiety pills, the sleeping pills, the amps; all of it… all of it to whore for your mom?"

The first few blows had sent him reeling like she'd meant to kill him, but she'd stopped at breaking his left arm – the arm he'd raised to protect himself till the fiery *snap!* She'd lowered the large wooden king nutcracker and wiped a strand of wrath-spittle from her retouched Hydian face. "I guess my mom was wrong," she'd said; "this was just a college fling after all. Take your shit and leave." *Take your shit and leave.* Her steel-reënforced door had shut behind him with the crisp impact of a guillotine.

The concierge had called for an ambulance, not police, after Finn had stepped out of the elevator, cradling his arm in the vaulted foyer. "You fell down the stairs? How terrible. I'll have maintenance check them immediately. Good luck." The best discrétion money could buy.

He stepped down to Jameson 12 for drink three. After a certain point, the nuances escape you.

No cat. Arm braced. He'd returned home by taxi, mounting losses. Saitō had lifted nearly every stitch he'd left behind. A few unworn gifts from the Countess aside, Saitō had reclaimed her things and taken the final vestiges of the It-girl along for the ride. He'd found his long-lost varsity jacket in the entry closet alongside his Buzz B-3 and a dusty note upstairs on his listening seat: —Text me if you want your Loubs back. C.

Taylor – or someone – had tossed his bicycle at his doorstep later that night, a pedal gashing the door and his wrought-iron décrottoir scratching its paint. He'd found the mint red-and-white Fuso frame on eBay and had it built up with premium Italian bicycle parts by a local shop. "Like trash", Taylor had said of the Countess and Morgen. Like trash.

Memory was a Burrovian virus: mutating, spreading, lying – killed by a forty percent solution of ethanol. Settled into his groove, he counted not drinks but hours; until the branes of spacetime opened like Euclidean flowers, and he was lost within the garden for a spell.

☆

HE awoke under pressure. He didn't recognise the austere moonlit bedroom, but Kristi was asleep next to him on the narrow bed, arms and neck aglow with the soft shimmer of ivory-pearl. He caught distorted flashes, fluid, melting in the amber nectar of Lethe – carry-dragged by someone, a legless amadán. Might've been an old memory, though, or one half-imagined in vacuo.

He staggered his way to the bedroom doorway; and curled up on a doggy bed, Twigs raised her head, tail thumping twice. A chill shivered him; the caress of shades within a waking Orphæan dream – did they cry to him, blame him? – and he cursed when he slipped and fell in the bathroom – explosion! His stung knee flared, a new heart throbbing in the compact fluorescent light. He washed his hands and face in the pedestal sink: an ablution of Avernian waters.

He returned to Kristi's bedroom without urgency, swaying

with the rolling tide of intoxication, and sank onto the bed with overthéâtric care not to wake her. She'd shifted in her sleep, her long ponytail an ebon rope across her throat. He brushed the silken noose away, the softness of her skin rising to his hand, and she sighed – the faintest breath falling to the underworld. Something lost for evermore.

He snatched his hand back and bit his thumb, then gathered a pillow unto himself stiffly, and regained his unsteady feet. He entered the unlit living room, cold in the air-conditioned night, and cast himself down on a scarlet catafalque. There, couched below lifeless fronds, he awaited darkness and rebirth, already in pieces.

☆

So much death. Drums quaked – an ō-daiko crescendo – building, louder, thrumming, here! Boom. Boom, boom. Boom, boom, boom. Boom-boom-boom-boom-boom-boom-boom! The lake shone, a frosted blue mirror; blue the sky, all still. Dead.

☆

GIGI, wake the fuck up already.

Kristi's voice, bright and sharp as a bayonet – a coarse string of Gallic expletives; then he was shaken again. He opened gritty eyes and croaked,

—Yo. Why are you swearing at me in French?

—Because you don't know Chinese.

—Lucky me.

He and his throbbing head were in no state for a verbal flensing with five millennia of verbal arms. He needed a drink. Seated beside him on the sofa, she was as fit as a track star in her elastane and chunky steel wristwatch, her eyes opalescent jewels narrowed in overt irritation behind new square-frame glasses. "I'm still mad at you for not telling me you were back. What happened with Taylor?"

"'List how I, *care wretched* …'"

"Gigi, cut the shit."

"H'mf. Thirty silver denarii."

"Less cryptic?"

He raised a plaintive hand.

—Later. I'm not ready to talk about it yet.

—Then what happened to your arm? Snowboarding in Dubai?

—A nightstick fracture. No big. I fell down the stairs.

—How did...

—How'd you find me last night? I was drinking at the pub; then, I don't know. I usually cut myself off before it gets too late. Did I text you?

—No. Paige called and told me you needed help; she's out of the country. But it works out since I have something else I've been waiting to talk to you about. Something significant.

—O, so that's why you didn't dump me at home.

—Yes, but I need you to dry out first. Can you stay put and out of trouble for a couple of hours while I go to the gym?

—What, the Corporation again?

—No. A different opportunity for the both of us. Take a shower and make some coffee.

Kristi bounced to her feet, hands on her hips; she looked down at him with military poise, eight-pack abs a reproachment of his post-dance laxity.

—Do you need anything while I'm out?

—A cybernetic body. Think I wrecked this one.

—What, that Terminator Three blonde? She is tall.

—The original Arnold model, please.

C·P·SERRET,
DIE THE VILLAIN.

WINTER,
DAWN,
V.

★

H E'D GIVEN TAYLOR everything and nothing, and so she'd done him. Soaking in Kristi's old-style clawfoot tub, the heat soothed, but his skull still pounded, his braced and plastic-bagged arm resting on the ledge. He'd checked the cupboards for something to drink, but the place was dry. His voice moved over clear water: "'at whiles the swan cries …'"

"Gigi?"

He responded, but Kristi called again, her keys ringing nearer like a cat bell. He cleared his throat and yelled:

—In the bathroom.

—Are you decent?

—No; in the tub.

The door opened a crack.

—Hurry up and towel off; there's work to do.

—Work?

—You'll see. But I need to shower, so hurry up and get out of the way. Wait for me in the living room.

She left the door ajar, and Twigs, her golden whippet, peered in with big Keane eyes. He pulled the drain plug.

Damp hair dishevelled, towel-bound, he shouted the bathroom was free and returned to the living room, bundled clothes in his arms. The ornate ancestral shrine cabinet, in high-polish sang-de-bœuf, stood apart from the pale rosewood glow of a polished Pleyel upright in one corner and the bold lines of her Eames and other Miller-catalogue furniture, letters patent hanging above the sole bookcase: to Wharton from Punahou. It recalled Saitō's place: an unhomely hollow, partial veneer of normal. Plastic plants.

He hung his damp towel from the back of the meshy suspension seat set before an otherwise chairless dining table and assorted desk detritus; a legal pad beneath a burgundy Montblanc, and two English words amid spidery hanzi: "Chocolate Mercury". He pulled his clothes on, then sat, resting his chin, and closed his eyes. He was shoved.

—I'm awake.

—Right. I told you to make some coffee.

She'd dressed for another workout, her dark hair up but more streamline than cloud. Her black 'n' tan Goyard briefcase had apparated onto the tabletop. She swept papers and pen to one side, then set a slim ultrabook before him. Her five-minute lecture on binge drinking became ten, no words in edgewise till the but:

—If you don't kill yourself with booze first, she was saying, I have something that will change your life – both our lives.

—What? You won the lotto, and you're splitting it with me?

—Close. ▮▮ read me in…

—▮▮?

—Sorry, I meant Saitō. Guess I need some coffee too. One minute.

Kristi stepped into the adjoined kitchen space, and he flipped open her laptop. Twigs lapped at a water bowl, and Kristi set two white cups on the counter next to the capsule-loaded works of her red-enamelled coffee artillery; it sang like lonesome cicadas.

—Saitō told me a little about what you really do behind your little logistics front. I knew there had to be more to you, though it surprised me, but I kept my eyes open for…

Consternation disrupted the elegant line of his eyebrows, his heart plunging into the whirlpit, and though his lips parted, he failed to make denials and counter-accusations. She made mollifying gestures too much like jazz hands.

—Don't freak out, don't freak out; it's fine. No, it's more than fine. As you know, the Corporation has its fingers in everyone's purse, and I managed to get my hands on something that should yield a significant return.

About to stand, he sank back in almost relief.

—It's way too risky to fence anything that can be traced back to you. Destroy it, whatever it is. I've already quit that line of work for good, and I'm not gonna do that whole one-last-job trope from the movies. I didn't hear a thing, and this never happened.

Kristi turned back to her buzzing Nespresso, talking over-shoulder:

—It's from a different division in the Corporation. Not mine. Even better, they have no idea anyone's copied the data. I've sat on this since before I left for Hong Kong in May, and there've been no alerts. No investigation. Not even a ripple.

His ripple of tension begged to differ.

—What is it?

—You'll have to see for yourself.

—You're done trying to recruit me, then.

—You took too long. They hired a Japanese-American kid over the summer, and it only took that long because we had too many applicants. The Great Recession has them lining up, and if he keeps hitting on me, he might need replacing soon.

Finn smirked at her back.

—Should I have him killed?

—Spoken like liumang.

—Huh? Don't know that one.

—A *gangster*, don't you remember? You might need help with the booze, huli jing; the girls teased you about liumang more than once. Some triad street thugs have tattoos like your yakuza: Guan Yu, dragons, Chinese phœnices. But the top-level triads – the kingpins – are all business. Could you really order a yakuza hit over here?

—I was joking. My old connexions don't work that way. I'm not a member of a syndicate. I can't be. At best, I was a hired hand, and as I said, it's over. I'm out. Besides, if you know where to go, you can order a hit online, like pizza. You don't need to be gokudō for that.

Kristi arrived with ceramic demitasses in both hands, evoking his mornings before class at a Shōwa-era kissaten near Imade-gawa station, chain-smoking spicy-sweet Seven's, the hot si-phoned coffee served with thick buttered toast. She presented his: «Due caffè.»

She pivoted the laptop and touch-typed her credentials too fast for him to catch her password. She retrieved a tiny flash drive from her briefcase without needing to look, clicked this 'n' that, then turned the laptop back to him.

—It'll take a minute to load. Don't mess with my work computer, or I'll kick your narrow butt.

He scalded his tongue, then blew on his coffee, heavy with crema, watching the slomo software show – though why would a corporate exec have a CAD-viewer on her sliver-of-magnesium ultrabook? – until the mystery CAT product loaded. A show stopper.

—Jesus, Mary, and Joseph.

A puttylike airframe with a pivotal mono-wing and an internal void for a compartmentalised payload that popped in like a cola can. He googled the "s//rd-sg …" encoded on every CAT part file. She brought a red-top Aalto stool from another room and sat, shoulder surfing with espressi raised.

—Amazing, isn't it?

—Amazing isn't the word I'd use. Maybe terrifying. I don't deal in DotGov IP. Never did. The risk is too high. What do you even know about this monstrosity?

—It's a joint contract between two of our subsidiaries, ███████ ███████████████████████████████████████ ████████ manufacturing in Arizona. A complete modernisation package: they strip off the original eighties-era ██████ and rebuild it into that. Treaty compliant. Micro-PNT guidance, dial-a-yield, stealth – all that and a bag o' chips.

He scrutinised her. She shrugged.

—What? I read the PowerPoint.

He shook his head.

—We'd have to flee the country if we tried fencing this. This is big-boy espionage. See that? Secret//Restricted Data–Sigma. This sort of thing is s'posed to be air-gapped on a secure military network. TACLANE'd an' all that. It should take deep HUMINT even to try to EXFIL a piece of this data.

—Hacker jargon aside, what's it worth on the Dark Web?

—Seven, maybe eight figures? Hard to spend in Guantánamo, but at least they have Starbucks and a Taco Bell.

—No one knows. They aren't even looking.

—Not that you know of, but they don't announce espionage investigations to the public unless the EXFIL got leaked to the press. Who else did you involve?

—No one. Just me.

—How'd you manage then? This Technical Data Package has the whole alphabet of Department of Energy and DoD restrictions.

Kristi pulled the stool up and folded her arms on the tabletop, demitasse down.

—Domestic, our North American division, did a closed-door presentation on the project for the top brass. They broke for lunch, and one of the visiting engineers left his laptop unlocked in the conference room, which they also left open. It was easy.

He blew wordless bafflement. "Like I said, I never dealt in military TDP, but someone did try to con me into it once. Most of our remaining industry is part of the Defense Industrial Base and work on military contracts, and all these big projects – commercial or not – run under code names; that's how we locate them. But the con was obvious as soon as we pulled the TDP, so I dealt with the guy who conned me, to make an example.

"No, I didn't have him taken out or anything sordid like that, but I organised a kind of hit team, and we burned him – let INTERPOL and Sûreté Nationale have the scraps. It made the newswires, but there was nothing left to lead them back to me. I don't mess around when it comes to this stuff."

"'Kill one'," she replied nodding, "'warn a hundred.' Sûreté Nationale? He was in, what, Morocco?"

"Algeria."

"Saitō never mentioned any of this."

"I never mentioned it. Told her I didn't trade in government IP, 'specially not ours, but she might not've believed me. The risk..."

"Is worth it. Look, this is a winning ticket. Grow a pair."

He reflected over his blackpool, then shot the remainder.

—Besides it being a bad idea, I've never fenced anything myself. I only organised and oversaw EXFIL for a percentage.

—Message to Garcia.

—Huh? My...

—Kingpins know the fences, or they know who knows; if you can't do it, then tell me who can, or I'll figure it out myself. I'd rather cut you in, but...

—Kristi, if you don't know what you're doing, they'll catch you, and then it's hard time. Federal time. Even if you do know what you're doing, it's the Wild West out there and...

She snapped the laptop shut.

—I'm going to throw the dice with or without you. I'll find...

In the real world, the mythical Big Score was like catching Moby-Dick; it pulled you under – no survivors. Kristi was in over her head, and if the Feds rolled her up while she fumbled in the dark, they would take an exacting look at her friends and associates, assuming she didn't turn state's evidence. Finn didn't expect to pass more than a cursory inspection after the overindulgences of the past year. Recooking the books would take several expensive calls to his lawyers, and time he might not have. He was cornered.

—Stop, stop, he said in hands-waved capitulation. Fine. I'll do it. This time and only this time. Don't expose yourself again – not for anything – and you have to follow my rules without arguing, or I'm on the next plane to a non-extradition country. Not joking.

—I knew you'd see reason.

C·P·SERRET,
DIE THE VILLAIN.

HE NET INVOICE, viewed in aggregate across several
T   cryptocoin wallets, stared back at him. No thrill. More
like the dead body after a hit: a mess to be cleaned up.
Kristi's Big Score wasn't that big, not in 2012 dollars, and she'd
already begun pestering him to do one more job. Her persistence
had raised other concerns and suspicions.

Muddying the blockchain had proved a tedious shell game
involving a byzantine web of wallets, tumbler accounts, and
altcoins. He'd gifted her a burner 'droid, paid for with cash, and
he messaged her over an OTR app: —Done.

Winelike, the fruity-bright acidity of the last mouthful swirled
beneath his palate, and he grimaced, musing over the lingering
floral finish. She'd offered to play chauffeuse instead of meeting
up at his place, and Three Clovers was near – but not too near – to
her office building. A flannelly coffee bar with a suited line out
the door, it had three pre-Starbucks-acquisition Clover machines
and a one-gallon tip jar – requests for espresso milkshakes were
referred to that donut shop around the corner. The financial
district had never fallen into his hotspot rotation due to the
difficulty in parking and the overabundant CCTV. You took an
overpriced taxi or the grimy metro.

He was sick of taxis, but vintage Porsche values had skyrock-
eted on a sudden, to his benefit in July and subsequent loss today.
He hadn't seen anything that wouldn't further increase his risk
of exposure – like the '76 930 Turbo he'd spotted last week. Six
figures. His matching burner buzzed with her reply: —OMW.

He crossed himself, then packed up, his old messenger bag
over one shoulder. He almost hacked on the throat hit of diesel
soot outside, the mid-August steam bath stifling in the scant
shade of glassed colossi. He adjusted his ballcap and rechecked
his burner, double-taking when a silver Range Rover pulled over
into the red-curbed fire lane, Kristi heiling him from behind the

wheel. He swore underbreath and tugged on the door handle, climbing up and up into refrigerated smugness. She forced her way through hostile congestion, cutting across lanes with supercharged v8 aggression. He struggled against the G-forces with his seatbelt, horns blaring on all sides.

—You ought to use your turn signal.

—O. Habit. If you signal in Hong Kong, it encourages them to cut you off. You have to strike first and without warning.

He hung on, grin constrained, holding his tongue as long as he could through the dirge cascading on the in-cab audio.

—So where'd this come from?

—You like it? I got a decent deal. Car dealers always think they can pull one over on you because you're a woman. He was very wrong, but "I didn't have him taken out or anything sordid like that."

—The timing's a little unfortunate, but at least your big trucks are tasteful. Most supersized sport-utes look like soccer-mom penis envy.

Kristi gave him a multifaceted black look.

—Gigi, sometimes a jeep is just a jeep.

—Sure.

—So says the girl that smokes cigars and only drives collector's cars. Freud would have a field day with you, and then Jung would have to figure out that tattoo.

—Like I said, I didn't pick it out. The tattoo artist came up with the design by himself; it's more traditional that way. This Chopin again?

She didn't challenge the change of subject.

« « Le vent d'hiver ». It's a classic.

—You never listen to anything that isn't de profundis, said Finn in his best remaining Latin. Why not something light-hearted like Shostakóvich?

—You're awful sensitive for a heartless pirate. But I wanted to ask you again about when I should use the prepaid phone versus my regular phone when texting you.

—Anything regarding the enterprise, use your burner to contact my burner; and don't use text, use the TextSecure app. Every time. For anything else, like shooting the breeze about your new big truck, use your iPhone to text or call my Galaxy. The two worlds can never touch.

—Thug-life is hard.

—Not even joking. All the preparation in the world doesn't guarantee victory.

—Spare me the fortune cookie platitudes and « Show me the money » ; I have a line on a like-new Birkin. O, don't look so sour. I didn't let Saitō take your Steve bag.

—We have to be careful. Extra careful. One small mistake and someone will be kicking in your door. Let's just finish this up so that I can have a drink. Been a long day. A long week.

—Didn't we talk about you laying off the sauce ?

—Laying off the sauce ? What are you ? Forty ? »

She'd look twentyish for decades yet – but if looks could kill, he'd've splattered all over her upholstery. She had some trouble finding parking for the British behemoth, leading to an extended walk back to his place. She was all business in a skirt suit of plum georgette and a white blouse, with modest but very nice leg; though he wasn't sure how she wasn't melting. He unlocked the front door of his rowhouse. She gave her Rolex a pointed glance.

—How long will this take?

—Not too long. You have to get back?

—I held off on going to lunch till you texted.

He led her into the library and set his laptop on the black 'n' chrome Laccio coffee table, his printer cabled and waiting after last night's test run. She settled in on the sofa.

—It's too quiet here without your cat. Not that she meowed a lot, but it feels sort of vacant now. Empty.

—I know; it's strange.

—What are you going to do with your hair? Are you staying auburn or changing with the season?

—Haven't decided yet, but I'm due for a change of some kind. OK, time to get paid.

—Those bit-things?

—Yeah. In a second, I'll have you enter that twenty-digit pass-phrase I told you to come up with. Don't tell me what it is, but be ready.

—I read up on bit-stuff, and it sounds like bullcrap. So why are we messing around? I'd prefer hard cash upfront.

—In a word? Distrust. I don't want to meet up with someone in person with aluminum suitcases full of C-notes like in the movies. Bitcoin allows for a secure transaction without ID from either party. In the drug trade, everybody knows everybody, but no one knows who I am – and I intend to keep it that way.

The last was a lie. Too many people knew too much. He should've bailed the moment he'd heard that Saitō had talked. He'd packed his bag. Cash. Passports. All of it. He'd put one foot out his door, but this place – the place he'd made here for himself – was the only thing he hadn't lost. And they were in the same boat now, him and Kristi; a mistake by either, and they'd both be wearing orange for life; he was no cat's paw. She tapped the toe of one black patent pump.

—But it looks like something anyone could make up; there's nothing real backing it. Nothing tangible, anyway. It's not even money. It's a commodity minus the commodity.

—I s'pose one person could make up Bitcoin and maybe did, but a lot of people – a lot of stakeholders – are building and sustaining the cryptocoin networks and exchanges and mining new Bitcoin. Think of it as virtual Krugerrand – a commodity minus the commodity.

Kristi snorted.

—How about real Krugerrand instead?

—Too heavy. Time for your passphrase.

He offered the tethered laptop, then stood and stretched as she typed with an extra-careful hunt-and-peck. She said she was done and shifted back on the sofa. He detached a small white iPodlike device from a USB cable and presented it to her.

—This digital wallet is your primary repository for now, but there've been some thefts recently, so don't plug it in unless we're doing a transaction – and don't leave any Bitcoin in an online account. I'll print a paper backup in a sec in case it fails or gets lost. You'll want to store them in separate secure locations. My cut already is. There is some risk of volatility, and we'll start the laundry over the next few months in small amounts, but Bitcoin's gone up over the summer; it was around five dollars for most of the year, and now it's eleven.

Kristi turned it over in her hands.

—It looks like a beeper. There's really seven million stored in this little thing?

—Not exactly. I won't get too technical, but holding Bitcoin is like having an allocation of serial-numbered bullion in a CO-MEX depository. Around six hundred thousand Bitcoins are

registered to that wallet, but the coins are inseparable from the multinational blockchain; so unlike bullion, you can never take the coins out of the vault. You can only transfer ownership to someone else, whether for goods or currency, but dropping that in your purse beats pushing a wheelbarrow of Krugerrand.
—On the one hand, it amazes me that we got almost nine million for one thumb drive of data. On the other hand, I thought it would be more. The engineering has loads of non-military applications. Anyone would want a piece of that.

He shrugged.
—It was over ten before the broker's fee and the cost of tumbling the coins; that's when the other bidders folded. These are huge numbers by darknet standards, and given that the total trading volume of Bitcoin is only around four hundred million, it's hard not to leave tracks with nine in play. I can spend another few days on it, but we'd lose another two or three percent – and we'll already be losing more when we exchange for dollars and begin laundering. You'll have five or six clean when it's all over, but if you reconsider placing some or even all of it offshore, you'll lose less in the wash.
—No, thanks; I prefer a bird in the hand. And we should do at least one or two more auctions; the Corporation has contracts here and in the EU that I could get access to, nothing traceable back to me.

The printer fired up. Sounded like she'd spent her share in her head, and her offer hinted she might've already collected such and intended to fence them, through him, at intervals. It was a daring heist, even if it had played out as she'd said; Chinese-agent daring. She could've passed a copy to Beijing on her recent trip and had only brought it to him after the fact. She was second-generation but spoke the language and identified with traditional Chinese culture more than her mainland friends – exactly whom China would ask for a technological leg up, per recent analysis. She fit the profile.

China rarely paid for intel, but some of their people – MSS, MID, 863 Program – knew the back-alleys of information and came to sell, like she was, here with him. Or was she a plant, working for private intel or another corporate interest? A hedge fund management company was a safe bet with short odds, but which? There were thousands of hooded cabals holding trillions, and █████████ Mgt had already blown him out of the water. Then, le Carré–dramatic, she might be a double or triple, playing all sides for personal gain. Had she worked Saitō for IP? In all, it was getting too spy novel.

—Don't push our luck, he said; one misstep and it's national infamy and leg irons, or if you're lucky, exile in a non-extradition country. You only have to roll snake eyes once in this game, and someday someone will use that technical data in a recognisable form. The Feds will scramble, looking for scalps, so you might want to plan a long-term exit strategy abroad. I hear Kazakhstan's nice this time of year.

—No, thanks. China doesn't extradite either – at least not to the U. S.

He frowned but shook it off. It was exactly the wrong response, but it made him feel better – a new itch between his shoulder blades – about hiring Centimani to pull Kristi's dirt; it had been too long since she'd added up. He'd included Chocolate Mercury in the request. You never knew what might come back.

C·P·SERRET,
DIE THE VILLAIN.

★

R   ED PENNANTS faced blue across a wide field, silks fluttering like unbattened sails, the wood beyond fallen into rust. Forests of black spears undulated, urchinlike, as cavalry circled, their hooves a low rolling thunder. A fox lay in swaying autumn grasses, white chin on dark paws. Golden eyes grave, three tails lay flat behind him, still as stone. The morning sun was dim through low clouds, screened from the rattle of lacquered iron plates and shaking quivers.

Drawn bows arced, asymmetric, and ten thousand arrows hissed, casting a river of shadows. The fox bolted – an orange flash against the green. Steely rain washed the plain with equine screams and the cries of men. Again, the iron-shod drums of thunder.

The treeline welcomed the fox with cool shade, birds screeching as they scattered. He glanced back upon the blooded sward of spreading death, then slinked into the underbrush, three tails tucked behind.

☆

FINN faced what remained him. Bedding stowed, his transposed pocket of Old Japan was tea-house tranquil, his open closet light with the husked wrack of an Oisínian tide, palm prints in the sand: here, Saitō; there, the Countess. He mulled over fractured and fading faëryland memories of the past year and more: from Trace's first smile to the bimestrial coda on Taylor's isle of discontent. It was time to clean house.

His Tigers cap sat atop the ishō-tansu, among an It-girl's dusty accoutrements: make-up, nail polish, &c. He dumped his satchel over it all. More of the same.

—Shit.

A near-empty amber glass vial of Vik's faëry dust, once five grams, metred to the second decimal. He tapped the remainder onto the ridge of his hand and inhaled the final brightness, a passing tightness in his chest. The vial went into the open trash bag, followed by a clattering fall of Gigi's personalia and the heated implements of hair torture. He swept it all away.

He stripped to sports bra and boyshorts, then slipped into the magical skin-feel of a silk polo and – of all things – chinos, weary of the dryer-accident fit of his post-Saitō band-shirt-and-jeans default. He dialled for a cab but hit END. Nudged by morbid curiosity, he called the number for the Countess's car – expecting nothing – and shivered, greeted by dead name. She'd had him forwarded to a local black car service and placed on account, despite everything, the bitch. Twenty minutes.

He stepped outside in his wedge sneakers into the final unforgiving furnace blast of August, a large black sedan waiting near the fire hydrant, shades of the oyabun's S600. A livery driver climbed out in a generic penguin suit and cap.

"Miss M——?"

Finn set him straight in no uncertain terms; then the contrite chauffeur opened and held a rear door, revealing an interior more akin to the first-class suite in an Airbus jetliner than terrestrial transport. Finn dropped into one of two diamond-quilted rear seats, and encoached within, he found a chilled bottle of Krug and two sterling flutes had been provisioned. He considered not opening it, but one drink wouldn't be the end of the world. Maybe two. A shame to waste the bottle. Pushing the recline button, he settled in and smiled to himself – back in Kansai, most taxi cabs were black.

The assorted upscale ladies in the waiting area of Taylor's salon all appeared to have just left a stylist, not in need of one's services. The two women behind the counter gave him dismissory looks down their upturned noses: the same failing assessment of his clothes and Japanese gangsta ink.

—Can I help you? asked one in a tone that assured him she could not.

—I'm here to see Charles.

She squinted over Finn's shoulder at the brazen black car stopped by the NO PARKING sign outside the front door, ZEPPELIN on one hindquarter. She didn't check the open book in front of her.

—We're booked solid.

—Is he here?

—You'll need to make an appointment.

Finn wasn't above making a scene for the richly upholstered ladies awaiting their spit 'n' polish, raising his voice in repeated demand till she retreated in an acrid huff, the other glaring silver-eyed poignards. He did his best to look bored, wishing he had some gum to chew for insouciant effect, and Charles arrived in tow two minutes later, devoid of flamboyance other than in sheer muscle mass, sculpted from the Tom of Finland school of æsthetics. Charles greeted him in a Sarumanian basso profundo and, after the pleasantries, asked how he could help.
—Something roughed-up, Finn replied. Fifties' edgy. Brando in Streetcar; Dean in Eden. Pick a colour.
—Bronde balayage and a spiky quiff. Edgy, but...

Charles explained the finer details, then returned to his work in progress, Silver-eyes on the phone, scrambling to rearrange his afternoon appointments. It was standing room only, because handbags, but a brief wait before Finn cut the line. He watched the friseur adjust his colour in the mirror: the final transformation in his féerie.

He left with pomade and a new hairspray for his "pixie pompadour", as Charles had dubbed it, and the hair changed everything and nothing, his faint reflexion on the inside of the passenger window recalling Chris: the boy's unrealised, little-spoken, and swift-belted projection beyond compulsory leotards and parochial skirts. At Pygmalion, he tried disparate things, dissatisfied with the sight of Peter Pan through the looking-glass – at the gamin as much as the gamine. Ugh. He growled sotto voce:
—Grow up already.

He went upstairs and tracked down Kristi's secret brand among the business wear, stepping into his revised rôle at the head of an expanded and fully realised FSSO. Kick in the door of Black Sea shipping in a big way. Mafiya? SVR? Whatever. There were millions to launder, but a life and future lay beyond that. A change in tack. A new default.

A salesgirl helped him pick out the first necktie, telling him breathily that the anis-green silk would bring out his eyes; she tied it for him and showed him the four-in-hand ropes. He tried a few different shades and styles on his own; until he found what beseemed him, and in a dawning moment, looped mid-knot, a recognition: Chris.

—I always was, wasn't I? Despite everything, she couldn't change it no matter what she did.

He spread his slim fingers and clenched his small fists in turn, then looked again at the silverspun « désert du réel » in reflexion. —That line from the second GITS, Saitō Ryokū-sensei: « A mirror should be looked down on, not through. »

Chris piled bagged Pallas suits, an assortment of « cool » shirts – like in that new *Gatsby* trailer – &c. on a low bench, then perused the shoe galley, recalibrating the envelope of his intentions. He pursed his underlip when it occurred to him he'd have to go elsewhere to find plain ole Oxfords sans stacked heels. Not every man could be six-three – or even six-zero. Not even Steve McQueen.

C·P·SERRET,
DIE THE VILLAIN.

WINTER,
DAWN,
VIII.

★

EWARE THE IDES of Virgo – seven, his luckless num-
B   ber. The elevator descended in silence to P2. A long and
wearisome day of waiting for nothing and rescheduled
delays, futile as Achilles tilting at tortoises, washing black money
white to fund Kristi's handbag habit, for now.

The IT contractor – from the outsourcer she'd tipped him
to – had proven a neckbeardy creep, leering through Coke-bottle
glasses, and Chris had brushed the revolver under his suit jacket
for reässurance more than once during the appointment. Hands
shaken twice, he'd scrubbed surgically – up past the wrist – in
the unfinished en suite, and hand sanitiser waited in the glove
box of his new car.

He'd found the showroom dust bunny within the industri-
al-Romantic new car lots, after leaving an art-gallerylike vintage
dealership empty-handed again, and had bewildered a slithy sales
rep by talking turkey. He mashed a button on his first keyless key
fob–thing and dropped into the black leather bucket seat of last
year's 911 Turbo, in a vivid pull-me-over red. It rang up the same
as that vintage 930, but leasing under his company was a standard
tax-minimisation strategy and read normal to the IRS – versus a
hundred large for the vintage car, in cash, raising a red flag. Its
five hundred horses chomped at the bit of white-knuckle traffic
in spitting rain, so he dropped out to hunt for new vinyl as the
band-aid on his shitty day. It was all grey through his defogged
windscreen.

He drifted through Midtown Records without aim, the odd man
out in his pinstriped pantsuit and burgundy trench, spot-checking
the bins. He stepped around a shopgirl in hipster-boy clothes and
Buddy Holly glasses, a labyrinthine sociosemiotic of glyphs and
pictograms etched into the occult tapestry of her visible skin: a
transhuman cave painting, her hollow on the outside instead of
within. She turned – across her throat in blackletter, EMETH. She
gave him a once-over.

—If you dyed your hair green, you'd look like the Joker. Y'know, from *Batman*?

His own laugh caught Chris off-guard like a hiccough.

—I don't tan well, but I'm not that pale or that smiley.

—Looking for anything in particular?

—Something darkish. Moody. Like today.

She flipped her short asymmetric hair, turquoise-blue, down to the roots.

—Dark? What do you usually listen to?

—Neo-psych, bluesy garage, some stoner. I still collect a lot of nineties punk, though I've been listening to it less. Nostalgia, I guess.

She thought for a long moment, blackest eyes on the ceiling, then back to him. Her look was speculative, but her tone wasn't.

—You like Jesse Sykes.

Another hiccough laugh.

—I'd have her baby.

—Come with me.

He left the shop clutching an extra-rare triple-LP box set of *Altar*, imported from Japan, with Jesse Sykes on vocals for one cut of "The Sinking Belle". Straight home, he dropped his umbrella into the stand to dry, untied his horsehide brogues, and hung his trench coat; then, he scooted upstairs, his new-old-stock gem underarm. Electrodes awakened ab intra – a fiery bloom. He removed the shrink wrap and sorted through heavyweight black records, placing disc one on the platter, B-side up. He slid the carriage down the steampunk aëroarm, cutting to Jesse, then sank into the causeuse within an unusual resonance, like buoy bells in heavy fog, sonorous with warning.

He loosened the knot of his sage-green tie and unbuttoned two key buttons, his breath pacing a new rhythm, aware he'd forgotten to pour himself a drink. He played through all six sides of the album while the grey light outside faded, then relit electric-bluey, and began to ponder a solo dinner, hankering for the convenience-store bentō he'd survived on for years at Shindai, but he started at a familiar female voice close by:

—Well, well, what's this? A dashing dandisette in place of our little Gigi? Whatever shall we do?

It was the first time he'd seen Paige dressed down: a fine-tuned *Grazia* editorial on the state of Milano street style, shot by a celebrity photog, her fedora well outside the contempo preppy girl code, Botkier bag. About to ask how she'd gotten in, a door closed – the bathroom. One plus one, equalling Kristi, he gained his stocking feet.

—What're you two doing here?

—Staging an abduction, birthday girl. Lucky you, it's a Friday.

He scowled, sure he hadn't told a soul. Not in ages. Nor had he gone through the pretense of celebration. Not since the friendless grim of his sixteenth – not even with Senpai. Paige tapped the furl of his brow.

—Time for preventative Botox. I'll email you a gift certificate.

—How'd you know? About my birthday, I mean.

—Have you forgotten that I never forget anything?

—But I didn't tell anyone…

—Your ring's in the ashtray, love.

It sat amid dead stubs and steel-grey crumbles, a sparkling clot of South African blood. He glanced from it to her.

—Back for law school?

—Yes; it's almost that time. I may even have to pay attention this year. Can you imagine?

—We're taking you out, said Kristi from the doorway. Turn that thing off, and let's go; the limo's waiting.

No DD. They were serious about drinking. He considered asking for his spare key back but complied, grumbling under-breath. Paige observed the esoteric power sequence, one step behind him.

—I hear your days as a solopreneur are ending. When will the new offices be open for a guided tour?

—Um, maybe next week? It's been hectic and aggravating. The effing stencil on the door is the only thing even done – ô, and the car lease, I guess. It's on the company tab.

—Yes; Kristi pointed it out. Rock Star Logistics, is it?

—Wish I'd thought of that before I incorporated.

—Delaware, I assume?

He yielded a curt nod at her guess-in-one but didn't mention Delaware was merely the first shell in a web of corporate proxies that curlicued around the globe, from haven to haven.

—Right now, everything is pending my licensing change from forwarder to non-vessel carrier. Then I'll hire one or two people and build from there.

Paige stopped him in the darkened doorway. She unravelled his necktie the rest of the way, pulled it free, and liberated one more button. Fanservice, she said, using his word. Kristi descended the stairs ahead of them, dressed for a fu'er dai brunch in powder-blue, her like-new Birkin hanging from the crook of one arm.

—You two can flirt at the bar. Let's go already.

He led Paige down, asking which bar.

—A new speakeasy-style pub, she said, midtown, on forty-second. Connie's Rage, it's called – I hear it's the cat's meow. I have some peeps meeting us there; only one or two blokes, so don't cry or try to run. But you'll need a new sobriquet now that our little Gigi is off in Paris.

—You know, I have a perfectly good name. Chris? Finn?

—Yes, but Gigi had flair. How about *ghee*?

—Ghee? O, you mean the French Guy.

—A guy's name, Kristi interjected from the front door. Everyone still calls her Gigi. Stick with that.

Chris retied his brogues. Paige stepped into her ankle boots.

—But it's perfect for a swag tomboy, don't you think? Very Georges Sand.

—She looks more yakuza than littérateur with that hair.

He rolled his eyes.

—Whatever, let's just go, long as they're not playing "Gangnam Style" at this place too.

C·P·SERRET,
DIE THE VILLAIN.

WINTER,
DAWN,
IX.

★

H   IS SHINY NEW Note II rang, and he stopped typing. It was a short call, the female voice on the other end sharp, impersonal, and efficient: the background package on Kristi would be hand-delivered by armed courier later today. He set the phone down. Huh. Sensitive. Super-sensitive. It had taken weeks – and many billable hours – longer than expected. He didn't look forward to the final invoice from Centimani.

His office suite was three-quarters there: French Grey walls blank but for a 3-D print of Kandinsky's *Winterlandschaft* I; the adjacent rooms, including his corner spot, also furnished but unstaffed. Alone at the front desk, Chris went back to processing a pending shipment on the thin client, *Throttle Elevator Music* playing on a stand-mounted Muji CD player. He started at a familiar female voice from the doorway:

FINN
STRATEGIC
SUPPLY &
OPERATIONS, INC.

EMC LICENSED

Damn, eoljjang, that look is hot.

Saitō's Gibson-tuck updo was even lighter. Caramel blonde. She was business dress coded in an iris-blue blouse, grey skirt and pumps, thin red line of heel. A large tote was askew one shoulder, the canvas leather-trimmed Prussian-blue against écru. She held the frosted glass door open, chewing gum, and the IT neckbeard he'd said good riddance to last month stepped in, manpursed nonthreatening jacketless white-collar, carrying a black duffel straight to the server closet.

Chris was on his feet in a cocaine heartbeat.

—Chloë, what are you doing here ¶? Hey, what are you... ?

—Sorry, Baby Doll, she cut in, but Chloë's bullshit. Where's the cash you got for the ███████ blueprints?

She pulled an oversized double zip-tie from her tote; Neckbeard was taking tools out of his duffel, open closet. The image rippled like fabric, her follow-on questions muffled underwater. It was over.

—Who are you? Chris interrupted. FBI?

She ignored his questions in turn and circled the front desk with a gleamy cartoon shark smile, black noose raised. Resistance was futile, and he didn't pretend, her firm grip on his wrists replaced by the practised cinch of hard-edged plastic. She patted him down, stopping at his snubbie, on-waistband at four-thirty; she dropped it – holster 'n' all – into her bulging tote, along with the speed loader from his front pocket, then pressed him against the desk, holding the crook of his suited arm.

—And where's the paper backup? she was asking overshoulder. Here or stashed someplace else? We're towing your sexy new car right now, and we'll take it apart bolt-by-bolt if we have to.

One thing stood out to him:

—The package was fake, wasn't it?

—A Trojan apple hiding a worm. We mapped the broker's network, cleaned out the buyer, then burned them to the ground – right out of your Algerian playbook. You should've been there. You were...

—Kristi a part of this, or did you switch out her IT guy?

—Kristi? You're funny. You should've come in when I asked – you know, one of the first dozen times. You're such a pain. You could've changed hats, no one the wiser, but things are heating up, and we have to take you out of play for now. Lucky for you, we intercepted chatter this morning and got here first, but they beat us to your place. Last I heard, the fire's under control, but didn't you have a cat? Hold on.

She tugged on his arm, turning behind him. She had a finger to one ear, highlighting a dangly gold earring and the earpiece tube coiled behind it.

—You heard the man. Let's go!

Neckbeard stuck his fuzzy head out of the closet.

—Claire, I need more time. The drives aren't hot-swappable.

—Didn't you set up the rack?

—Well, yes.

—Christ, use thermite. Or donut charges if you brought enough det cord. We have to go. Now.

They argued. Neckbeard lost. She pushed Chris out into the empty hallway.

—Claire? he asked.

—Move it, Aphid Grin. What does that even mean anyway?

Claire pushed till she pulled him to a sudden stop in front of the empty suite next door. The building was an all-but-vacant casualty of the last derivatives scandal and a consumptive economy on negative-interest life support. No movement was visible down orthogonal corridors. Her racking cough echoed.

She still hadn't identified whom she was with, leaving CIA the too-obvious conclusion. It began falling into place – his explosion in reverse. That surge of guys chatting him up last fall, he'd rebuffed them all, and then the so-called Chloë had sat at his table. Her hot pursuit. Amadán... Should've known something was wrong from day one. It was too fast. Too easy. She'd had access to his place. Access to his laptop. Complete pwnage.

The patter of water spray on glass was followed by the shrill bray of fire alarms and the onset of flashing strobes. Grey smoke billowed from below his office door, spreading the commingled stench of molten metal and burning plastic. Claire spat her gum and – ping! – lit a stud.

She reached back into her tote and pulled out the little black submachine gun he'd googled at her place. He cursed. Pwned himself. She dropped a stubby silencer over the flash hider and locked it in place with ready skill, then extended the foregrip and stock, her stud at a rakish dangle.

Neckbeard waded to them through sooty fog-machine smoke, a matching silenced machinenpistole slung and extended before him, fake Coke-bottles shed. Claire looked towards the near exit through a blocky holographic sight.

—Weapons free.

She rubbed out the remains of her cigarette, then led the way in short, cautious steps, hunched low over her gun. Neckbeard tried to push Chris along from behind, MP7 held high-ready overshoulder, but he shrugged off the unwanted touch.

—Where's our backup? asked Neckbeard. I didn't hear.

—Too busy chatting around the bonfire. Five mikes out.

—Shee-it. Maybe we should call the fucking cops.

Claire shook her head.

—Posse Comitatus. I shouldn't be here without a nanny from DOJ or Homeland Security, and neither should you, Company man.

—Green badge.

—Call your lawyer and ask, but we need to extract the asset in one piece – maybe two – right the fuck now.

She held up a braking hand at the fire door, then reached for the handle, her MP7 pulled back, but the door swung wide, a moving shade – black – the crack of dry branches underfoot, bellowing into the muffled beat of a woodpecker-on-oak over a tuneless crash 'n' gong and the tinkling wind chime of brass acorns off the wall and across Chris's bow –

the sirens' relentless shout – *snick-snack*

snickersnee,   picine thrum.

He opened his   eyes the blood

wretched dry   against the wall

Claire shoving back   other way, hard

stumbling, lifted,   pulled, shoved again:

—Keepgoingkeepgoing   keepgoingDown!

woodpecker woodpecker   puffpuff ring

smoke of purest white: almost pretty

—GogogoMove!   —Getdown!

ducked-head   *doki doki*

—ContactfrontContactrear!   *woodpeckers,*

falling trees   taiko drums, buzzing bees –

screaming richochet

—Shit! Mags? Mags!   —My last one!

—Stayfucking…!   poundingsound

too close, too loud

—Shit! Man down…

Man down. Ears ringing in the wake of a percussive Dies Iræ, a voice muffled by cotton balls:

—Are you hit? Are you hit?

Claire was spilt on the floor, the front of her blouse saturated red in overlapping blooms, his Rhino in her white-clenched fingers. She dropped his empty speed loader and flicked the revolver's hexagonal cylinder shut with an awkward winged flip. She fired at something he couldn't see past the corner, then again, the flashing alarms an insistent white noise.

Her gun hand dropped to the floor. Sledgy *thunk*. He couldn't look away, not to that groaning sound nearer by. Her eyes were wide, staring at nothing through streaming tears. He twisted at his bonds, wrists and knees burning. Pink foam trickled from the corner of her red lips, pooled blood reaching towards him. She struggled to breathe, then rasped through her gurgling cough:
—Where's Nick? Mom...

Claire gagged, choking. A wet sound. A helpless soprano soubrette like his reached no one:
—Help her, please!

Her gasping heaves quickened, then stopped, empty brass scattered around her like powder-burnt petals. Still and shuddering heaps choked the corridors and risen to a listing kneel, Neckbeard swept the scene with his off-hand, the walls Swiss-cheesed with through-and-through holes. A final woodpecker–whuff of white smoke and the sub-machine gun snapped empty – *jingle, jingle*, little bells – the wail of fire trucks rising in the distance.

He set the gun down, and his other hand, shaking, tore open a packet of Kerlix with his teeth. On Claire's curled left hand, a gold ring – Chris twitched with an odd tremor, breathing the chemi-metallic air of an indoor range and the metallic stench of something else. The far emergency exit they'd almost reached opened a few inches, and gloved fingers signalled through the gap. Neckbeard spoke into the mic at his wrist:
—Bravo-two-niner. I have visual. Over.

A ballistic shield preceded a balaclava'd file of squat black rifles. Muzzles sweeping every corner, they spread out, shouting tactical jargon and cuffing the mostly dead. Kristi followed through the guarded doorway, her blocky pistol held isosceles low-ready. She'd hidden her long hair under a high-cut black helmet and wore a matching plate carrier over long sleeves and trim cargoes in a bluish wet-concrete grey. There was a U. S. flag patched in reverse on her right arm but no badge or other unit-marking. Not on her. Not on them. Electronic earmuffs mounted to her helm, a boom mic hovered before compressed lips. She stepped with care around the flex-cuffed fallen: bodies, blood, and bits of pulverised meat.

Neckbeard called her Anne. She holstered her sidearm and squatted next to him, ignoring Chris.
—Sorry, incompatible radios. SITREP?

Neckbeard winced and shook his head, mid-triage with a grey-clad medic.

—██ is gone, but the asset wasn't hit. I secured the hard drives, but the paper backup wasn't there.

Anne glanced at Chris and Claire through yellow-lensed wrap-arounds, then back to Neckbeard, her voice too loud when the alarms cut mid-sentence.

—What are ██ and the other ninjas even doing stateside? Checking atmospherics again?

—Classified, Neckbeard grumbled with a significant glance at Chris; I'd bet, but she didn't tell me, and neither did the Agency – if they even know. But blindfold the asset, Kim said...

—What? You're not rendering her or whatever else NSA thinks. Remind CIA that we have lead here: not DoD; not you. And where's your HSI liaison? – nevermind, we'll sort it out at the debrief. I'll take the detainee down; she's not your problem anymore.

Anne stood, pulling Chris up by a twisted arm, then past the rising abattoir stench to the emergency exit.

—Fucking contractors.

They squeezed past two uniforms carrying a folded stretcher and began to circle the stairwell down, the furore of sirens ringing up from an open door at the very bottom. His condemnation lay in a single word. No question.

—Anne.

—Anaïs, but no one calls me that. Americans can't pronounce French names any more than they can Chinese ones.

Her sang-froid chilled him, and he shivered as her nebulous exoticism snapped into focus: the melting pot of French Indochina – another child born of a dead empire. Chinese? Check. French? Safe bet. Vietnamese? Maybe, probably, or something else. Velcro 'Merica.

—You're not part-Japanese, he said, are you? Or even from Hawai'i?

—None of that was my idea, but I was overruled.

—And – lemme guess – ██, Claire ██, was what? Korean?

—You said it, kid, not me. If only you'd come in voluntarily, it didn't have to go down like this. They were hot to recruit you for their joint OCO – offensive cyber – shitshow at ██. Fucking *cyber*, it's the new blank cheque, but you blew it. Sure, they could've pulled you in last year, but Deutch Rules or no, you can't trust someone who's only compliant with a gun to their head. They offered you the keys to the kingdom, but you kept putting them off, so here you are: a counterintel discard. They weren't expecting blowback this soon, but they got their win. All that's left for you now is lawyers and hard time – Federal time – like you said yourself. But there won't be an FBI/espionage media circus; this has to go away, no one the wiser.

—But that fake data package...

—Doesn't matter; they'll charge you with tax evasion like Capone. The Trojan horse op never happened. None of this ever happened. I don't contract for corporate NSA, like ██, and you won't see me again after today – not even in court.

—So for a corsair, « corsaire et demi ».

—Ou, she stopped and rebutted, « à trompeur, trompeur et demi ». « All war is deception. » You know that. Besides, I'm only here to rubber-stamp this clusterfuck; though at first, I was supposed to give the bride away.

The heavy steel door to the street locked in the open position, Anaïs pulled him towards the light, but he caught the steel door frame with his shoulder.

—Wait, what's *Chocolate Mercury*?

—Where'd you hear that one, ██? It doesn't matter now, but it was CIA's codename for an advanced persistent threat identified a few years ago. One of the top three most destructive economic espionage actors in history, depending on whose math you used. It was billions either way. There were lots of theories: Iranian econo-terrorist? Russian cyber-spy? But they've retired that APT. You were in over your head, and you'll go down as a smalltime trafficker and tax cheat once we hand you and your redacted file over to HSI and the IRS. They'll report this as a mass-shooter spree and pin it on one of the bodies. Let's go, huli jing. It's time.

She yanked him out into the Winterfull sun, and he blinked through blinding glare. Black 'n' whites cordoned the commotion of fire trucks to the front of the office building, traffic piling up faster than they could divert it, while a slicktop convoy of taupe-grey Tahoes on black steelies crowded the fire lane, their low-profile e-lights flashing blue and red. Several more paramilitary types in uniform grey held ready formation near the open doorway, stacked behind another black scutum, and a separate group of unsmiling faces approached along the cleared sidewalk, speckled-camo plate carriers over their killer-spook plain clothes, no visible badges or ID, their carbines held low-ready. "Ninjas", she'd said, American plural.

An insistent buzz resolved through the apocalyptic ambience – a hummingbird sweeping in from above. It hovered, indifferent to the cacophony, its wings vorpal arcs of frumious vibration: a plumed machine.

—Get that thing away from me, yelled Anaïs.

She lit a Gitanes with the flash and ping! of her red-enamelled lighter, gathering a laquearian mob around him. It loomed, a dark wall closing in; "No, we're detaining her," insisted in turns, contending for a slice of his spoofed-fingerprints pie. More vehicles pulled up, blue jackets, yellow lettering. They argued among themselves and on bleeping radios, stabbing at each other with their forefingers, more cigs lighting up. He lifted his face to the cloudless vault, up through the toothy portal of high rises, awaiting hang-'em-high judgement's fall, tri-letter cowboys locked 'n' loaded.

Anaïs cursed and flicked a sparking stub into the gutter. He was pulled away from the picket of black rifles by an iron-gripped wo-man of the plain-clothed set, a large blue transit van – ██████ ELECTRIC – awaiting them, greyed-out within. "Atmospherics", she'd said. He was searched, then lifted like sacked potatoes into the dim screen-lit hold, voices murmuring over the idling engine and the crackle of radios. He was forcibly sat on the low grey-padded bench to one side, a black vinyl body bag lying be-fore him on the powder-coated diamond plate, its sarcophagian profile sharply creased with square folds.

Blackout goggles were secured over his eyes, straight out of the Afghan war, and naught else was said to him ere earmuffs clamped tight over his hung head, followed by a hood with a plasticky reek. Sound wasn't sealed but veiled, and he flinched when the van doors slammed shut like steely curtains drawn – "it's a kidnapping" in Claire's laughing voice.

Brought forth and kept in darkness,
cold tears spilt free: unseen,
inconsolate: they fell
below him.

★

Printed in Great Britain
by Amazon

d396a6e4-5684-480c-b45c-3666656c1d2fR01